PSYCLONE

A Novel By
ROGER SHARP

Published By
Barclay Books, LLC

St. Petersburg Florida
www.barclaybooks.com

A Spectral Visions Imprint

PUBLISHED BY BARCLAY BOOKS, LLC
6161 51ST STREET SOUTH
ST. PETERSBURG, FLORIDA 33715
www.barclaybooks.com
A Spectral Visions Imprint

Printed and bound in the United States of America
Cover design by Barclay Books, LLC

ISBN: 1-931402-01-9

send feedback

roger_sharp2@excite.com

I would like to dedicate this book to Gail, for all of her
encouragement and contributions.

Ruth,
   I hope you enjoy the book.
Merry Christmas!

          Roger Sharp

Prologue

Tears streamed down a little boy's face as he sat next to his mother on a solid oak church pew. She was the last member left in his family now. His father had just passed away three days ago and his twin brother, Darryl, had been missing for the last six months. He was only ten years old and already had the responsibility of being the man in the house.

While his mother wondered how she could comfort him now, he wondered how he could comfort her. All they had left in the world was each other and a dark presence. David might have mistaken the dark presence for gloom or depression, but it had been there for six months, even before his brother's disappearance.

He remembered his father's last words to him, "David, I need you to be strong. Your mother will need you. Be there for her and let her be there for you." His father had been the local sheriff and had been very well respected by others in their small Pennsylvania community. Medically speaking, he had died of a severe case of pneumonia, though close friends said they believed that he had grieved himself to death after being unable to find his missing son.

David held a picture in his hands. It was the last family photo that had ever or would ever be taken. In the picture, the twin boys had dark brown hair and dark brown eyes like their father, and his mother was smiling. This had been the last time David had seen her smile.

Now, she lowered her head sadly and let her auburn hair cover her trembling lips.

He wondered if Darryl was still alive. Maybe if he were here now, things wouldn't seem quite as bad.

Twenty-Two Years Later

Chapter One

Just after the break of dawn, Dr. Brooks carefully injected the genetically altered mouse's DNA into the unfertilized egg. He watched in amazement as the egg cell swelled. Within mere seconds, it split into two and then three cells. The cells began to form into a peculiar looking embryo as Dr. Brooks continued monitoring the accelerated growth rate. He moved the microscope; it was no longer needed. The embryo was already the size of a newborn mouse, yet it was still a nearly shapeless blob. Watching patiently with a great degree of interest, he observed the expanding mass beneath the fluorescent lights that illuminated the small room. His smile was hidden beneath a sterile cloth mask, which took on a deeper shade of blue along its edges as it dampened with the perspiration from the doctor's face. The clean hospital-like smell of the room was drowned out by the warm stagnate smell of his breath as he breathed a proud sigh of success as the cell mass took an oblong shape.

He regretted the fact that he had to leave the laboratory and miss even a few hours of the rodent's metamorphosis, but he couldn't have anyone, even his wife, Gayla, getting suspicious of his experiment or the reasons behind it.

By late evening of the next day, the cluster of cells had taken on the shape of a mouse. David looked around anxiously as paranoia struck him, as it had many times before, while he worked alone in the laboratory. He stood up from the raised stool near the island counter in the center of the room and proceeded to walk through the rest of the laboratory. There was no one in the larger room. Not even in the far corner, where Professor Williams normally sat conducting his neurological research. The long narrow observation room was empty. David shook his head as he looked in his own office. Though he couldn't see anyone else in the building, he certainly didn't feel alone. Normally, Jim Turner, a recent addition to the small team at the lab, would have been watching his every move. David knew that the reason he usually felt like he was being watched was because he really was being watched. He would almost be comforted by Jim's presence now, however; at least he wouldn't be taking a momentary break to question his own sanity. Yet, in the lab this evening there was just David Brooks, a cloned mouse, and a presence invisible to the naked eye, but undeniably there.

Out of the carefully monitored one-quart container of amniotic fluid crawled a slimy white mouse. This mouse was not a typical mouse; he had been cloned. Furthermore, he wasn't a typical clone, as the usual clone would have been transplanted into a surrogate mother. In addition to being brought into the world through a heated amniotic fluid tank, this clone was not at the newborn stage of all previous clones. In fact, he was at the exact same growth stage as his "twin" brother when the DNA had been collected. Though this small mouse had been Dr. Brooks' greatest discovery, neither Brooks nor the rodent would take credit for this accomplishment. Nor would the scientific world or his closest friends learn of this experiment. He would continue to work on less important projects with a façade of interest.

Dr. Brooks scooped up the tiny mouse in his left hand, while holding a needle with black ink in his right hand, and carefully placed a tiny and inconspicuous tattoo on the second toe of the mouse's right hind foot. The mouse would go into the cage with the others, but Dr. Brooks would discreetly follow the progress of the cloned rodent on a daily basis. Other than the daily checkups, Dr. Brooks would never let on that he had made such a discovery; that would hinder his future projects, and he was already being watched closely enough.

Glancing towards the picture on his desk, he thought about his brother Darryl. Would Darryl support his decisions if he were here? Surely, he would; they had the same mind.

Sweat beaded on Dr. Brooks' forehead as he peered through the microscope. He was confident that this project would go well. Unknown to his assistant, he had already successfully completed a more complicated experiment two days prior. He had worked meticulously for three years waiting for this moment. Sure, cloning was old news, but it had not been perfected to this level until this moment. His newest clone, a mole, was completely identical, with no flaws; it didn't even age faster. It was so perfect! The inherent flaws from the original sheep clone, "Dolly," had now been circumvented. Though the mole had grown from infancy in the same manner that Dolly had, Dolly had been just a discovery experiment— never intended to be perfect. Perfection was the only acceptable result for David Brooks.

He smiled and rose from his slump to converse with his counterpart Dr. Turner who had just entered the lab. "Well, Jim, congratulations!" said Dr. Brooks as he thrust his hand forward. "We've just made history."

Dr. Turner breathed a sigh of relief as he grasped his mentor's hand. Earlier that month, the laboratory had threatened to cut funding on the cloning project and possibly his position. This suddenly changed everything. Now he intended to pursue his original goal of cloning one organ at a time. He could save thousands of lives. *I can do it! My purpose in life will be fulfilled shortly*, he thought to himself. The two men stood smiling at each other, neither saying a word as each pondered what their discovery meant to themselves and each other.

At last, Jim Turner spoke, "How soon until we proceed to cloning lungs?" This was most important to Jim. He had promised his uncle he would someday find a cure for lung cancer less than five minutes before he drew his last breath. If he could clone healthy lung tissue, he would have a cure of sorts.

As Dr. Brooks contemplated his own plans, he responded to Jim's question through his own goal. "As soon as we have cloned a human we will begin cloning individual organs . . ."

Dr. Turner interrupted "We can't do that Dave. You know damn good and well that's illegal. And what would we do with this clone anyway?"

"Britain made it legal to clone human embryos over a year ago," Brooks argued.

"And that was a tragic mistake." Turner spoke barely above a whisper before continuing. "Six billion people in the world are sufficient. I just want to keep the ones we already have healthy."

Brooks nodded his head understandingly. "I agree with you. We *do* have enough people already, but think of the knowledge we could gain from this. To have a clone of Albert Einstein working with us would be . . ."

"Ridiculous!" argued Turner. Their debate halted only for a moment as they heard the door open.

A large-framed black man with kind eyes hidden behind a rough, natural scowl walked in. It was Professor Williams, a man with strong opinions about everything.

"Trevor," Jim addressed Professor Williams by his first name while he looked for an ally in his battle, "what do you think about cloning humans?"

As predicted, Williams began with a typical disgusted look on his face. "And who would we clone? Starving kids in Africa or homeless people in America? Oh wait, let's create more of the idiots that I have to drive around on my way to work."

"Exactly," agreed Jim. They were all well aware of the world's problems and that's what kept them employed.

"Besides," continued Williams, "all you can clone is the

flesh. The clone will not have the knowledge of its' host. You would have a six foot tall infant on your hands, and you're crazy if you think I'm gonna change it's diaper." He continued with a sly grin.

"Alright! I just think it would be a major breakthrough if we could begin cloning human organs," growled David Brooks. He desperately tried to defend his position with any logical argument that might convince his peers.

"Wait a minute, Dave," said Jim, "Don't try to use cloning organs as an excuse to clone people and turn around and kill them the next day. We can't play God and you know that."

"Spare me your semi-Catholic bullshit, Jim. Your logic escapes me. In one breath, you gripe that the world is being over-populated and next you say we're all going to hell if we do anything about it. Your views change with every conversation." By now, David had become irritated and was ready to vent his frustrations however he could.

"There are differences," Jim protested. "Every situation is unique. We are over populated, but that does not mean we shouldn't try to save lives. Furthermore, I don't agree with killing anyone whether they were created by man or God, period."

Williams chuckled. Then he said, sarcastically, "Preaching again. How can you guys believe in God? You're scientists. Has years of research taught you nothing? At least science can be proven."

Now Williams had gone too far; Jim had become offended by the professor's blasphemous remarks. "The reason science exists is because of God! God does not have to be proven. He simply IS!"

Suddenly, the three men realized that their conversation had gone astray and would be better off forgotten. They glanced back and forth at each other. No one would apologize. After all, each man was right in his own mind.

David whispered, "I have to get home. It's been a long day."

Williams and Turner made eye contact once again. Nothing was said, but they each took pity on the other for his misguided views.

Brooks reached across his desk for his briefcase. Before he turned away, he stopped long enough to pick up a picture on his desk—that last picture of the twins together. As David rolled a small toy car back and forth across the top of his desk, he reflected on the last time that he had seen his brother before his disappearance. He had kept this car ready to give it back to Darryl the next time he saw him. That was twenty-two years ago. He wondered what had happened to Darryl, but there was no way to bring him back . . . *or was there*? Could he ever relieve the pain his mother had felt for over two decades? Could she love a clone as her own son? Would she ever have to know that it wasn't really Darryl after all these years? Too many questions, and no one understood anyway. He placed the picture back on the desk and walked out the door.

Brooks pondered the concept of human cloning all the way home. Everyone was against it. If only he could find someone who agreed with him.

At the lab, Professor Williams' day had only started. He too, was on the brink of his greatest work, both as an accomplished neurologist and a computer programmer. By himself, he was a one-man team of scientists. Not only did he have a vision, he had the capability to conduct his work exactly as he had imagined. A team of other neurologists had already proven that the human brain worked as a series of electrical pulses, much like that of a computer. Unfortunately, the human brain did not code in binary. However, other devices that translated signals at high speeds had been around for almost two decades. He reasoned that it had to be possible to record thoughts, memories, and even emotions in the brain if they were merely electrical signals.

William's hoped that his work would earn him the title he deserved. Last year he was recognized as being the most successful African-American scientist in history. While this should have been a great moment in his life, he was somewhat offended by the recognition. He wanted to be recognized as the most successful *scientist* in history regardless of race, color, or creed. He felt the award was a slight insult to his entire race; it was segregation. He knew that he would eventually accomplish more than any Caucasian scientist, including Einstein himself.

The silence that had overcome the lab had become unbearable for Jim Turner. When he looked at his watch, he noticed that over ten hours had passed since this morning when he had met Brooks at the lab to check the progress of their specimen. *I should go home*, he thought, *but to what?* This small lab had been his life for over two years. It was one of the smallest laboratories in the country, yet so many great things were happening here. Despite the fact that his theological views were different from his co-workers, he had to respect their knowledge as well as their accomplishments. They were both relatively young considering what they had already contributed to history and the scientific community. Now, it was his turn to do something great and he was honored to be able to work with David Brooks on the cloning project.

David had grown accustomed to the splendors of his life. He no longer stopped to notice the beauty of the nearby mansion that he lived in. From the brick archways above the windows to the lead crystals that dangled from the chandeliers inside, it was immaculate. It was more than a couple would ever need. When it had been built, David had planned for an expansion to the family, but he and Gayla had put off the addition somewhat indefinitely.

As David walked in the front door of his home, he saw his wife, Gayla, already on her way to greet him. He felt guilty about spending so many hours at work lately. They were both very busy and he knew he needed to take precautions to keep them from growing apart. As he put his arms around her, he asked, "How would you like to go out on the town tonight?"

She seemed surprised by his proposal.

"On a Tuesday night? What has come over you?" she joked.

PSYCLONE

"We can play hooky in the morning," he assured her.

She eagerly accepted his proposal with a nod and a smile.

As they headed upstairs to freshen up for their evening, he remembered their first date. The gaze of her cat-like, aqua colored eyes had made him such a blundering fool that night. He had been surprised when she had accepted his offer for another date.

Gayla was still as lovely as that first time he had seen her nine years ago, he thought while watching intently as her dress slid down her delicate body. It had been far too long since they had had time for romance in their lives.

David moved close to her to assist her with the removal of her undergarments. She smiled knowingly. Who needed romance when it had been so long since they had had true passion in their lives? One tender kiss led to another, heating the room, apparently rising at a rapid pace. They made love tenderly, gently, and, moreover, passionately. All previous plans of the evening's adventures would be postponed.

Fluids spewed all over the table as a tiny cauldron over-heated. Jim turned the propane off and began to clean up the mess. He was preoccupied with his visions of the future, when his work would save the lives of thousands of people each year. Now, he was growing weary from the long day and it was time for him to leave as well. He regretted the fact that he did not have a significant other to welcome him home in the evenings. He was envious of David; David had the perfect life. Still, he should go home, lonely or not.

As Jim walked toward the door, he cautiously approached Williams. He wanted to say something; he needed closure to the dispute. "So," he paused, "Are you still making progress?"

Trevor turned to face him. "Yes, however backwards. I can read signals from the brain of a mouse . . . but since a mouse can't speak, it's a little hard to decipher exactly what it means. Times like this, I guess I could use one of these human clones Dave was babbling about."

14

Jim shook his head with distorted amusement. Had Dave actually influenced Trevor? Trevor had always been so stubborn that Jim found it hard to imagine that anyone could change his mind.

"I will be going to Dallas to experiment with a human subject next month," Trevor added quickly in an attempt to keep the conversation from reverting back to its predecessor. "Obviously, it's a dangerous procedure and we just don't have the resources here to conduct that type of test safely."

"What's the purpose of this anyway? You can't save anyone's life by recording his thoughts. I mean, sure it's neat but . . ." Jim shrugged.

Trevor's project, as complicated and impressive as it might be, didn't seem to have the impact on life that his own did. He had no doubt that Trevor was indeed a brilliant man, but why waste his talents on such a project with limited value?

"Contrary," Trevor said arrogantly, despite his recent attempts to be polite. "It will change education. It will even change justice. It could be the greatest accomplishment ever."

Jim realized that he was a novice on the subject and had little insight into Trevor's project, but he found his last statement a bit hard to believe.

"What could be greater than saving the life of a child?" Jim asked righteously.

"To educate every child in a single day more than he or she would learn in twelve years of school. If we could read memories, it's only a matter of time until we can write them also." Trevor was eager to support his position again. "And . . ." he continued, "think about this, if we could read a murder victim's last thoughts, there is a pretty good chance that we could find the killer."

Again, Jim was amazed at the man's foresight. He would have never considered these possibilities.

"Impressive. I'll admit that would make a difference," Jim was forced to agree. He knew that there were good intentions inside Trevor, despite his lack of spirituality.

The two men were on speaking terms again. Now, Jim could

call it a day without carrying home the weight of bitter feelings towards his co-worker. "Good luck," said Jim as he closed the door behind him.

David grasped Gayla's hand as they walked out the door of their home. They had been married for five years now, and were at a point where some men would have lost interest in their wives, David found Gayla even more intriguing. Gayla was absolutely adorable, and as successful as she was beautiful. Further, he knew how dedicated she was to him. He made it a point to turn on the charm as he opened the passenger side door of their Jaguar. Still, his life left one thing to be desired . . . time. He craved the ability to slow down enough to enjoy his luxuries. Tonight the world would wait. Gayla was the single most important aspect of his life. Tomorrow . . . well, that was different. He was haunted by his own ambitions. Soon he would take a long vacation; they would travel to their condo in Florida for an entire week with no interruptions. It was her favorite place; they referred to it as their 'sacred retreat,' and they had only been there once since they bought it nearly two years ago. He just needed time to finish one more project.

As David closed the door and started the car, he looked at his wife and asked nonchalantly, "How do you feel about human cloning?"

A bizarre question, it took Gayla off guard. "I don't put much thought into that kind of stuff," she said with a look of confusion. "Why would you want to, though?" she asked attempting to sound interested.

David chose his words carefully. After all, Gayla was a psychologist, and he didn't want to draw suspicions to his intentions. "Oh, well, for organs to save the lives of other people," he stammered.

Gayla gazed at him. "For spare parts? And what if the clones don't want to just give up their organs? Whose decision is it to let one or the other live?" Gayla hadn't had the time to put much thought into it, but some questions seemed obvious at even the slightest thought of the matter. David could tell he wasn't going to get his much needed support even from his own wife. He knew it would be best to give up now and enjoy this rare time with his wife rather than relive the same arguments with his co-workers.

"Just a question," he stated blankly, then smiled. "Where would you like to eat?" he asked to change the subject.

A pile of shaven dead mice filled the container on the table next to Trevor. Obviously, neurology had been more challenging on the tiny subjects. The mice had frantically attempted to rid themselves of the tiny needle inserted precisely under the backs of their skulls. In their feeble attempts, all but one had unwittingly driven the needle further into their brains. Trevor had already collected plenty of information on the emotion of panic from his subjects. He still needed to go into other emotions, though. The lone survivor of this experiment would be compensated well. His eyes quickly darted from the mouse to the monitor in front of him and back to the mouse again. Trevor introduced the mouse to a large chunk of cheese. As he recorded the results, he wondered if the emotion was excitement or hunger. He needed to try another method.

Trevor examined the remaining mice carefully until he found a female mouse in heat. This could distinguish some of the possible thoughts, he concluded. He began to prepare a maze for his mouse so that he could examine the creature while it was lost and confused.

It had been a long day. Trevor looked at the clock. He had been at the lab for fifteen hours. "Quitting time," he announced, though he knew no one was present to hear his words. He subdued the mouse with ether and gently removed the tape, then the needle, from the poor rodent. "Fine job! I guess I could use a pet anyway," Trevor told the unconscious mouse. The professor placed the rodent in a separate cage, "What kind of name should I come up with for you? How about Rambo?" He smiled.

Chapter 2

As the first beam of light passed through the window, David woke up thinking about the perfect clone. It was time to get back to the lab. There was much to do. He showered quickly, threw on his clothes and leaned over to kiss Gayla good morning.

Gayla awoke, instinctively disappointed. "What happened to playing hooky?" she inquired.

David knew that one evening had not been enough to make up for three years of eighty hour work weeks which had become the norm.

"I forgot about an important meeting with Professor Cook this morning," he lied. Any excuse that would ease her disappointment might make the situation just a little closer to acceptable. "I'm already running late. But last night was wonderful," he whispered with a mischievous grin. "Two more months . . . I promise . . . and then we'll go on a vacation. And when we get back, no more than ten hours a day five days a week." He prodded.

She nodded understandingly. Through her disappointment,

she still saw the ambitious young doctor that she had fallen in love with.

"I'll see you tonight?" she asked.

David nodded back at her, then leaned forward to place a gentle kiss on her forehead. "I love you more than anything. You know that, right?" David's conscience started to speak for him.

"Yes, and I love you too. That's *why* I miss you," she pouted solemnly.

Another quick peck on the cheek and David was out the door. He knew he could make it up to her later.

David remained somewhat bitter that no one else shared his views on human cloning. "Even Gayla doesn't understand," he growled knowing that there was no one else in the car. In fact, if someone else was in the car he couldn't talk about it. His idea was not that bizarre. He was just surrounded by close-minded worrywarts. Did they doubt him? His colleagues recognized him as a brilliant man. He found it hard to believe that suddenly his ideas were *that* far left field.

David unlocked the door to the laboratory and burst through. He had to confirm that the clone of the mole had not been a cruel dream mocking his work. He rushed to the counter, looked at the twin moles and began to double-check his work.

David soon realized that he wasn't going to have an opportunity to conduct any "other" tests. Jim had also made it to work quite early that morning. David knew that Jim was a fast learner and was his own equal in ambition, but it didn't change the fact that he would relish even a short break from his shadow. David was already growing irritated knowing that Jim would be watching his every move. He shook his head in annoyance. *Next thing you know he'll be following me to the bathroom*, he thought to himself as Jim drew nearer.

"Hey Dave, any changes?" Jim chirped in his usual happy-go-lucky tone.

"Same old shit every day. Nothing changes around here." David replied coarsely.

Jim backed off a bit as his smile quickly faded into a trace of confusion. Jim briefly reflected back, wondering how he could have possibly infuriated David in the twelve seconds he had been in the lab.

"I was referring to changes in the mole clone," Jim said somewhat apologetically, though he wasn't sure why. David realized that Jim was oblivious to the fact that he was smothering him.

It's not really his fault, he reminded himself. "No, she's an exact duplicate," David replied more calmly this time.

Jim walked away, sure that he could find something else to occupy his time.

An hour and a half later, Jim walked toward David again. This time he had news David would like. "I just got off the phone with Dr. Lease. She wants me to join a team in Boston to continue my research on cloning organs. She also told me to pass along her congratulations to you for the 'Gemini Mole' project."

David made a valiant effort to hide his joy that Jim would be gone for a while. "Well that sounds great! I'm really happy for you." He beamed with a newfound joy.

Jim neglected to inform David that he had made the call and the reassignment was at his own request. He respected David and Trevor for their knowledge, but he was afraid their personalities might start to wear off on him if he stayed much longer. Jim could tell it was a much-needed break for all of them.

David found a new tolerance for Jim's presence. He knew that he only needed to be patient, for the time was coming that he could work alone and unrestricted. David and Jim started researching chromosome nine. It was clear to each of the men that this would be a long drawn out project from which any results would be slow in manifesting. Jim was focused on his work, unlike his mentor. David had no *real* interest in chromosome nine, so he daydreamed as his apprentice studied on his own. "It is ten o'clock now," David regretted quietly. He should be just getting out of bed at this time.

Gayla would be leaving for work soon and valuable time

had been wasted this morning. It wouldn't have been a total waste if Jim hadn't shown up . . . but he had. He lied to her. *And for what?* Guilt and anger teamed up on the young doctor. David grew irritable and grouchy again, but this time he made it a point not to take it out on Jim. Jim had suffered enough lately, despite all his good intentions. David would continue mindlessly looking at charts and books, taking care to put up a facade of researching while he drifted back in time, tormenting himself with memories of bad decisions. He dwelt on his sour emotions so much that he failed to even acknowledge Trevor's arrival as he walked through the door. How could he have rushed out on Gayla? This would consume his mind for at least the rest of the day.

Rambo began to stir about and lazily creep around in his cage. It was different than where he had been before the experiment yesterday. No other mice and enough food to keep him content for a week. The bald rodent looked through the glass wall of his cage and saw Trevor analyzing data from another mouse.

Trevor turned at hearing the rustle in the cage. "Good morning," Trevor said to his new sidekick. Trevor reached down into a plastic bag and produced a handful of treats for the mouse. After letting Rambo devour some of the morsels, Trevor picked him up and stroked the miniature whiskers growing on his back. "Don't worry, I won't be experimenting with you little guys much longer," he confided to the pet.

Trevor continued his testing, and then composed new information on his recent studies. He was ready to test human subjects now. Unfortunately, volunteers for this experiment were in short supply. Until he could proceed with his other studies he could work out the bugs of his new program. "Come see this, Jim," Trevor said as he noticed Dr. Turner headed in his direction. "Fear, fear, and fear," continued Trevor as he pointed to three separate graphs. "And on these I recorded hunger," he said as he held up another set of graphs.

"Impressive," Jim encouraged, though the charts had little meaning to him.

"I wanted to inform you of my relocation to Boston, Trevor. It's only temporary, but I will be part of a team experimenting with organ cloning. I leave tomorrow and I wanted to wish you luck on your project," Jim announced as he extended his hand.

Trevor smiled and shook Jim's hand. "How long will you be gone?"

"Could be three or four weeks . . . could be years, depending on what we can accomplish," Jim replied as he gave a mock salute to his co-worker and walked away.

At ten minutes till four o'clock, David reached for his briefcase. He could surprise Gayla by picking her up from work and going out for a drink. Then she would forget all about his broken promise this morning. David sprang from his chair and lifted his briefcase, preparing to race to the other side of town before Gayla concluded her last interview of the evening.

"Don't run away because you saw me coming!" A familiar voice boomed from behind. "Gayla said you were psychic." Fate was cruel; what could possibly be worse than an alibi coming true?

"Professor Cook!" David gasped in astonishment.

"I called your house this morning to let you know I was coming in today to discuss your findings. Gayla said you had already left to meet me. That was pretty intuitive since we haven't talked to each other in months." He laughed, the round sweaty man. "So, show me the moles, Dave. What did you do different?" Cook interrogated.

David's mood changed to an entirely different type of frustration. He stumbled through his explanation to Professor Cook wondering how much of his time would be wasted in the process; so much for the idea of surprising Gayla. *Did Gayla catch me in my lie? She can see through anyone; it is her profession.*

Questions continued being asked for another three hours. It

was late and David needed to get home to see how much of a lie he had been caught in. He couldn't leave after Professor Cook had flown over eight hundred miles to get the information for the medical board. David disguised his panic to the best of his ability as he engaged in the politically necessary chitchat with Professor Cook.

Before David walked Cook out of the building, he checked to be sure that Trevor was still there. He was. At least David didn't have to stay and lock up the lab, not that an extra ten minutes would make much difference at this point.

Tires screeching around every other corner, David wasted no time in getting home.

Should he gamble a misunderstanding—digging himself deeper with every word? Should he confess that he had just lied to get back to work on his project? No acceptable option presented itself.

Just as she had the night before, Gayla met David at the door. "So, did you make the meeting in time?"

She knows.

"Look honey, I . . . I'm sorry . . . I was just anxious to finish this project because I knew he would be coming out soon . . ." *That sounded okay*, he reassured himself.

"Soon? I thought you said you were late this morning," Gayla said with a puzzled look on her face.

If she didn't know before she does now. Damn it!

"This morning, I didn't have a meeting with Professor Cook. I wasn't even sure when he would be coming out, but I had to be prepared for when he did," he admitted, though patching it with a different lie. "I told you I was late to try to get you to understand."

"I think I've been pretty understanding for years now David Brooks. If work is more important to you than I am, then I can understand that too." Amazingly, she had a knack for picking out any given word of a sentence and proving him guilty of everything she had ever suspected. David concluded that it was wise to accept his guilt and remain silent.

The house remained quite. Gayla was irate, and rightfully so. David ate his cold dinner, searching for something to say to her. It wasn't happening.

When they retired for the night, Gayla lay on the far right side of the bed that night, facing away from him. "Goodnight," David said softly.

"Goodnight," she repeated in a monotone voice.

She had not expected much from David. She knew his career was highly demanding. But he had lied, and she wondered if he was getting used to being away from her. Had they already grown apart? Was this the beginning of the end? Gayla knew the statistics. Five years was a dangerous time for couples. Did he even go to the lab this morning or was he elsewhere? Was the lie, he assumed he was caught in, merely a cover for another darker lie that he was still hiding?

Beams of light pierced through the window again. This morning David would not rush off to work. Instead, David started a pot of coffee and rushed out the door to get some doughnuts for breakfast. David was not gifted when it came to cooking but he wanted to give Gayla some type of breakfast in bed this morning. As he rushed back in, he grabbed her favorite mug and poured her coffee. In another attempt to be a gentleman he carried her breakfast upstairs.

Gayla awoke surprised, but not impressed. "I stopped drinking coffee three weeks ago, but I guess you would have had to have been here to notice." Her imagination had fed her bitterness. She needed time, and above all, proof. Gayla wanted him there, but his presence was as welcome as flies at a picnic.

Completely aware that his every move seemed to draw his wife's wrath, David headed for work in order to avoid an awkward situation.

The laboratory doors were still locked at nine thirty. With

Jim gone, David was free to work on his long awaited project, though it seemed a little less important today.

David looked around the room. For the first time in his adult life, he was lonely. I wish Jim were here he thought and then pondered the irony of it. "No one will know what species this clone is until the later stages," he whispered to himself needing someone to share in his experience. David examined his body looking for a painless place to draw blood. He picked a finger at random, thrust a razor into it, and dripped his blood onto a narrow piece of glass.

David jerked, knocking the microscope and slide off of the table as Trevor said "Good morning, Dave"

"What are you doing here so early?" David gasped. He curled his left hand into a fist and slid it inside his pocket to keep from showing his bloodied finger.

"I needed to check on Rambo," Trevor replied holding up a small wheel for the rodent's entertainment. *Too close.* David was growing paranoid. Everything seemed to be against him.

Sensing that David was not quite himself, Trevor asked, "What's wrong?"

"Nothing . . . well, Gayla's kind of got me in the dog house."

Trevor attempted to lighten the gloom "Ah, ancient Chinese proverb say 'woman who keep man in dog house eventually find him in cat house.'" Trevor replied with a smile.

This attempt at humor didn't solve David's problems, but despite having his plans fowled again, he was happy *someone* would talk to him.

"I received a call last night after you left, Dave. I'm going to Dallas this weekend. I have several volunteers for the next few weeks, so I'll be gone for awhile and I suppose you'll be alone after today."

"Who's going to keep me out of trouble then?" David replied, only half joking.

Trevor gave David a quick grin and made his way to the other side of the lab.

Two months, possibly, to myself, David schemed. He looked

at his agenda for the next month—chromosome nine—ho hum, who would notice if any significant data was or was not attained on that?

Chapter 3

In comparison to the tiny lab in Phoenix, the Dallas laboratory was immense. The observation deck alone was as large as the entire facility to which Trevor had grown accustomed. As he gazed upward at the observation deck, his eyes met with those of Diana Martinez, an old girlfriend whom he had met while studying to become a neurologist. His lips began to form a sly smile until he noticed Dr. Green standing beside her.

Dr. Green was his successor, so to speak. Too many times Trevor had put Diana off in favor of his work. Dr. Green was not incredibly ambitious as a neurologist, but he had been more persistent with Diana.

Trevor's head instinctively spun away as the serrated edges of his memories plunged deep into his soul. Subconsciously, Trevor began to compare his past to his last conversation with David. Was David making the same mistake? Trevor wondered. No matter, he had waited for this moment a long time and there was much to accomplish. To isolate a single human thought or emotion could take years and Trevor hoped to do much more within the next couple of months.

David had several weeks alone on his hands. However, cloning took time; how much time, even David wasn't entirely sure. Human cloning had never been done before, and cloning beyond the fetal stage could prolong the project as well. Researching the matter had been impossible.

David walked over to Rambo's cage and gently scooped up the rodent with both hands. Trevor had asked him to feed the mouse while he was away, but that wasn't the *only* reason David had come to the cage. He flipped the rodent over and examined his rear right foot. David was thankful that Rambo had not died during Trevor's experiment; it had been a necessary risk. Though he had been distraught that Trevor had used Rambo, Trevor hadn't known that Rambo was significant—the clone—as he had randomly grabbed one mouse after another, insistent on achieving his own goals.

David put the mouse back into his cage and proceeded to his own area of the lab. He would need to begin his work now if he were to have any chance of completing the clone in the near future.

The large tub he had constructed was ready to be filled with amniotic fluid and warmed to the ninety-eight point six degrees common to a natural womb. Already he had purchased the replacement door locks to keep the others who had keys from randomly discovering the curious looking tank. Would it all be in vain? He might not even be close to completing the clone by the time either *or both* of his co-workers returned to the lab.

Again, he held the razor to his finger, gritted his teeth, and thrust the sharp corner through his skin. After squeezing the blood onto the glass plate, he examined it carefully.

The DNA was extracted and introduced to the oocyte. Now, all he could do after the quick and relatively simple procedure was wait. Thus being done, he would carry on with the research on chromosome nine without all his previous distractions.

ROGER SHARP

More attractive than his usual subjects, Trevor watched the young woman wake from her chemically induced nap. She would be introduced to a series of graphic pictures while Trevor recorded the results. A name had never been accurately placed for the feelings Trevor was attempting to capture. Disgust, sorrow, and sadness most accurately described the state of mind in words, but Trevor got a crystal clear recording of the signals from her mind.

While she watched a variety of movies, Trevor watched the meter that recorded her chemical levels and reactions to situations. Laughter, love, spite, hatred, relief, one by one he would learn her emotions thoroughly.

Satisfied with his day's work, Trevor entered the room of his subject. For all he knew about her by this time, he still did not know her name. "Hi there, my name is Professor Williams. I wasn't given the opportunity to meet with you before the implant, but I wanted to thank you for your contributions to our research." Trevor leaned forward to shake the hand of his first human subject.

"Well, the money persuaded me a bit," she replied honestly. "Oh, and my name is Sareena," she added, as she felt the firmness of his handshake.

Gayla was on speaking terms with David once more. She didn't rush to the front door upon his arrival, but she was nonetheless, happy to see him.

"Do you think we could spend Christmas in Vermont this year?" she asked, knowing that he was already somewhat indebted to her.

"With your parents?" he replied with his own question.

"Um hmm" she mumbled anxiously. "I just got off the phone with Mom and she laid a guilt trip on me about how her 'good' daughter was coming in and how nice it would be to have the family together again."

David quickly calculated the projected growth of his clone and took into consideration the absence of his co-workers.

"That sounds great," he started with Gayla already anticipating the *but*. "But Trevor is in Dallas and Jim is in Boston . . ." David proceeded, realizing that he was putting her off once again. "I'll see what I can do," he tried to recover.

"I'm going," she said coldly, then added, "I'm not sure when I'll be back."

"Okay, I'll . . . I'll figure something out," David stuttered back desperately. Gayla was less than impressed with his sensitivity to her desires.

A chart containing seven words was placed in front of Sareena.

"Pick a word, don't tell me what it is." Instructed Trevor.

Sareena carefully reviewed the words and made her choice, "struggle."

"Now, I want you to think about your word and associate a memory with that word and continue thinking about it until I tell you to stop."

As she followed the professor's instructions, Trevor noticed great similarities to the recordings of fear and panic. It had been less than ten seconds since she begun to recollect the old memory when Trevor announced, "You can stop now." He walked around to face her.

"Struggle," he crowed confidently, ". . . was the word you chose."

"Wow! Yeah," replied his youthful subject. This was rapid progress, but it was only the beginning, and many more obstacles still needed to be overcome. Without taking time to dwell on this success, he advanced to other studies.

As the wheel in Rambo's cage turned, so too, did the wheels in David's brain. The gestation period of a mouse was far less than that of a human.

I can do this, he reasoned as he flipped through the pages of the calendar. Two phone calls later, he had formed his plan. He sighed in relief as he picked up the phone to call his wife.

"I called Jim. He said it looks like he will be in Boston until next summer. Then I called Trevor. He won't be back until February of next year . . ."

"So, are you telling me that I'll have to spend Christmas without you?" she moaned impatiently.

"No, not at all, if you'll let me finish. I told Trevor I would take Rambo to Vermont with us and give the other mice to a pet store."

"You're going to take a mouse to my mother's house," she giggled. "Oh well, I'm still glad you're coming with me, mouse or no mouse."

At last, David had been able to make Gayla happy without completely interrupting his "alternative project."

While contemplating the thought of whether he could ever safely reveal the nature of his clone, David reflected on Trevor's words. ". . . A six foot tall infant . . ." For all Trevor's knowledge as a neurologist, teacher, and computer programmer, he knew nothing about traditional cloning. The only method of cloning that had been used outside of David's lone experiment was that of cloning to the sub-fetal stage. Still, Trevor's uneducated slur hit dangerously close to the reality of David's intentions.

In the synthetic womb, the clone was growing steadily and considerably faster than it would have in a natural womb. *Maybe it's because of the adult growth stage that the clone is growing so large and so rapidly,* David rationalized. He was pleased with the progress and felt that it would be safe to let "nature" take it's course as the clone needed no assistance in it's growth. He estimated that the clone would be complete near the end of January, just before Trevor would return. From there, well, he'd figure it out.

Sareena shook Trevor's hand as she left. It was time for Trevor to begin studying another subject, this one male. It was doubtful that he could learn as much this time around as he had from his debut experiment with Sareena. Time proved him tragically wrong. Trevor began to draw actual words and vague descriptions of memories out of his new subject within the first week. Similar, in many ways, to the polygraph, there was no hiding private thoughts or opinions from the chemical measuring device that Trevor had constructed. He only needed to ask the subject a question. Responses were not necessary as Trevor read the charts and observed key words that the program had deciphered from the frequencies of the electronic pulses.

Anyone with less patience, persistence, or dedication could not have made such an incredible degree of progress. The ability to decipher particular words had been achieved at the rate of one word per a dozen lines of computer code. The program had a vocabulary of less than fifty words and Trevor began to grow weary. He looked forward to the holidays, as he would be forced to take a break while the lab was closed.

Gayla looked out the small rectangular window of the plane. From here she could see the geometric shapes of multiple irrigated fields where a variety of crops had grown the previous summer. These geometric shapes reminded her of the pieces of children's puzzles in the lobby outside her office. On slow days, she would step outside and watch the children fumble the pieces around and into their appropriate places. She had considered having a child several times in recent months but had not mentioned the subject to David in over a year. She averted her gaze from the surface below when she heard the voice of a young boy directly behind her. "Mommy, how much longer 'till we get to grandma and grandpa's house?" the boy asked.

"After you wake up from your nap," The mother replied.

Gayla knew that her parents would be sure to inquire about the possibilities of grandchildren at some point during the visit, while David wondered about the clone's progress. He had been contemplating the "miracle of life" but had not found the right opportunity to discuss the issue with his wife. He wondered how speculating about the growth of his own child would compare to his interest on the clone's progress. As soon as he completed the cloning project, he planned to discuss the possibilities of children with Gayla. He knew that· if he mentioned it beforehand, she would be sure to remind him of how he was never home and how hard it would be for her to raise the child by herself. He could only hope that, between his own mother and his in-laws, he would not be forced into the conversation prematurely.

A layover in Chicago, and the better half of the following day, the couple arrived at their destination in Montpelier, Vermont. David looked out the window and regretted that another precious day away from the lab had been wasted. They had left Arizona just after the break of dawn that morning and between the length of their journey and the loss of two hours, they were surrounded by darkness again.

A chilling breeze swept through the crowded tunnel as they waited to exit. Gayla had grown up in this climate and David was also used to the cold from the few years he had lived in Pennsylvania, but their five years in Arizona had thinned their skin considerably. Gayla's eyes lit up as she saw her mother standing near the door.

The petite old lady's arms reached forth as if preparing to hug her daughter even though she was fifteen feet away and behind several of the other passengers. Behind her frail mother stood her father, a robust man with salt and pepper hair that formed a crescent from ear to ear behind his head.

After her parents had greeted Gayla, her father turned his focus back to David.

"How have you been, David?" Gayla's father inquired with a broad grin as he clenched David's hand with a firm handshake.

"Busy, as always, but Gayla's keeping me straight," David replied.

He remembered the first time he had seen Gayla's father. For two hours, he had sat silently across from him in a quiet living room, trying to figure out how to engage him in conversation. There had never been much to say between the two men. David originally thought that Richard didn't like him, but even then, Richard approved of his career ambition and was glad that his daughter had met a decent man. They both held a great deal of respect for each other; they were just two totally different men with different interests.

David reached to open the back door of a light blue Volvo.

"I'll sit in the back. Gayla and I have some more catching up to do." Barbara said with a gentle smile.

After Gayla got into the car she leaned close to Barbara's ear. "So is Phil coming?" Gayla asked her mother in a whisper. She didn't want her father to overhear the question. The last time her brother had been mentioned, Richard and his son Phillip were not on speaking terms. While Richard was a passionate man and a good father, he hadn't reacted well to his son's announcement that he was homosexual.

"Yes, dear, it will be the first time he has been home in three years. But can you believe that he asked if he could bring his . . . boyfriend?" her mother replied with a shiver of disgust.

Christmas was still three days away and Gayla already began dreading the imminent tension at the dinner table.

As the car pulled into the driveway, David looked at the house his wife had grown up in. Like their home, it was just shy of being a mansion. David realized that his wife had never known poverty. She had lived a pampered life and continued to do so with him. He wanted her to experience life without ever having to deal with real trouble. If only he could spare her from the reality of what he had come to know as "life," maybe she could spend the rest of her life only having to help other people through their problems.

Others at the laboratory in Dallas finished projects and secured their areas before leaving the office and preparing for the holidays. Trevor, however, saved his work on his laptop computer and gathered several folders containing readouts produced from his prior experiments. He intended to take a break over the holidays, but wanted to wrap up another couple of hour's work from his hotel room after the lab had closed.

Dr. Diana Martinez took notice as he gathered up his working files. She wanted to invite him over for the holidays, but she remembered how Trevor had not shown interest in the holiday season before. She knew that he was an atheist and imagined that he would continue working through Christmas without feeling that peaceful joy that she did. She felt sorry for him, but didn't know what to say, so she said nothing. Diana shook her head sadly and turned away before Trevor even noticed her standing behind him.

Christmas Eve had arrived without any mention of children. David had considered himself lucky so far, and hoped that he could continue to avoid the subject for another six months. He sat next to Gayla with his arm lying atop the back of the couch behind her.

Gayla was interested in hearing what her mother was talking about over the telephone. So far, she had only heard things like, "That's great," and "Congratulations," but the words had been spoken with enthusiasm and there was a gleam in her mother's eyes.

After Barbara pushed the button on her cordless phone she turned to Gayla and said, "That was your Aunt Jackie. She's now a grandmother!"

Gayla smiled, "I'll bet she's so proud."

"Oh, yes, she couldn't stop talking about her new grandson. I was beginning to believe that she was rubbing it in that she is nine years younger than me and has grandchildren."

The remark ran through David as if it were a bolt of electricity. It was inevitable that the dreaded conversation would take place now. Gayla forced a weak smile to her face and placed her hand on David's knee.

"I'm sure you'll have grandchildren . . . someday," Gayla said as she turned her focus from her mother to her husband.

"Yeah," David said blankly before he forced a smile back at Gayla.

Later that night, David lay in bed staring at the ceiling; he could almost count the few remaining seconds before the imminent conversation would take place.

"David," Gayla cooed, "we need to talk about something."

David swallowed hard and squinted his eyes until they shut, looking as if he had just stubbed his toe.

"Okay, let's talk," David replied as if oblivious to the nature of the upcoming conversation.

"We've talked before about having children. What are we waiting for?"

"Well, I don't know, I suppose we could, but you know how busy our schedules are right now," David said, trying to defend the time he spent at the lab before Gayla had the chance to attack him over it.

"We could get by on your income for awhile. I'm afraid that if we keep putting it off it will never happen. We're so much more prepared for this than the average parents today."

David couldn't argue her point and he was surprised that she had not mentioned his time away from home. He'd known that at some point in the future it would become an issue. Looking back at her, he smiled as he caressed her face with the back of his hand and said, "Well, I guess we're going to have to do a few rehearsals for the conception."

Gayla returned a seductive, mischievous grin as she reached to turn off the bedside lamp.

As Diana had predicted, Trevor continued working on his massive program throughout another evening. Trevor became so involved in his work that he failed to notice the passing of midnight and the arrival of Christmas. There was no tree, no gifts, and no nativity scenes, just Trevor and his laptop computer.

David woke up to the feel of Gayla's fingertips barely touching his skin as they slid down his chest.

"Wouldn't it be nice to have the pitter patter of little feet coming in to tell us what Santa had left for them?" Gayla said as she continued the conversation from the previous night.

"Yeah," David answered with a gentle smile as he imagined the moment that Gayla spoke of. "Of course, that could be at least a couple of years before we hear that 'pitter patter.' But who knows, maybe next Christmas we will be parents."

David remembered his last Christmas with his twin as he pondered the concept of children and Christmas morning. Then he wondered about the clone. How was *he* doing this morning.

In a room without music or flashing lights, a child lay. His heart beat rapidly and his eyelids thickened. He would receive no presents today. He was alone in what he knew as the world. Alone, with one exception—that of a dark presence.

"Merry Christmas," David greeted his own mother over the telephone.

"So are you coming down to see me?" his mother asked.

"Next Christmas, I promise."

"I never hear from you anymore. Occasionally, I get to talk to Gayla, but you're always at work."

"I know, I stay pretty busy, but if you would like to come see us in a couple of months I will take as much time off as I can."

"Well, I would like a chance to see my son and it would be nice if I had grandchildren, but I guess that would be asking entirely too much."

"Actually, Gayla and I were discussing that last night. I think the time has come."

"I certainly hope so," she replied hopefully. David was her only surviving child and lately she had felt as if he had forgotten about her.

David continued his conversation with his mother as he watched Gayla and Barbara place heaps of food on the dining room table.

He finished his phone call and then walked over to the table. By now, the entire family was waiting for him to join them before they asked the blessing. He had just noticed that Gayla's younger brother Phillip and her older sister Linda had arrived while he had been talking on the phone. He noticed that Barbara had placed his drink at the opposite end of the long table from where Richard sat. He remembered that this used to be where Phillip sat. It had been a status thing, as if to say, "sitting here proves that I am one of the men of the house." He barely glanced at Phillip as he sat down.

"Naturally, my mother also inquired about when we would have children," David said quietly to Gayla.

"Hey, when you get to be our age, grandchildren are all you have left," Richard replied with a smile. Then continued almost under his breath, "Linda can't have kids, so, I guess we'll have to depend on you and Gayla for that."

Phillip slung his fork down against his plate. He was bothered by the fact that his father had not accepted his sexual preference and didn't want to be provoked any further. He looked at his mother and shook his head,

"Let me know when I'll be accepted again," Phillip stated coldly before rising and walking out the door.

Barbara looked at Richard in dismay,

"Why did you have to make that remark?"

"Hey, it's the truth. I can't help it if queers can't have kids. I certainly didn't want him to turn out gay and I'm trying to deal with it. But I know that he isn't going to have any children if he continues with *that* life style," Richard replied angrily. "I shouldn't have to worry about every little thing I say offending him. He needs to be a real man and get over it."

Dinner continued quieter than it had began. The tension was thicker than the gravy that David smothered his potatoes with. No one was going to rush after Phillip. Barbara and Gayla wished that he hadn't left, but they didn't want to continue to make today an unpleasant experience. David looked forward to going back to Arizona and getting back to his less stressful, normal life.

The next few days had gone by without mention of Phillip or his lifestyle. Gayla had made the best of her time with her parents before she had to return to Arizona.

"Are you and Mom going to come to Arizona to see us next Christmas?" Gayla asked her father as she stretched her arms around him to hug him good-bye.

"On one condition, if I have a grandson or granddaughter. If I do, then we'll be there. If not, you have to come to Vermont to see us. Deal?" Richard replied.

"It sounds like a deal," Gayla said with a smile.

An announcement over the intercom for boarding signaled the end of her time with her parents. Two hugs and a handshake later, the younger couple grabbed their luggage and dashed away.

Chapter 4

The plane had not yet landed, when David began to anticipate the metamorphosis of his clone while he was on the other side of the country. What would the fetus of a thirty-two-year-old man look like? He stretched his arm upward and behind Gayla's neck, pulling her close to him. Despite all the knowledge he had lost from his forced vacation, she was worth it. The flame had been rekindled.

"I just need to run to the lab for a few minutes to check on things and then I'll come right back home." David whispered as though he were asking permission.

She smiled and nodded in approval. She knew he was dying to get back to the lab. He had spent the last nine days with her without mention of the place. The compromise seemed acceptable.

"I'll be waiting," replied Gayla with a seductive wink.

The amniotic fluid level in the tank was dangerously low. The clone had grown far more than David had estimated. A fully formed man lay in the shallow tank covered in a thick, milky slime.

David unlocked the door to the laboratory and rushed to his "conception room." He began to panic when he saw the clone with such a low food supply. How could he have known that the clone would have grown so fast? David heated the last of his amniotic fluid supply to body temperature and watched carefully for any sign of life.

The clone kicked!

This was more than he expected. The force of the blow nearly cracked the large sturdy container. He would be fine until morning, hopefully. David knew that he would need to be in as early as possible. As fast as the clone had grown so far, he could be "born" by lunchtime tomorrow.

Gayla lay in bed waiting for David. Two hours had passed. Finally, she heard David's car pull into the driveway.

David walked into the room with a sly smile. "I'm not in the mood any more." Gayla spoke as though she were trying to prevent global warming.

"I had things to do. I needed to do a quick inventory of the equipment since no one had been there in over a week," David explained, confident that he would not get caught in this lie.

"Then why didn't you say from the beginning that you would be gone for two hours?" she questioned bitterly.

David threw his hands in the air. "I give up. There's no pleasing you."

Gayla reconsidered. He had given her his undivided attention for the past nine days, and maybe she was overreacting. "Well, I'm glad you are home now and that's what counts," she said as she placed her hand on the back of his shoulder.

David was confused by her sudden change of tone but decided to leave well enough alone. "Good night," she cooed as she kissed his cheek.

"Good night," he replied as he attempted to adjust to her latest mood.

While Gayla slept soundly beside him, David lay on his back staring at the ceiling pondering the fate of his clone. He also pondered the amount of progress that Trevor had made on his project. Trevor's invention, if successful, would allow David to clone his own mind for Darryl. This recreation of his twin would be virtually undetectable to anyone excluding himself and his man made twin. The possible applications of these two projects could have an infinite amount of uses. One could raise an army of genetically enhanced, highly skilled warriors in less than a year. It was a concept that could bring him wealth without limits if the Department of Defense became interested. He glanced over at Gayla; even when she slept, she was remarkably beautiful. Then, deep within the more perverse areas of his mind he considered cloning beautiful women and giving them the mind of a completely subservient woman. The thought merely flashed through his mind before he dispelled it, but nevertheless, the thought had passed through his mind. It would be a restless night only to be followed with a busy morning.

Patiently, David watched as the clone began to thrash about. Was it time? Natural childbirth was much easier, in that it had clear distinct signs that the moment had arrived. Here, David would have to guess. Not a popular concept for this scientist; he preferred to work with proof. If he removed the clone from the tank too early, could he save him? The answers would be discovered soon.

David reached under the edge of the tank and released the valve that had kept the amniotic fluid from spilling into the lower tank during the three-month experiment.

The clone wiggled as David reached inside the tank, clearing the breathing way with his gloved hand. The clone cried as if he were an infant. David tried to stand the clone up.

"Oh yeah, no sense of balance yet," he uttered in a panicked, yet loving voice. As David began wiping the thick, gooey mucus away with moist towels, he reached for the warm milk he had brought in for the occasion. "Hungry?" he asked, as he presented the bottle to the thirsty lips of his clone.

Unlike a normal infant, this "newborn" guzzled down half a gallon of milk before he was satisfied. After a grueling five hours, the clone had been cleaned and fed, and was ready to take a nap.

David had tried to move the clone out of the tank, but he was extremely heavy. After putting the clone into a fireman's carry position, he stumbled across the room to place him onto a cot. "Whew!" David gasped for breath, as he laid Babyzilla onto the cot. Now, many of David's questions had been answered. That task being completed the next thing to think about was getting through the night. Gayla would surely grow suspicious if David spent the night at the lab for two or three consecutive days. Taking the man-child home was not an acceptable option. *Now what?*

"Oh my God, what have I done?" David declared with a newfound sobriety. He looked carefully at the clone. His hair was shorter and softer; his skin was also softer with soft blonde fuzz in other areas where David's hair was thicker, darker and coarser. David stepped back and gazed at his creation.

"I guess I'll call you Darryl," David said quietly. "I love you." And it was true—David did love Darryl, but not as a brother, more as a newborn son.

Gayla sat quietly after a stressful day at work. She was actually happy that David was not home yet. She wondered if David could ever have to deal with pressure on *his* job. She had to deal with teenagers threatening to commit suicide; what kind of life or death situations did David ever have to deal with, yet he acted as though *his* work could change the world. She knew he would be home eventually; she just had to get used to it. A smile came to her face when she heard the phone ring; she knew it would be David with some excuse as to why he would be late. She answered the phone and David began to explain

"Honey, I'll be stuck here really late tonight . . ."

"It's okay," she interjected.

Relieved, David decided to finish his thoughts with, "Thanks for understanding." A wail pierced the air throughout the lab, as Darryl became frustrated.

"What was that?" Gayla exclaimed.

"Oh, it's the TV. I had to have something to break the silence," he fibbed.

"Try the radio. It's a bit more relaxing than the sci-fi channel."

David said a quick good bye, rushed to Darryl's side, grabbed Darryl's hands, and sat him up on the table, trying to teach him to balance himself. There was no one who would even attempt to teach a newborn how to sit up within six hours of his birth. However, given his intellectual level, Darryl was an exceptional learner. Even so, unfortunately David was entirely dependent upon an extraordinary learning curve on Darryl's part. If he left Darryl unattended throughout the night, what would happen? Any decent parent wouldn't leave a baby alone over night and just 'hope for the best.' But David was not his *Father* . . . well, not technically. "I should have put more thought into *this* date," David said, regretfully. Before he prepared to leave, David removed all sharp objects from the room. He would get safety plugs for the electrical outlets when he went to the store.

As Darryl began to doze again, David locked the door to the "conception room," which would henceforth be known as the nursery from the outside.

David scurried to the store and grabbed several packs of adult diapers, four gallons of milk, safety plugs, and a variety of snacks. Nearing the check out register, he felt awkward about his purchase. Months ago, when he had bought the first pack of diapers, he had also purchased a bottle of Geritol, as if to say,

"They're not for me." Now, with this combination, it was slightly more embarrassing. No matter, it had to be done.

Upon his return to the laboratory, David quickly finished "baby proofing" the room. *Maybe*, he thought, *it's too soon to bother with that*, but then again, he had already learned to sit up. How fast could he learn to crawl?

Having awakened when David had entered the room, Darryl watched David intently as he moved around securing the drawers of the cabinets. Before securing the last drawer, David pulled a pair of his sweats out of the drawer and dressed Darryl warmly for the night. The experience reminded David of his college days when his friends would drink themselves to idiocy.

Finished, David could go home and rest. He kissed Darryl on the forehead and said goodnight. He started to turn off the lights as usual, but decided against it. Looking back into Darryl's innocent eyes, David felt horrible about leaving. As the door closed, Darryl's cries only amplified the emotion.

Alone, or so it appeared to Darryl's weak eyes, David's comforting presence had left, only to be replaced by a terrifyingly different presence.

Trevor had not taken full advantage of his opportunity to rest during the holidays. Instead he had continued to work feverishly on expanding the vocabulary of the program that associated the brain signals into recognizable words or thoughts and emotions. By the time the lab reopened, he was ready to press forth and with continued progress. He couldn't complain about the time taken to gain such information; he had never dreamed that this amount of data could be collected in only a few months. He had expected less from years of work.

He contemplated what David could have possibly achieved in the past three months that could change the world as his creation would. Trevor and David had always had an unspoken "one-up" relationship, regardless of their vastly different scientific fields. Each felt compelled to be better than the other.

An elderly woman lay back in a chair reminiscing about her second husband. While she explained the first time she met him to the technician by her side, Trevor recorded an enormous variety of brain signals. The signals varied in frequency, amplitude, and period. Trevor realized it would be challenging to extract any valuable information from these signals. As the elderly lady finished her story, Trevor walked into the room, signaling to Diana that the experiment was concluded.

"Dr. Martinez and . . . excuse me," Trevor apologized and corrected himself. "Dr. Green and I would like to thank you for your participation, Mrs. Boyster. You have been a great help to us, but we will not need you for the rest of the week as originally scheduled. You will still receive the full amount of money for your cooperation."

The old woman smiled kindly and nodded before exiting the lab.

As the door closed behind her, Diana turned to Trevor and replied to his earlier remark, "Actually, it is Dr. Martinez," she cooed. "Jack and I divorced over two years ago. We still get along though we never had children, so we didn't have much to disagree on after we decided that we weren't as perfect for each other as we first thought."

Pleasantly surprised at this revelation, Trevor asked, "So are you still single?"

"Very," replied Diana with a sly, yet lonely smile. "I thought about asking you what you were doing for the holidays, but when I went by your office I saw you working so hard that you didn't even notice I was there. I guess you could say that was my answer. I *know* you Trevor, you still don't take any time off, do you?"

Trevor lowered his head, listening to the truth in Diana's words, reminding him of why she had left years ago.

"I would for you," he pleaded.

Diana did admire Trevor. He was an incredible scientist, and undeniably a genius. She had wondered an infinite number of times what her life would have been like if they could have worked through their differences.

"You've always been ambitious. That's one of the things that attracted me to you. But ambition was the wedge you drove between us. You love your work so much that you don't take the time to love anything or *anyone* else. When that old lady was telling me stories about her past, I was jealous. When I'm seventy-six years old, I want to remember a good life. I don't want my past to sound like a job interview. We're just too different, Trevor."

Diana tried to retain her composure. She hoped she wouldn't regret this opportunity to make amends on the past. Still, some sort of closure was needed.

Trevor took a deep breath. He never thought Diana could possibly give him a good reason for the abrupt end of their relationship. Now, he realized that he could have been *partly* to blame, also. Her words were filled with both truth and passion. Briefly reflecting on his past, Trevor tried to remember his last birthday. There was no party; he didn't take the day off. *I worked in the lab all day, by myself,* he remembered remorsefully. *Perhaps she's completely right.*

"I have time now," he spoke as if he had just been beaten. He considered his earlier plans of how he would work through the night trying to decipher the old lady's thoughts. His work could change the entire course of life for millions of people. Still, tonight might be his last chance to change the course of his own.

With a doubting smile, Diana probed, "Time to keep me from eating alone tonight?"

"Yes, and dessert too, if you eat fast," Trevor joked, trying to lighten the mood.

Instinctively frightened, Darryl needed help. *Where did that man go? Is he ever coming back?* Darryl kicked and thrashed frantically trying to get to the door. If he could just make it to the door, surely David would still be there to keep him safe. With all his energy, Darryl continued to thrash about. Finally, he was able to roll over, falling off the small cot and bringing it down on top of himself. Squirming underneath, Darryl learned to maneuver from beneath the cot. He continued his journey towards the door in a belly crawl fashion. Once there, he reached up, grasping the knob and trying to pull himself up. Still, the threatening presence loomed all over the room. Darryl continued wailing, waiting for David to come back and rescue him. David would not come to his aid. Five hours later, Darryl would pass out from a combination of exhaustion and dehydration from the endless crying.

Chapter 5

The song of a blue jay woke Trevor from his peaceful sleep. Trevor sat up in his bed remembering that he had abandoned his project the night before. While he was decades ahead of schedule, as far as his peers were concerned, he was now behind according to his own schedule. Without a second thought, he sprang out of bed and began to prepare for another busy day.

Once back at the lab, he began his seemingly endless task, comparing each signal to those already collected and associated with various vocabulary words. The most challenging portion of the entire experiment was near. To deduce actual memories from these overlapping groups of signals would require the removal of all spoken words. He rewound the videotape from the interview with the elderly woman and watched, carefully recording her body movements. Movement also required thought, subconscious or not, it would still create a signal and these must be extracted as well, he concluded.

As Trevor reached for the phone, he decided that his

dismissal of Mrs. Boyster had been a bit premature. In his haste he had neglected to consider all these possibilities. He knew that Dr. Kang, the lab director, would not be pleased with the additional expense, but he had to have Mrs. Boyster return to the lab for further observation, regardless of cost. "I need you to contact Mrs. Boyster and have her return to the lab. Offer her another thousand dollars if necessary," Trevor told the receptionist in no uncertain terms.

Eerie quietness filled the Phoenix laboratory as David dashed across the floor. When the door opened, Darryl fell to the floor unconscious. After checking for vital signs, David retrieved some water and began to revive his creation. "How could I do this to you?" David whimpered, feeling ashamed of his neglectfulness. Being careful not to drown the unconscious clone, David dripped the water into Darryl's mouth. As Darryl's eye began to twitch, David breathed a sigh of relief.

After Darryl became hydrated, David unlocked and opened the drawers containing his research papers. Looking at the modified chromosomes, David considered that the chromosome affecting his learning ability could have been enhanced more than he had intended. *It's natural for some animals to walk on their first day after being born,* David attempted to comfort himself.

"Probably won't be long until you're smarter than I am," David told the enormous infant.

Darryl crawled toward David, happy to see that he had not permanently vanished. He grasped David's arm tightly, as if to say, "Don't leave me again." His fear had eased. The threatening presence was gone again now that David had returned.

David looked deeply into Darryl's eyes. He saw the innocence that he knew he had lost with the passage of time.

"What makes the world such a harsh place?" David asked philosophically. "I only wish I could be a better role model." David continued, still feeling guilty about the abandonment.

"Raise your right hand, Mrs. Boyster." Trevor said as he monitored the results. "Wave your left hand." He motioned.

Recording these basic movements kept Trevor busy for another three hours. He studied every twitch of her finger, every blink of her eye until at last he again concluded that the testing was complete.

"I deeply apologize for having to call you back. I was a little distracted yesterday," he said, glancing at Diana and remembering the main reason for his distraction. "I hope we do not have to trouble you again."

As Diana led the old lady away, Trevor pondered Diana's words regarding the woman's youthful memories.

"When this project is complete, I'll give you a life full of memories," Trevor said under his breath, aware that she wouldn't hear his vow.

Trevor turned and gathered the printouts from the latest study. He had work to do. The sooner this was over, the sooner he could spend more time with Diana, he reminded himself.

David assembled a crude walker, similar to one used by an elderly or otherwise disabled person.

"Here," he motioned to Darryl.

He lifted Darryl up by his arms, placing his hands on the horizontal bar and bracing his knees. The results were not surprising for David. He had expected nothing less than almost instantaneous success.

Within a matter of fifteen minutes Darryl began clomping the contraption in front of himself and moving around the room almost as fast as David.

David ran in front of him, counting from one to ten repeatedly, occasionally breaking the monotony with the alphabet song.

David already worried about the upcoming night. He couldn't neglect Darryl again, even though he knew Gayla wouldn't be happy when he announced that he was going to go back to spend the night at the lab. Admittedly, it would sound suspicious. He couldn't blame her for being frustrated.

"I wish I could just let her know about you," he said softly to Darryl.

"Why in hell do you need to spend the night at the lab?" Gayla exclaimed accusingly. "Why don't you just come right out and say it David? Who is the little bitch? Am I not good enough for you anymore?"

Perhaps she's taking it better than I expected, David reasoned. "Look, you can call me every half hour if it will make you feel better. I just have things to take care of throughout the night," David replied calmly and innocently.

Gayla grew no less suspicious hearing his weak explanation. "Things to take care of throughout the night," she dwelt. "Fine. And I *will* call every half hour."

"Great!" David glowed with a smile as he slipped a quick kiss to her numb cheek and rushed back out the door.

Darryl had crawled to the walker and pulled himself upward. It was back! As he scanned the room in sheer terror, Darryl was unable to determine the exact nature of the presence in the room. He could not comprehend the concept of evil but his instinct told him to flee. As he backed the walker near the door, he grasped the knob as he had seen David do several times during the day. The door still would not open. He slammed against the door harder and harder, to no avail; he was trapped. Again, David had abandoned him in his time of need.

The voices . . . from where were they coming? Darryl walked to the counter where David had placed the television. He pushed the button that David had shown him would turn the device on and off. The television was now off, but the voices continued. Darryl looked at the TV with confusion. Finally, he leaned against the counter and swung his walker with all his might. The TV burst into sheets of flame, sparks, and smoke. Darryl seemed convinced that he had set himself free of the dark force in the room. He stepped back from the smoldering debris. His superior intellect caused him to question the connection with this device and the presence in the room the night before. The TV wasn't in the room until earlier today. Darryl walked to the corner nearest the door and lay down in a fetal position hoping that David would come back soon.

David unlocked the door and entered the room. Darryl scrambled to be near him as he entered, clinging tightly, afraid that he would leave again if he let go.

When David saw the smashed TV, his mind filled with thoughts as to what sort of behavioral problems that Darryl might have. Should he discipline him? This was beyond logic.

"Darryl!" he pointed to the smoldering television set. "Why did you do that?" Darryl had to learn that this type of behavior was unacceptable even if there were no consequences.

Darryl looked back with innocent eyes. He wanted to defend himself but lacked the ability to communicate his thoughts in a way that David would understand.

Pile after pile of papers surrounded the room that Trevor had called home for the past three months. He had deciphered a vast vocabulary, most major muscle movements, and vague mental pictures of objects. He paused momentarily from his work to envision scenes from gothic horror movies where two people had several wires running from their heads while strapped down to tables. Was he a mad scientist? A small grin seeped across his face as he found a slight degree of humor in his comparison. Would he ever be able to find a volunteer, better still, two volunteers for such bizarre research tactics? Years ago it was fantasy, now it was becoming reality.

With a sigh of utter exhaustion, Trevor decided to look for other programmers he could hire. This was more work than even he could do alone. After all, he would make a fortune from the invention. If not, he had invested his money well; he no longer worked for the sake of more wealth, but for the only love he had known since Diana.

Oh yes, and then we have Diana, Trevor's mind drifted even further. *I can have more time to spend with Diana if I hire additional programmers,* he concluded. Satisfied with his work for the night, Trevor put all the charts, graphs, and notes to the side.

"I'm through for now," he whispered to himself.

As she finished her first "check-up" call of the night, Gayla grabbed her cellular phone and scurried out the door. Future calls would be made from her cell phone as she staked out the laboratory parking lot. She was as sure that she would catch David in whatever scheme he was trying to pull off as she was that the scheme existed.

Five hours and ten phone calls later, Gayla began to grow drowsy. She had not seen anyone enter or exit the lab. His car was parked out front. What was he doing? She wondered. She had been reluctant to present herself before the "evidence" had arrived, as she couldn't prove anything. *Is she in there now?* Her temper kindled. At last, her curiosity betrayed her.

Gayla approached the lab quietly and inconspicuously. The main door to the lab was locked; not a problem, for she had expected as much. She retrieved her set of David's emergency keys, those that he had given her in case he locked his own away. Opening the door as quietly as possible, she crept into the lab. She didn't see David anywhere. *Is he really even here or did he have the phones forwarded?* Suspicions grew hotter as she listened carefully. She heard David's voice. *He's talking to someone in the next room, but who? He said he would be working alone.*

Three computer programmers listened intently to Trevor's

instructions. Each man realized that this would be a lengthy and tedious job. Trevor concluded his conference with the eager, if not overwhelmed programmers and gazed at Diana.

"I told you I would make more time for you," he said with a loving smile. "But . . . I do have some bad news," he added.

Somehow, Diana was prepared for the omnipresent "but" that Trevor was sure to continue.

"Next week I will go back to Phoenix for another couple of weeks. After that, I will request a permanent reassignment back to here. I'll call you two or three times each week. I won't disappoint you again," he promised.

With cat-like stealth, Gayla approached the door to the nursery. As she reached for the knob, the door opened, pushing her hand back.

David leaped with fright. No one else was supposed to be in the laboratory. More importantly, it was Gayla. What was she doing here? She couldn't find out about Darryl. She was certain that cloning would lead to too many complications and had previously expressed her concerns on the matter.

David stood in the doorway blocking her passage.

"Let me in," she demanded.

"Honey, wait . . . I don't know how you're going to react to this."

"We'll find out, won't we?" She slipped past him and burst into the room. To her surprise, there was no gorgeous woman in the room. She noticed an adult-sized man wearing a diaper and playing with simple toys in the corner. His back was turned and she could not see his face. Looking around the room she noticed the adult diapers on the counter. David would make the most of her partial discovery.

"Please, come out here," David begged as he tugged at Gayla's arm. She followed anticipating David's explanation.

"He has Down's syndrome." David explained falsely. "I didn't want you to know because I knew you would be worried about me. I've been working with chromosome twelve lately and I'm trying to prevent the disease. I realize that I've been spending too much time at work lately, but I needed to complete my projects so I could take you on a vacation to our condo in Florida. I had intended to be done with this by now, but the vacation to Vermont threw my schedule off. I'm sorry that I have seemed so sneaky lately. I just wanted to surprise you."

Satisfied with his answer, she began to feel guilty about her baseless accusations. David had been planning a romantic vacation and she had just ruined her own future surprise. "You'd think I would be a little more rational, given my line of work, huh?" she was ashamed of her distrusting actions. David *had* been neglecting her, but why? He was attempting to improve the lives of multitudes of people. Those same people she tried to help after the fact. Conversely, David was *really* the one who would make *permanent* changes for future generations with mental problems. She had been selfish.

"I'm sorry. Go ahead and do whatever you need to do. I thought you had lost interest in spending time with me." Gayla gave David a gentle kiss. "I've got to get some sleep," she whispered drowsily.

After Gayla left, his words hit him like a guillotine. "Two weeks! What am I going to do about you for two weeks?" David said as he looked pathetically in Darryl's direction.

"Two weeks," Darryl repeated.

"Wow, you're talking," David exclaimed with a proud sense of joy as he moved closer to Darryl. His worries had given way in the excitement of Darryl's progress. *Maybe*, David reconsidered his dilemma, *he'll be capable of taking care of himself by then.*

Chapter 6

The program was complete. Trevor had numerous bugs to work out now, but the actual program was completed within four days of hiring the other programmers. They had worked ridiculous hours on the project and Trevor had been impressed by their dedication. After a good night's sleep he would go back to the laboratory and begin his final touches, ensuring total perfection mere hours before his discovery would make world wide news. *I could be awarded the Nobel Prize this year.* He daydreamed as the airliner's wheels made contact with the Phoenix airstrip.

Long hours had made David grow weary. Even though Gayla's misinterpretation of the truth had bought David a vast amount of time and understanding, the time had come for Darryl to spend the night alone again. Darryl had made significant progress. Even so, he had a limited vocabulary and was unable to express most of his thoughts adequately.

David explained to Darryl that he would be going away for the night.

Darryl expressed his disapproval by pouting.

David grew frustrated. He needed the break. A full night of sleep in a comfortable bed had almost escaped his memory. He couldn't stay here forever, and Darryl would need to adjust if David were to take Gayla on the poorly conceived yet promised vacation.

The telephone rang again. This time he could tell Gayla that he would be coming home tonight. Deep down, he understood that even her newfound patience would be growing thin. Much to his surprise, the voice on the other end of the connection was not that of Gayla, but Trevor.

"Hey, I'm back in town. I'll be coming in tomorrow. Wait till you see what I've done now," Trevor boasted.

"That's great. When will you be coming in?" David casually inquired.

"Probably around eight," he replied.

"Okay. I look forward to seeing what kind of progress you've made. I'll see you then."

This news fell entirely short of pleasing David; it meant that he would be getting up early again to rush in, hide Darryl, and restore the room to it's usual look.

"Goodnight, Darryl." David whispered softly.

"Goodnight," replied Darryl in his pouting, childish tone.

David turned half the lights off and locked the building for the night.

The room was soundless and motionless. Darryl sat alone. He had lost interest in the pile of toys that had occupied his attention for the past few days. *Where is David going? Why can't I ever leave?* Darryl questioned the nature of his relationship to David. A memory from a television show—a western—flashed through Darryl's mind. It seemed peculiar, nothing like this room that Darryl knew as home. *Is there more out there? How much more?*

Darryl stood up and looked in the mirror; he looked to the side, cutting his eyes so that he could admire his profile. He looked just like David. *Do all people look the same? The people on the TV all looked different.* His hair had grown coarser, like

David's, but his face was getting hairy. *How does David keep his face from getting hairy?* So many more questions remained unanswered.

Darryl's questions lost importance as he felt the threatening presence re-enter the room. *How? The TV is gone!* The presence, however, seemed less frightening now. It had not brought any harm to him yet. David was gone, period. Crying for him had never helped before. *Why worry about it*, he decided.

The room was soundless and motionless.

Gayla remarked, "I'm glad to see you again even if it is for only a few minutes."

"Actually, I'll be here for the entire night," David defended his position. He held her tightly. "Just two more weeks, believe me. I need the break too."

The night went too quickly. For the first time in months, David slept until the alarm went off. He would have pressed the snooze button, but he had to arrive at the lab at least a few minutes before Trevor. He rushed out of bed and began his preparations for the day.

"I should be back tonight," David announced to his wife, hoping that he wouldn't regret the statement.

After a quick peck on the cheek, David continued his hasty exit.

The night had been uneventful for Darryl, and he wished this strange presence had a face. It had kept him from being alone throughout the night, and that was a lot more than David had accomplished.

David raced through the lab removing and hiding all signs of Darryl's existence.

"We're going to play a game called hide and seek," David

explained to Darryl. "While someone else is in the lab, I need you to hide and hopefully they won't find you," he continued as he led Darryl to the storage room. "I'll help you find a place to hide this time."

Trevor entered the lab as David exited the storage room.

Rambo nibbled nervously on the edge of a sunflower seed as he peered through the glass at the two humans that occupied the room outside his tiny cage.

The two men discussed their latest findings.

David admitted, "Well, it certainly sounds like you've beaten me this time. I can't top this." *Not legally,* he thought to himself.

"I'll be in and out of here for most of the day. When I'm finished with the program, I'll be relocating to Dallas on a permanent basis. I ran into an old friend back there and she has convinced me that the move would be a good opportunity," explained Trevor, relishing another of his many recent successes.

"I see. Well, congratulations!"

Not wanting to make light of Trevor's moment, but needing to move onto matters that *did* concern himself, he inquired, "Are you going to be needing access to the observatory room? I was about to place some extremely light sensitive cultures in the room and lock it up, to prevent any accidental exposure."

"No, I'm through. In fact, I'm going to be removing most of my personal items from my office today," Trevor replied.

As Trevor went to his car to retrieve a box of papers, David raced to the storage room to relocate Darryl to the observatory room.

Seeing the different rooms had fascinated Darryl. He now realized that the lab was a much larger place than he had thought. *Which one of the places does David call home?* Darryl wondered. The observatory room was longer and narrower than his old room.

"This is where I'll need you to stay for awhile," David

informed him. "You can even watch me and the other guy while we work. It's only temporary though."

David was comfortable with this arrangement. Darryl could see him through the one-way mirror, while Trevor could not see into the room.

The day seemed to go on without end for David. He wanted to go home early tonight to finish getting caught up on the rest he had been cheated out of lately, but Trevor continued working until the latter hours of the evening. Finally, Trevor was through with his work.

"Now it's perfect," he bragged. "I think I'll come in and clean out the rest of my belongings tomorrow. Maybe I can have everything packed and be on my way to Texas by the end of this week. It's been a pleasure, Dave," Trevor said as he reached out to shake David's hand.

David grasped his counterpart's hand. "Hey, its not like I won't be seeing you again. I'll be here to help you clean out your things tomorrow," David replied.

"Just in case . . ." Trevor said gallantly.

David glanced at Rambo's cage. "Can I keep Rambo? He and I have become attached to each other while you were away."

"Sure. I intend to be spending less time at the lab. This mouse is quite symbolic for me though," Trevor continued.

"I know what you mean," David said, as he considered the mouse's significance to himself.

Before leaving, David stepped in to check on Darryl.

"Do you want me to get you another TV tomorrow? You're not going to destroy another one are you?"

Darryl didn't fully understand what David was asking so he just stared at him blankly. David gathered the trash from Darryl's lunch and brought him some more food.

"Next week I'll take you out to see the world, Okay?"

"Okay."

"Here. I ordered pizza earlier. I'm sorry that it got cold

while I was waiting for Trevor to leave."

"Why can't anybody see me?" Darryl inquired as to the nature of his imprisonment.

David tried to explain honestly at a level that Darryl could fully comprehend. "Because I created you, and that's illegal. If someone sees you I could get in trouble. After you have learned how to take care of yourself, though, I'll be introducing you as my twin brother. It won't be long until you can meet lots of people and go lots of places."

David moved the cot into the room and tried to make the observatory as comfortable as possible for Darryl. *Food, drink, bed.* David made sure that Darryl had everything he would need to make it through another night without him. While he changed Darryl's diaper, he determined his next objective, potty training.

David was confident that everything was in place as he said goodnight to Darryl and completed the lock-up of the laboratory.

Gayla smiled as David walked in the door.

"I was beginning to think you had decided not to show up tonight."

"Trevor's leaving tomorrow and we had some catching up to do." It was a bit of an exaggeration, but truer than most of what he had told her lately. "Speaking of leaving. How do you feel about leaving later this week, instead of next week?" David was comfortable with Darryl's progress. He estimated potty training would take a single day at his supernatural learning rate.

"Wow! That's unusual for you. I was expecting you to postpone it. I can have my secretary reschedule all my appointments if you think you can finish up in time." She was eager to leave before some unforeseen event disrupted the trip altogether.

At the lab, David had secured all areas well with one

exception. The door to the observatory had failed to lock when David departed.

Darryl was not alone in the room. A far darker presence had joined him. This was usual, and almost expected by Darryl. He made himself comfortable and babbled to himself until he fell into a deep sleep.

David woke in the middle of the night sweating profusely. It was the end of January and far from hot in the room. He had had a nightmare about Darryl killing someone. David knew that this dream was meaningless. Darryl had the uncorrupted mind of a toddler. The dream was no less disturbing, however. He began to toss and turn, awaiting the horrid thought to pass.

Chapter 7

Darryl's eyes snapped open. He looked at his hands. Though his body remained physically free, his mind was oppressed, being held captive by the dark and threatening presence that had shared his quarters in David's absence. The dark presence had a name, Hephanaethus, an evil spirit, or more accurately, a demon.

Dawn split the darkness of the winter morning sky. Trevor packed his few belongings in his modest apartment. He had lived a squalid lifestyle of only bare necessities. Despite his healthy bank account, he didn't have time to enjoy many luxuries and therefore hadn't bothered acquiring them. Besides, it made packing a quick and painless task for the bachelor.

After loading his belongings into his car, he drove to the lab to collect his research papers and a few precious knick-knacks related to his past discoveries. He had it all planned. After removing his possessions from the lab, he would turn his key into the landlord and be back in Dallas by nightfall. Diana would be surprised.

I'll be homeless. I'll have to stay at her place for awhile, Trevor schemed.

Trevor unlocked the doors to the laboratory for the last time. He strolled across the floor in sheer glee. Suddenly he noticed the door to the observatory standing wide open. As he walked around the corner, he saw Hephanaethus holding a mirror over a sink and shaving with a straight razor. "Hey Dave, I thought you said that you were going to lock up the observ . . ." he paused with confusion when he saw the wet clumps of hair in the sink. He knew that David had been clean-shaven the day before.

Without the utterance of a single word, Hephanaethus brought the razor around in a single motion and sliced through Trevor's throat, nearly decapitating the man.

As Trevor's blood flooded his own lungs, two thoughts waged war for his consideration. One was about Diana and the other was about the afterlife. Who this man that resembled David was, was irrelevant and wouldn't matter in a few short moments. Trevor didn't waste his precious time debating the issue. In his dying thought he tied his emotions together into a single question,

If there is an afterlife, will I get a chance to see Diana one last time?

David kissed Gayla lovingly before he walked out the door. "I don't know when I'll get home. It's probably gonna be a rough day," David told her, ignorant as to what he would be faced with.

Upon his arrival, David noticed that Trevor had already arrived. *I sure hope Darryl stays quiet so Trevor doesn't find out about him,* David thought to himself.

The air had a vaguely familiar smell to it, bearing a sharp contrast to the typical clinical smell of the lab. Upon seeing the observatory door opened, David became paralyzed with fear. No matter what, David was surely going to have some explaining to do. His pace accelerated into a sprint until he saw Darryl hunched over Trevor's body.

"Oh, God, no! What have you done, Darryl? You've killed him . . . he's dead!"

David's knees weakened with fear. David knelt down to raise Trevor up to check his vital signs. As he lifted on Trevor's shoulder, his head plunged back revealing how large the gash really was. His head would have fallen off had it not been for two muscles in the back of his neck.

"I didn't want anyone to find out about me. I didn't want you to get into any trouble," Darryl explained through a teary and still innocent gaze.

David was speechless, his mind flooded with questions that he was too distraught to form into words that Darryl might or might not understand. David ran to the door, making sure it was locked. He certainly could not afford to have any unexpected visitors this time.

He couldn't bring Trevor back. That much he could take out of the equation. The best possible solution from this point was to cause an explosion that would destroy the entire lab and hopefully any incriminating evidence, which would reveal David's folly along with it.

David looked at Darryl. What about Darryl? Would it be safe to hide Darryl elsewhere? Did he even realize what he had done?

He couldn't just let him die in the explosion. It would be like killing a child. That would be worse than any punishment he could receive for Trevor's death. If he hid Darryl, where could he hide him? Furthermore, would he kill again? "What have I done!" David screamed as he looked upwards tugging his hair towards the back of his scalp.

After David scrambled through piles of documents that would otherwise be forever lost, he sorted through a variety of chemicals.

Looking onward, Darryl inquired, "What are you doing?"

David replied in a disparaged voice. "I'm going to destroy the lab. I'll have to hide you out in this little place south of the border for awhile, but I'll be back for you in a couple of weeks."

David himself wondered how much truth was in the statement he had pulled out of thin air.

Hephanaethus would not sit idly by while the foolish mortal destroyed both the lab and the much-needed ingredients for Hephanaethus' future plans. He had yet to benefit from Trevor's work. He stood up and approached David quietly. He grasped David's shoulder and spun him around to face him. With lightning speed, he jutted his open hand upward, clinching David's jaws between his abnormally powerful fingers and pinned him firmly against the wall.

"That's unacceptable," Hephanaethus announced.

David's mind again numbed with fear, but this time for his own life.

What has happened to Darryl? "Wait . . . what's wrong, Darryl? What's unacceptable?"

"My name is not Darryl, it's Hephanaethus, you incompetent idiot. I don't shit my pants and I know far more than you could ever teach me, *brother.* I have spent six millennia waiting for imbeciles like you to make use of the knowledge I delivered to your dense minds."

A sudden epiphany hit David as if a mountain had crumbled on top of him. True enough, he was no longer dealing with an uneducated child-like clone. This was a terrifyingly different situation.

Hephanaethus reached towards the counter for the hypodermic needle he had prepared as he had premeditated this moment.

David felt the sharp needle pierce his skin. The fluid seared deep into his deltoid muscle, as the colors of the surrounding room faded. Suddenly, all was dark.

"Prepare to reschedule my appointments, Jessica," Gayla told her receptionist. "I believe we'll be leaving for Florida some time this week. Nothing is confirmed yet. I just need you to help me plan in case our schedule does change."

"I wish I could afford to be that spontaneous," the receptionist replied jealously.

"It comes with a different kind of cost," Gayla answered. "I'll let you know as soon as I find out when were leaving."

As Hephanaethus looked at Trevor's corpse, he formulated his next move. He needed some place to store the cloning tank and supplies before the laboratory was to be destroyed. After an instantaneous debate with his logic, he decided against using Trevor's apartment for the storage of his newly acquired gadgets. *The police may investigate after they discover the body,* he concluded.

He stacked two large tubs, one inside the other, and flipped them upside down on top of Trevor's car and secured them with elastic cords. He was somewhat irritated to find all of Trevor's belongings packed tightly within the vehicle. *Really, now. How inconsiderate*, he thought to himself, as he jerked the contents from the car and slung them through the laboratory doorway.

Money, he thought. *I'd better go by the bank.* Hephanaethus chose not to use David's credit cards because he didn't want any connections with the name after David's disposal.

Proceeding calmly into the bank, Hephanaethus eyed the teller as he slipped her the account number and David's driver's license. "I would like to withdraw four thousand dollars," he said casually. As the teller took the identification and looked up the account balance, Hephanaethus considered, *It's not as fun as robbing the bank, but I am a bit rushed.*

She glanced back with a friendly smile as she slid the identification and bankcard back across the counter. "Large bills, Mr. Brooks?"

"This is absolutely pointless!" boiled Jim Turner. "Pointless and *ridiculous*," he emphasized. He glared at the team of other scientists around him and before returning his gaze to the dish of headless tadpoles on the counter between them. "Just what do you hope to accomplish here, Dr. Trader?" Jim ended his furious explosion looking for an acceptable reason for the wasted time.

"We could clone organs from headless, brainless bodies, Dr. Turner, don't you see?" the man argued as though it were the perfect solution.

Brainless, thought Jim. *Trader is the only one here that is brainless.* Looking around the room, Jim felt different than he had with David Brooks and Trevor Williams. *Those men were true scientists; these people discredit the title by even referring to themselves as scientists*, he reflected quietly.

"I'm telling you that there *has to be* a better way. If we can copy an organ cell by cell, then, and only then, will this work."

"But it *won't* work that way, Turner!" Dr. Trader replied confidently and all-knowingly. "If you duplicate your lung cell, then duplicate those two lung cells, do you know what you'll *really* have?" he paused but not long enough for Jim to answer. "You'll eventually have five million *identical* lung cells without form or function. I repeat, 'It will *not* work!'" Trader finished, making a point to show an equal amount of hostility.

The men scowled at each other for a moment, each one writhing in complete disgust at the other's incompetence and ignorance.

If it were David or Trevor, I would apologize, Jim considered, *but he's not worthy of it.*

Changing to another, and hopefully neutral method, "We could use human embryonic stem cells," offered Dr. Keller.

"And how would you acquire those," Jim asked, already feeling animosity for the suggestion as he predicted the response.

"Well, from aborted fetuses," Keller replied nonchalantly.

Jim's hand drew near his stomach; this conversation had made him become nauseous.

"So, now we're going to promote abortion in the name of research? I see that my suggestions are *too stupid* to even try. Perhaps I should go home for the day," Jim stated coldly and remorsefully as he turned to walk away.

The others were at a loss for words, except Trader, of course, who decided to remain quiet only because he had felt a victory in the outcome of events.

The apartment was small, only a single bedroom, but sufficient to meet his needs.

"No pets and no wild parties," the rotund landlord warned.

"You won't even know I'm here." Hephanaethus smiled. *Who does this fat bastard think he is?* Hephanaethus wondered. *Apparently, he is not yet aware that I make the rules. I'll enjoy reminding him of that when the time comes,* he concluded.

"You'll have to sign a six-month lease and I expect to be paid promptly," the landlord stated firmly.

Hephanaethus reached inside his jacket and produced the stack of one hundred-dollar-bills. "Would it be okay if I paid all six months in advance?" he asked politely.

The large man's disposition began to change as Hephanaethus counted the money.

"Well, yes, but I'm still going to need a deposit."

Hephanaethus nodded as he continued counting.

The landlord smiled as he accepted the money. He knew that the apartment in its current condition was barely worth the money that he was receiving for the six-month lease.

"I hope you enjoy your stay here, sir." He beamed as he folded the wad of money into his pant's pocket.

Chapter 8

David's eyes opened slowly. He soon realized that his eyelids were one of the very few muscles he could move. Wide straps pinned his naked body snugly to the cot, which was Darryl's former bed.

"Good morning, David, or more accurately good afternoon," Hephanaethus taunted. "After considerable deliberation, I have decided to carry through with your earlier plans. The lab *will* explode. But first, I needed to make use of the nifty little invention that I patiently waited for Trevor to complete. The eagerness that the two of you shared in the completion of *my* work is appreciated. But now that is over and *your* usefulness, like Trevor's . . . has expired."

David attempted to reply to the remarks but the tight-fitting gag prevented even most of his muffled screams.

"You have an interesting mind, David. I only hope that wife of yours is as attractive in person as she is in your memories. Oh, and let's not forget the valuable knowledge of chemistry you have." He pointed to a bucket with an electrical wire from the ceiling dangling into its center. From opposing sides of the bucket, volatile fluids dripped one drop at a time.

David understood the nature of this reaction well, for he had been the first to create it. It was the same project that had made him financially successful after selling it to the Department of Defense. Once the foam from the reaction reached the electrical wire, a simple spark was all that was needed to make the compound explode as if a truckload of dynamite were ignited. The liquid compound was a form of raw plastic explosives covered by an equally lethal lather similar to napalm, only ten times the effective strength.

"To insure my success," he continued, "I've also set other bombs. Hopefully, the blast will completely consume your corpse, if not . . . well . . . that could lead to an embarrassing situation on my part."

A ring of the phone interrupted the taunting.

"Hello. I'll be home soon, honey. I have a special surprise for you."

Hephanaethus grinned evilly as he seduced Gayla before David's very eyes.

Even more tormenting than Hephanaethus could be capable of, David knew this was *his* fault. Every one had discouraged the idea of cloning a human being. His closest friend had already died from the experiment and he grew nauseous as he imagined his wife's fate. *Why didn't I listen to them?*

Hopelessness and helplessness consumed David. Rationally, he accepted the fact that he would probably never see Gayla again. *Will she realize that it isn't me as he's killing her? Did Trevor ever know? Will they all die with their last thoughts being of why I killed them?* David finally began to grasp a tiny portion of the catastrophe that he had created. *Gayla wanted me to spend more time with her and I put her off in favor of creating the very beast, which will kill her horribly.*

Guilt and remorse wracked David's pinned body as Hephanaethus looked on. This was what had powered the corrupt being for thousands of years. The regretful, self-loathing emotions fed the beast as if they were a delicious, gourmet feast.

"You realize that men like yourself have served me for many centuries," Hephanaethus posed as a wicked, rhetorical question. "Technology," he continued in an attempt to cause David even more mental anguish, "will always be used for the purpose of evil, regardless of the good intentions of their inventors. Albert Einstein had only honorable intentions as *we* discovered atomic power. Only the backward societies such as the Quakers and Amish seem to understand this. The rest of you only feed the fire with your slothful creations, your pathetic attempts to take the easy path instead of dealing with your own problems."

Hephanaethus possessed a foul, and cruel wisdom from his extensive life. He felt it appropriate to reveal some of the mortal follies to David as he lay helplessly on his deathbed.

"And as for Darryl, do you really want to know, I mean, do you *really* want to know what become of your true twin?"

David lay motionless and attempted to answer with a series of blinks.

"Ah, where do I start?" Hephanaethus continued. "Some spoiled little rich bastard had recently inherited a fortune from his parents' estate. He had it all—the women, the drugs, the works. To make a long story short, he hit the cocaine a little to hard one night. As I watched him lay in a pool of his own filth, I decided to do him a favor. He had no control over his own life, so I decided to control it for a while. I would take control as the drugs set in and leave him to deal with the resulting circumstances when the drugs lost their effect. Screwing all the coke hungry whores on a nightly basis started growing old after a couple of weeks, though. I needed a little more excitement."

"I took off exploring one day when I saw two young boys. Can you guess who those two boys were?" Hephanaethus asked his mute victim. "That's right," he continued, "it was you and Darryl. I waited for hours watching the two of you play that afternoon. Do you remember, David? Do you remember what the two of you started arguing over? It was a little car, wasn't it?"

A tear swelled up in David's eye and rolled over his cheek

and into his ear. The memories of the last moment he saw Darryl were overwhelming. Further, he was well aware how this story would end. All hopes of ever being reunited with his twin brother were now gone.

"Do you remember going to tell your mommy that Darryl was being selfish? Do you remember being so angry with him that you wanted to see him punished? Well, guess what? He did get punished and it was because you told your mommy. When you ran into the house, that was when I made my move. I drove my car near where he was sitting and I offered him a soda if he could help me find my puppy. You didn't see him again, did you?"

The tears now poured from David's eyes. He was being forced to relive the day all over again. The muscles in his face jerked uncontrollably as he cried through the bittersweet memories.

"I was quite impressed with his stamina. Why, I guess it took me nearly fourteen hours of continuous beatings and sodomy to convince him to take the pills. That's right, David, your brother committed suicide. You've always seemed quite confident that people who commit suicide would be condemned to hell haven't you? Someday, maybe, I can beat him and force him into sodomy again. Until then, I suppose I'll just have to relive the excitement with Gayla won't I?"

"Oh, there I go getting sidetracked again. As I was saying, Darryl committed suicide and then it seemed like an appropriate time for me to evacuate the body that I had possessed. Naturally, the wealthy brat was shocked to see what he had done during his 'cocaine-induced blackout,' and therefore began to panic. He hauled the corpse around in the trunk of his car for hours trying to find some place to put it where no one would ever find it. He eventually found a place suitable for your brother's burial in a wooded area a few miles south of a little town called White Horse, Pennsylvania. Ultimately, he took more drugs to deal with his paranoia of being caught and convicted for his crime. In less than three weeks from that time, the young man had overdosed on his beloved 'nose candy.' It was truly a shame. I did enjoy taking control of his life from time to time." Hephanaethus concluded his story with a satisfied smile, as if it were a great accomplishment.

Again, Hephanaethus posed another rhetorical question to his muted victim, "Do you know why I am not going to kill you now, David?"

David wiggled his head as much as the tight cloth strap would allow.

"I want you to have time to suffer properly."

After having acquired David's memories, Hephanaethus understood David's way of thinking. David was very intelligent and might figure out a way to escape the lab. *But then what?* He would have no real reason to live. The guilt for being primarily responsible for the deaths of his closest friends and family would eventually drive him insane, quite possibly to suicide, and that would be even better, Hephanaethus decided.

Looking at his watch, which was formerly David's watch, Hephanaethus stated, "Well, I have to be getting *home* now. I need to take care of Gayla. You know David, I think I'll fuck the *hell* out of her tonight!"

Hephanaethus spun on his left heel and proceeded towards the door, being satisfied with the verbal torment thus far inflicted upon David.

Gayla began to pack after her earlier conversation with David. She had concluded that the "special surprise" David had mentioned earlier could very well be taking off for Florida tonight. That would be just like David to . . . Making her think she would have to wait longer from the beginning, so he could "surprise" her if his schedule went smoothly. With their anniversary only a few days away, she wondered if "the surprise" was in any way related to the upcoming date.

As *David* walked upstairs, Gayla left the half packed suitcase lying open on the bed.

"And the surprise is . . ." Gayla beamed with anticipation.

"Patience," replied Hephanaethus as he approached her in a

predator like fashion.

David tried to get his mind off of what was about to happen to Gayla and focus instead, on what he might be able to do to prevent it. Since the moment that Hephanaethus had left the building, David had been sawing away at the edge of the single strap that had been binding his hands, flatly against the table. Hephanaethus had positioned the straps so that every other strap alternated from going over his chest with the others pinning his arms under his back. At last, a minor success, a single thread of the strap had broken. With the corner of his fingernail he began to unravel the thread. This would take a long time. Maybe longer than he had. But his only alternative was to lay immobilized and think of the lives he would be responsible for destroying. *Even if,* he couldn't save Gayla, someone would have to stop him for the brutal slaying of others.

Hephanaethus took Gayla into his arms gently. Lowering his head to give her a passionate kiss, he slid his right hand toward her well-shaped buttocks. His finger wrapped into a small fold of her sheer, silky blue dress. Gently, his hand formed a fist, gathering the material and making it increasingly shorter. His left hand caressed the back of her delicate neck, then migrated to the top of the zipper of her dress. Within seconds, the zipper sped down her back, revealing the lean, tanned flesh underneath.

Gayla had longed for this sensation. Lately, when she and David had taken the opportunity to enjoy sex, something seemed to be missing, but not tonight. The dress slipped off her shoulders and crashed silently to the ground.

Hephanaethus lifted her gently and carried her to the foot of the bed, dropping her scantly clad body roughly on the mattress. He ripped his own shirt open, propelling the buttons in different directions.

He is a wild man, Gayla thought.

This reminded her of David in his premarital college days; it was a dangerously pleasant memory.

As Gayla's undergarments were peeled off her body, Hephanaethus kissed passionately down her torso.

For Hephanaethus, this wasn't for her pleasure but rather his own. It wasn't even a sexual pleasure, more a sinister one. He was *trespassing*, preparing for the cold violation of her body as she lay there willingly. *She doesn't even realize that she is committing adultery,* he thought as he began to ravage her.

The thread had just started to unravel when it broke. David cut his eyes toward the clock on the wall. *Why bother? She's probably already dead.* David told himself. Weakened by sorrow, David continued his relentless plucking, if nothing else, he now wanted revenge. Tears of frustration began to stream down his cheeks. He wanted to scream, but he was gagged. He wanted to punch something, but he was bound tightly. Like a raging bull, he twisted and squirmed with all his adrenaline filled strength. Finally, his thumb popped free from beneath the strap, relaxing it, however slightly. It was progress nonetheless.

The joints of David's hips ached from the unnatural position his feet and ankles had been pinned in for the past few hours. He tried to ignore the pain. *Perhaps I deserve it,* he concluded. He attempted to slide his forefinger from beneath the strap; the attempt was useless. Despite the minimal movement he had made, he had become exhausted from the efforts.

Gayla shoved her lover's head between her thighs; she gripped his hair tightly in both her hands. The experience was breathtaking, to say the least. Her entire body quivered in anticipation of his next movement.

Hephanaethus continued his actions, relishing the power he received from blind sin.

The irony humored him as Gayla exclaimed, "Oh, God!"

Not exactly, he thought, q*uite the contrary.*

If only David could see this show before he died. I should have used the camcorder, Hephanaethus realized as he delivered Gayla into a darker ecstasy.

Gayla drug her long brown hair down Hephanaethus' chest as she prepared to return the erotic favor. For an instant, she felt as if she were doing something wrong. It almost seemed as if she was having an affair. She had grown accustomed to the tamer, gentler version of sex that she and David evolved into shortly after their marriage. This was different, more exciting than ever before. Her tongue squeezed from between her lips split seconds before she opened her mouth widely.

I hope she's not still suffering, David thought as he wiggled his finger, one digit at a time. The man who his duplicate had become was not the "Darryl" he had taken care of for the past two weeks. Darryl had the mind of an infant. It was inconceivable that he could have learned so much so quickly, regardless of any genetic enhancement. David began to piece together the full truth of the matter. *But Darryl has thoughts, emotions, how could he not have a soul?* The issue had little bearing on the fate of Trevor's life. David wished he could apologize to Trevor for what had happened. He pitied Trevor. Would Trevor *ever* know that it was not David who had killed him? Trevor had already met his maker, whether he believed in him or not. For all his intelligence, Trevor, much like David, always learned the truth too late.

Hephanaethus had not enjoyed pleasures of the flesh for a few years. Further, his partners were seldom so willing or as physically attractive. The combination of his demented rewards coupled with this experience made the entire sequence of events better. He ran his fingers through the curls of her hair, raking the strands to the side of her face as he watched her take him further still.

Gayla rose from her curled position and crawled above him.

Her knees were placed snugly against his ribs as she lowered her body to meld with his. At last, penetration—another distorted victory for Hephanaethus.

Hephanaethus had already achieved a fate worse than death, in the event that David did escape his confinement at the lab. "His wife done the nasty with the boogie man," he mused.

David had gradually walked his forefinger to the edge of the cloth strap. With this, the band had loosened enough for David's other fingers to squeeze their way upward also. He bent his wrist as much as possible. *If I could just move my elbow,* he thought to himself.

It had been nearly two hours since Hephanaethus had left the lab. David wondered what disturbing thoughts Gayla was thinking at this moment, if she was still alive.

Gayla thought that no future sexual experience would ever compare to this one. Sweat beaded and trickled between her breasts as she fell backwards.

Hephanaethus pushed his torso upward and clasped his hands behind her back. Lifting her as he went, he stood erectly and pulled her up to him. Their bodies moved as if they were a single sweating and throbbing organism. In an explosion of sexual fury, he slammed her against the wall of the bedroom.

Her legs wrapped around his back, locking at the ankles, as if she were afraid he would escape. Her smooth sweat slicked skin slithered across his. Gayla's hair became damp from her own perspiration. It clung to the moist skin of her face as she attempted to rake it away.

He grinned sadistically with satisfaction as he watched her upper body bounce with his every thrust. The tips of his fingers dug deeply into the cheeks of her buttocks as he spread them apart. This was what evil was all about, he thought. *I doubt that being an angel could possibly compare*, he decided in his foul and corrupted mind. With a final earth shattering thrust,

Hephanaethus' thirst had been quenched.

Her slick legs slid smoothly down his back as she regained her stance on the floor. Stretching her neck upward, she ended the moment with one last passionate kiss.

All of David's fingers were now free from the strap. The straps were so tight that his entire body felt as if he were wearing multiple tourniquets. Circulation had been practically cut off from most of his extremities. The pressure of his blood soared to the point of making him drowsy. He wondered what the wicked clone had done to make the straps so taut and unbearable. Manipulating his wrist as much as possible, he scooted his newly freed right hand towards the edge of the cot. The nearer his hand got to the cot, the more circulation he lost from the strap binding his wrist.

His head pounded. He tried to take deeper breaths but the straps over his chest limited the expansion of his lungs. With what he thought would be his dying burst of energy, he forced his hand to the edge of the cot and twisted his wrist. Miraculously, his flailing finger caught the edge of the clip that had bound his wrist. He had escaped from the first strap. He estimated that there were at least a dozen more. He flipped his wrist and caught the edge of yet another clip. This one had bound his hands and fingers and still held his left hand motionless. With a pop, that strap also snapped loose.

Though he had made considerable progress, the man still suffered human limitations. He needed to rest as his drowsiness grew in intensity. Though he thought it would be a momentary rest, David lost consciousness.

Catching her breath, Gayla confessed, "I thought you were just going to tell me that you wanted to leave for Florida sooner."

As Hephanaethus gazed upon Gayla, he decided that killing her now would be senseless. Not that Hephanaethus had a problem with senseless killing, but letting her live a little longer might actually further his twisted plans.

"When would you like to leave?" he asked.

Glancing at the suitcase that had been knocked off the bed spilling its contents, she replied "Tomorrow morning."

Perfect, he thought.

Not yet finished with his path of destruction he told her, "I just need to take care of something at the lab."

She dared not even ask what that something was. She was happy and they were finally going on vacation and that's all that mattered at the moment.

"Fine. I need the rest," she said with a pleasant smile.

Before leaving, Hephanaethus stepped into the bathroom. He scanned over the surface of the wide vanity, picked up Gayla's hairbrush, and slid it into his pocket.

Chapter 9

Although the experience had been invigorating, Hephanaethus had not fulfilled the rape aspect he had planned for Gayla. His intentions for her had changed due to her willingness to comply and even help him weave the tangled web of deceit and betrayal. He would simply find another object for his brutal desires and save Gayla for another time. He sat inside David's Jaguar and drove toward the lab.

As he drove through a more rural area, his attention was drawn to an old farmhouse. White paint peeled off the narrow wooden siding of the house. The screens in the windows were worn thin and had several small holes in them. Through one of the windows, he could see directly into the kitchen. There, he could see a shapely young woman with streaked, bleach blonde hair and dark eyes walking across the floor. A thin white night gown adorned her breasts with lace before dangling gently from the features of her lower body.

He pulled the car to the side of the road.

"Intriguing," he muttered to himself as he approached the house.

He took a small detour on his journey to the door as he opened a small gray box on the side of the house and disconnected the phone lines. Then he knocked softly on the door and waited.

Forty minutes of shallow breathing later, David regained consciousness. Both hands were now free, but this really had not accomplished as much as David had hoped. He still lacked the ability to bend his elbows, and sliding down to loosen the strap pinning his head was made impossible by his inability to bend his knees. He reached for one of the straps he had already removed and placed the stiff metal end between the tip of his forefinger and that of his middle finger. With this extension, he pried the clip off of a third strap.

An old, bearded man with coke-bottle thick glasses came to the door. He was suspicious of visitors at this time of night, but noticed that the man was clean cut and well dressed and so asked, "Can I help you mister?"

"Yes. My car started making a clicking sound. I was wondering if I could use your phone and borrow a flashlight. I think I've broken a belt." He lied without a hint of conscience.

"Michelle," the old man called to his daughter. "Go down to the basement and get this man a flashlight." The old man smiled kindly and nodded at him. "I'll go get you the phone," he said.

As the scantly clad nineteen-year-old neared the door, her father scolded, "Either get in bed or put some clothes on."

Shaking his head as he opened the door to hand Hephanaethus the flashlight, the old man held the cordless telephone to his ear and noticed that there was no dial tone. The mystery was quickly solved as Hephanaethus snatched the flashlight from the old man's hand and knocked him unconscious within the same swift movement.

As Michelle folded her covers back, she heard a loud thud. Curious, she went back out and into the hallway and peeped around the corner. Hephanaethus casually shut the door behind him and barred it.

At the lab, David glared hopelessly at the bucket containing the volatile mixture. Three straps had been removed, but in vain he couldn't possibly reach any others without bending his elbows. Suddenly, David reverted to his original idea. He grabbed the metal end of one of the loosened straps and curled his wrist upward. Powered by a glimmer of hope, he began sawing away at the strap binding his elbows.

At the same instant that Hephanaethus bent down and grabbed the old man by the back of his overalls, Michelle made a desperate and useless dive for the telephone laying on the floor. Laughing sinisterly, Hephanaethus placed his right hand on the old man's left shoulder and cupped his bearded chin in his left hand, twisting his head to the side.

"Do *exactly* as I say or I'll kill him," he commanded.

She noticed the phone was dead and feared she might soon share the same fate. Out of fear, she obeyed.

She retrieved a lightweight kitchen chair and carried it to her bedroom as directed. As she stepped through the doorway, she spun in an attempt to slam the door shut, but Hephanaethus had anticipated her move and shoved the old man's limp body forward. The door hit his head even harder than the flashlight had. Dark red blood oozed and dripped from the man's scalp.

"Don't humor me," Hephanaethus warned.

Taking the cord of a vacuum cleaner, Hephanaethus bound the old man where he sat on the chair. By the time he had finished securing the final loop, the old man eventually began to regain consciousness.

The old man sat confused, trying to piece together the events that had taken place while he had been subdued.

Michelle's trembling intensified as Hephanaethus drew closer. She knew what was about to happen. Huge tears streaked down her soft cheeks as he caressed her chin.

"Aww, don't be sad. Just be a good little girl and it'll be over soon."

She gained no comfort from the sadistic encouragement.

He pulled the loose fitting, white lace gown up beneath her arms.

She levitated her arms unwillingly but helplessly. Her long, blonde hair fell back to her shoulders as he removed the gown, revealing her young, perky, voluptuous breasts.

Hephanaethus deliberately took his time and savored the moment as he moved down her body, rolling her panties into perfectly round tubes as he went. The suspense ended as they rolled over the tops of her knees and dropped to the floor.

She thought about her boyfriend whom she had refused to have sex with. She had told him she was waiting for marriage. This had made her the exception, one in a million in today's society. She wished he were here. Better still, she wished that she weren't here tonight. She wished that the house had been empty tonight when the stranger had arrived.

Michelle looked at her father as if asking for help.

The old man struggled to get free of the cord but failed. He gazed back at her in pity and blurted, "I'm so sorry," as he began to bawl hysterically.

She wondered what her chances of survival would be if she continued to go along without a struggle. She wondered what her mother would do if she were still alive.

Hephanaethus stood in front of her and placed his hands on her shoulders and softly traced down her chest with the tips of his fingers. He massaged her breasts gently as she sobbed.

"What's wrong?" he inquired ignorantly, as if she should be enjoying the experience.

"I'm a virgin," she blurted, "I was saving myself for marriage."

She raised her hands to her face and began weeping beyond her control.

"Would you like to marry me?" he proposed as a wicked smile raced across his face.

His proposal had the desired effect; she fell to the floor and continued crying even louder. Hephanaethus watched her display for well over a minute as he absorbed the power from her anguish. Finally, he grew impatient. After all, he didn't just come here to watch some teenage girl cry.

He reached down and put his hand on top of her head with his fingers spread outward. Digging his fingers through the tangles of her hair, he grasped a handful of her hair and lifted her back to her feet.

"Now shut up."

He spoke calmly and coldly. He fingered the hair back out of her face and again placed his hands on her shoulders. Firmly, he pressed downward on her shoulders; she knew what he wanted, despite her inexperience.

Falling back to her knees, she wiped the teary snot from her nose, and opened her trembling mouth. She placed her hand beneath his penis and moved forward feeling helplessly trapped.

A small ragged tear began to form on the strap as David realized the he couldn't go much further due to his limited reach. Oily sweat had begun to form on his forehead, giving it a slight lubrication. He tilted his head as much as the strap across his mouth and chin would allow. His forehead started to clear the strap as David endured the pain as the three-inch wide strap over his mouth cut into his cheek. As the strap cleared his forehead, it caught on his ear, feeling as if it had been yanked off of his head. With the heels of his hands, he pushed his body upward, a fraction of an inch at a time.

As Michelle moved closer, she determined her chances of survival would be best if she resisted. As her open mouth moved forward, she clamped her teeth together ferociously in an attempt to desexualize her attacker as she pressed with all her strength on his groin area.

With a wail of long forgotten pain, Hephanaethus drove his

thumbs into her jawbones, prying them apart. "You little bitch!" he screamed angrily at her. "It could've been easy for you." He lied only to cause her to regret her actions. His closed fist plunged downward into her cheek as he grabbed her hair and smashed her mouth against the bedpost. Pulling her head back to observe the damage sustained by the teeth that had bitten him, he saw her mouth fill with bright red blood.

Michelle lunged upward, extending her fingers, managing a quick jab to his right eye. She knew she was now fighting for her life; she had to try to inflict as much pain as possible.

The old man squirmed helplessly, as he bounced the chair closer trying to assist his daughter in some way. Leaning forward he made a desperate attempt to spin the chair around and trip Hephanaethus. His efforts fell short as the chair leg struck Hephanaethus' ankle and the man crashed to the floor on his side, still bound in the chair by the cord.

Hephanaethus backhanded the girl, and with a quick jab of his thumb, imparted an equal, if not greater, amount of damage to her eye as she had to his. Then he raised his knee sharply into her abdomen, leaving her nearly breathless.

Now, injured and temporarily unable to engage in any sexual activities, Hephanaethus pushed the girl down to the floor and then examined her for an instant. Her eye had already began to swell shut, four of her teeth had been shattered, and her hair fell raggedly in several directions.

"Funny, you don't seem that attractive anymore," he slurred as he tugged at her hair again.

With her chin cupped in his hand, he gave her neck a quick and sudden jerk, then dropped her lifeless body to the floor.

The old man had freed his left hand as he saw Michelle drop to the floor with her lifeless brown eyes staring back at him. He reached for her as Hephanaethus turned and brought the heel of his shoe solidly into his temple.

Hephanaethus proceeded out the door, leaving the old man for dead. *No matter at this point,* Hephanaethus decided carelessly.

As the strap covering David's chin slipped downward, it pressed firmly on his neck causing him to choke. He rolled his head to the side. The choking was replaced by another familiar discomfort. The taut strap restricted the blood flow in his jugular vein, bringing back the blood-rushing dizziness he had experienced earlier. Simultaneously to this new dilemma, he made another giant leap of progress. His elbows were now slightly above the strap that had pinned them down. He still remained unable to bend his arms due to one remaining strap pinning his lower arm and the two confining his upper arms. But he could at least rotate his elbows now. Pinching the edge of the metal strap end in his curled right hand, he tapped for his life at the clip beneath the cot that held the strap pinning the lower portions of both his arms.

Hephanaethus turned the car around and retreated to the small apartment he had rented earlier that day. Upon his arrival, he removed Gayla's hairbrush from his pocket and began to pull the tangles of her hair free. He separated a single strand of her hair from the tangles and placed it beneath a powerful microscopic lens. Carefully, he began to isolate her genetic makeup from the small strand of hair.

Blood dripped down the old man's forehead as he freed his right arm and began wrestling the electrical cord away from his body. If he were lucky, he would lay down and die from grief here, by his daughter's side. His survival was pointless to him now. After removing the cord from around his leg, he crawled to Michelle's side. "I lied to you. I told you that I would *always* be there to help you out of any situation. I'm sorry," he pleaded to the corpse. He clung tightly to the corpse as if it would somehow bring her back.

As he moved through the doorway of the master bedroom, Hephanaethus watched Gayla sleep. *I could kill her now,* he contemplated. *She would die in her sleep without ever knowing.*

"No," he whispered. "It would be like eating green apples. Fear and the knowledge of betrayal would sweeten the moment. The fruit *must* be ripe," he continued as he lay down next to Gayla.

He looked at her and smiled wickedly. He contemplated David's current position.

I hope he escapes soon, he thought. *I want to kill her in front of him.*

Gayla had already packed their suitcases. He only needed to load them into the car and drive to the airport. It hardly seemed worth falling asleep since the couple would be getting up for their next day in less than two hours. Hephanaethus closed his eyes; the weakness of his human body needed rest.

With another life sustaining snap the clip sprang loose and released another strap. It was only a matter of time until he would be free. David looked at the bucket of chemicals. Thick, foamy suds continually rose dangerously close to the live copper wire. It was also only a matter of time until the laboratory would explode. His elbow now free, he swung his lower arm quickly upwards towards the strap constricting around his neck. Wiggling his fingers desperately, his thumb managed to catch the bottom portion of the clip beneath the cot. Blood flow was restored. Now that blood rushed quickly through his jugular veins, David was relaxed—overly relaxed. The bright lights of the room began to dim one more time.

Gayla woke pleasantly and bursting with energy. "David, David, we have to get up. Our plane leaves at seven forty five."

Hephanaethus rolled out of bed and roamed toward the shower behind her.

Where is David? He pondered. *Apparently he's as frail and weak as the other mortals*, he concluded.

Now he would continue the charade on the other side of the country. Taking lives without discretion never to receive any punishment. Sure they could convict his body to prison and after twenty or so years maybe even death, but Hephanaethus had already lost five bodies to the 'hands of justice.' It was merely a way of passing his somewhat infinite time. Killings, rapes, child abuse—these were all mere hobbies.

He listened closely to Gayla's words as she spoke on the phone while drying her body.

"Jessica, its Dr. Brooks. I need you to go ahead and reschedule the appointments. David and I are leaving this morning."

The irony of it all, thought Hephanaethus, as she spoke.

David will ultimately receive the punishment for killing Gayla. I'll bet they'll use DNA tests in the court trials to prove his guilt.

David's eyes opened wide with terror. *What a horrible dream,* David thought as the constrictive cloth straps reminded him of the cruel reality of his current situation. His eyes darted towards the bucket and then to the clock. Time was short in more ways than one. Pressing further up the cot with the heels of his hands, David proceeded his backward crawl towards freedom from his "deathbed."

One of the straps previously confining his upper arms loosened, however slightly, as it slid down past his elbows and onto his lower arms. His hips continued to ache at the joints from the discomfort of their unnatural position.

Hephanaethus stowed the luggage and shut the trunk as Gayla insured that the house was properly locked and secured.

"We have to hurry," she said.

"You should relax and enjoy what little time you have left here," came the reply. He knew she would perceive the remark in a different manner from which he had conceived it.

Both his upper and his lower arms were restricted again. David debated on the successfulness of his attempts. After hours of struggling, David was in an all too familiar position. He had escaped five straps now and was really not much better off than he was ten hours ago, yet he continued his slow and rigorous journey upward on the cot. The cot was no longer supporting his head and he had maneuvered his shoulder blades onto the hard metal railing. Another push later, the heels of his feet began to emerge from beneath the lowest strap.

Gayla swung the door open and retrieved her carry-on bag from the back seat of the car. As she turned, her beeper caught on the edge of the seatbelt and fell silently. In her haste, she failed to notice the occurrence.

Chapter 10

The time had come. David had needed to relieve himself hours ago. He could wait no longer. David tried to twist his body at the waist and hips as much as possible, but ultimately found himself lying in a puddle of his own urine. He throat was parched; he envied Rambo as he watched the simple, ignorant rodent drink water from his bottle as if nothing were wrong.

He dug the recently freed heels of his feet into the cot in concert with his former efforts with the heels of his hands. Within five minutes, and with one great movement after another he found himself four inches closer to freedom. The straps now bound his elbow joints and his lower arms. He glared at the clock helplessly and continued his exhausting efforts.

The foamy mixture already appeared to be touching the wire. Had Hephanaethus mixed the chemicals incorrectly? Was this some kind of cruel joke of his? David pushed his body further, and finally both his elbows and shoulders were free of the straps. He quickly slid his lower arms up through the straps one at a time. Reaching beneath the cot, he worked feverishly unclipping the remaining straps. He then spun off the bed to take a closer look at the contraption that Hephanaethus had prepared. The foam was mere millimeters from the end of the copper wire. The electricity could arc the minute distance at any second.

He backed away and reached for the telephone. If he had only a few seconds remaining of his life he would choose to warn Gayla before escaping with what pitiful remainder he had left. His heart sank as the phone pressed against his ear and he realized that there was no sign of a connection. He could not warn her by telephone. *I need clothes and a car*, he decided. He raced to Trevor's corpse and began digging through his pockets for the keys to his car. They were gone. Next, he unfastened Trevor's belt and tried to remove his pants, but rigor mortis had already set in and the body was stiff and rigid. David knew that he lacked the time necessary to retrieve the clothing. He removed the shoes and took a smock from a hanger in his office as he headed towards the door. Then he looked back at the picture of the twins. This time he didn't grab the picture; instead, he grabbed the toy car in front of it and tossed it into one of the shoes. As he sprinted toward the door he hooked his fingers along the edge of Rambo's cage.

Less than ten feet out the door, David risked his life for a drink of water. He removed the bottle from the mouse's cage and funneled the remainder of its contents in a single gulp. Tilting the cage on its side, he looked at Rambo and said, "You're on your own now," and jogged away barefooted and naked at top speed, trying to ignore the pain wracking through his hips.

After fleeing a safe distance of nearly two hundred feet, David stopped to don the stolen shoes and the lab smock. He removed the toy car and placed it into one of the pockets of the smock. The shoes were considerably larger than he was used to wearing. He wondered if the blisters on his heels would be more painful than the gravels piercing the soles of his feet.

As he glanced back at the lab, he saw a wave of glass and fire racing toward him. In fear, he stumbled backwards a few feet further, underestimating the force of the explosion.

With no time to spare, David knew he had to find some way home quickly. If emergency vehicles saw him here, it would only delay his arrival. With all his might, he ran along the side of the road toward his home.

A distant but bright flash of light caught Hephanaethus' eye. Apparently no one else on the airplane had noticed, but then again, no one else had reason to stare intently at that particular area of the brownish surface below.

"Don't worry. Your precious lab will still be there when we get back," Gayla said in ignorance to what Hephanaethus had just witnessed. She placed her hand on top of his. "It's time for you to have some fun again."

Hephanaethus smiled deviously and nodded.

The old man climbed to his feet and stumbled towards the front door of his home. As he stood in the doorway, he reminded himself that his poor judgment in choosing to open the door was to blame for his daughter's death. Now, he only wanted to avenge the death of his only daughter before he died. He fumbled for the keys in his pocket and slumbered towards his truck.

A loud explosion-like sound rumbled in the distance only about a mile or so away. He stopped to peer in that direction for only a moment before climbing into his truck and starting the engine. Regardless of what it was, it could not possibly be as important as finding the man who had slain his daughter.

As he took the vehicle out of reverse, he noticed a man in the distance running waving his arms wildly for his attention. He really didn't have the time to help someone else right now, but if Michelle were still alive she would want him to. He pulled the truck back into the driveway and backed out in the opposite direction to see what the man wanted. Perhaps he had seen the man with the black Jaguar.

The rumble of an inadequate exhaust system grew louder as

the truck proceeded in David's direction; David began to feel some relief. Maybe this man could help him get home. Maybe Gayla was still alive, though he thought the odds against it.

Noticing a striking resemblance between the man up the road wearing a smock and wing tips and that of the stranger who had betrayed him, the old man steered the truck directly towards him and increased his acceleration.

David moved to the side of the road as the truck drew near. Unfortunately, the truck was matching his moves with every step he took. When David leaped away from the road, the truck continued to compensate for his movement. Was Hephanaethus the driver of this truck? He darted from side to side trying to avoid the truck's deadly path. Saving his efforts for the last possible second, David faked a move to his left and then leapt to his right. The front of the old truck hit David's airborne leg with enough force to crack his knee and spin his entire body around as the truck blared past.

The old man knew that he had not killed him but he was injured enough for the revenge to be prolonged, so he slammed on the brakes. The truck came to a halt and a cloud of loose dirt concealed the man's exit from the vehicle.

David looked up to see the old man reaching for a gas can in the back of his truck as he approached.

"Why?" David cried. "I've done nothing to you."

"Why you good for nothin' son-of-a-bitch," the man started, "You'll leave this world the same way you enter the next."

The old man splashed gasoline over David's body as David tried to roll away amidst the confusion. The old man chased after David ensuring that his smock was well saturated with the gasoline.

Gasoline splashed into David's eyes. The fluid burned his eyes as if it had already been lit. The scenery around him became blurrier.

Then, the old man removed a pack of matches from the bib of his overalls and pulled one of them across the rough surface to ignite it. He threw the match, but the wind extinguished the flame before it could reach David's body.

A deputy sheriff raced by as he responded to a call about the laboratory's explosion. He noticed the vehicle off to the side of the road and the old man standing above David with a gas can. Torn between the importance of the two events, he pulled his vehicle to the side of the road to investigate the problem.

"Halt," the deputy warned the old man as he drew his semi-automatic weapon from its' holster. "Step away from him."

"He killed my daughter; he deserves it!" the old man pleaded for the deputy's blind eye.

David was astounded by the accusation. What was the man talking about? The realization of the truth tugged on David's heart; it was Hephanaethus. The old man was another victim of the foul monster that had destroyed his life as well.

"Is that true," the deputy said, his weapon changing direction.

"No! I swear it's not!" David argued.

"Get down on the ground. I'll have to take you to the station for questioning."

The deputy knew not to ask any further questions until after the rights were read. He replaced his weapon loosely in the holster as presented the handcuffs. "Put your right hand behind your back," continued the officer as the shiny new bracelet of presumed guilt tightened snugly around David's wrist.

"I swear it wasn't me, please!" David pleaded as he saw his hope of saving Gayla dwindle.

"You have the right to remain silent," the deputy said firmly.

David had already failed Gayla once. He couldn't risk this loss of time, which might completely determine her survival of his mistake. As the officer grabbed David's left wrist, David knew he didn't have time to the weigh options, this time he had to react on gut instinct.

David yanked his right cuffed wrist from the deputy's grip. Rolling to his right side, he balled his right fist tightly and jabbed the officer in the neck while pulling the gun from the officer's holster with his left hand.

Deputy Johnson fell back, certain that this would be the last few seconds of his life.

David stepped up waving the gun back and forth from the deputy to the old man. He didn't have any intentions of harming the men but he couldn't let them stop him from seeing Gayla.

With a burst of adrenaline-powered speed, he sprinted directly to the car with an excruciatingly painful wobble resulting from his shattered knee. With a quick swipe of the wheel, he reversed the vehicle's direction and began accelerating. Another police car and a fire engine raced past him on their way toward the inferno, which had formerly been David's laboratory. David gripped the firearm beside him; he would need this for correcting his cloning mistake and saving Gayla's life.

He killed the old man's daughter. Has he already killed Gayla? David writhed in despair as he contemplated the usefulness of his efforts. *I could have explained to the policeman that I needed him to take me home to see about Gayla. But how long would it have taken for me to explain the situation. Cops never listen anyway.* David's internal debate was silenced by the announcement over the police radio.

"All units. An armed man has stolen Deputy Johnson's car. The man is considered to be dangerous and suspected of at least one murder and possibly arson."

David was overwhelmed at the amount of evidence that had built up against him.

"The man was last seen wearing only a smock and brown wingtip shoes. The car is northbound on route 87 . . ." continued the advisory.

David glanced downward. He was driving a hundred and fifteen miles an hour in a stolen police car, dressed in a smock and wingtips. Of course he looked like a fruitcake. He couldn't very well argue their point of trying to stop him. But nothing on earth was as important as Gayla. He wouldn't mind fourteen hours of explanations if only he could have a chance to save her.

Hephanaethus looked around the plane; it reminded him of one in which a previous earthly body of his had perished.

That was an interesting life, he reflected as the vivid memories of his life as an Arabian terrorist rushed back into his darkest thoughts. Hephanaethus had suffered tremendous pain for a few brief seconds from the event, but had received great comfort from the knowledge that he had been surrounded by another one hundred forty six other passengers and crew that suffered equal amounts of agony.

His life, or in mortal terms, lives, had been enough to send an entire nation into the depths of hell. Among his favorite recollections was a Vietnamese officer in charge of a prisoner of war camp, a seventeenth century slave trader, a General of the Hun army, and last, but certainly not least, a Roman soldier at the crucifixion.

Less than a mile away, David saw the police cars on the shoulders of the road. *What are they going to do?* He contemplated as his foot pressed solidly against the floor, accelerating the vehicle past one hundred forty miles per hour.

The patrolmen watched in terror, fearing for their own lives at the crazed maniac's next move. *Would he swerve to one side or another, killing one of the officers?* The patrolmen glanced at each other knowing that they might be the last ones to see the other alive or even worse . . .

Thinking quickly, two of the officers pulled out their guns, taking careful and calculated aim, and shot at the tires moments before the stolen cruiser barreled past at a hundred-fifty-seven miles per hour. At least one bullet ripped through the tread of the front driver's side tire; the force of the incident jerked the steering wheel from David's tight grasp. Large chunks of black rubber flew free from the orbit of the wheel as he continued his journey towards his home. Sparks flew over the vehicle's own roof as the metal burrowed itself into newly formed grooves in the pavement of the road.

David continued to push the car to its limits. However, the

limits were now significantly lower than before. He watched in the rearview mirror as the other cars began to close in on the disabled automobile. An intersection ahead would be his Waterloo. The light was red and several cars blocked his path. *Gayla,* he thought as he reached for the firearm.

A failed attempt to bring the car to the top of the curb meant that the last two miles of David's journey would be on foot, if at all. He flung the door open and started to run to the best of his recently crippled ability. A deputy and a state trooper slid their own cruisers to a screeching halt behind the decrepit car David had abandoned.

"Halt! Drop the weapon!" the men shouted as they took cover.

Neither officer would fire on David, despite their mutual conclusion of his insanity. Too many civilians passed by on the road behind him for the men to feel comfortable to take a shot. David continued his hobbling at top speed. Under different circumstances, he would have found humor in the ironic similarities between his gait and the maneuverability of the car he had left behind.

The officer's moved in closer, but cautiously. David continued hobbling towards his home. One by one the men approached him within fifteen feet. By now they seemed to have gained some confidence that he lacked with the intentions of firing the weapon upon them.

"Drop the weapon!" the Deputy repeated after positioning himself for a lethal shot.

"But she's gonna die," he babbled helplessly, continuing his journey. "I've got to kill him. I have to save her. She's probably already dead." He sobbed, realizing that at his current rate it would take him close to an hour to reach his destination, even if the policemen were not pestering him.

Suddenly, a pain shot up from his shattered knee wracking his entire body. As he reached to brace himself, he lost his grip on the weapon. As the weapon tumbled across the concrete sidewalk, Deputy Wilkins moved in, retrieved the weapon, and forced David to the ground. Again, David struggled for his freedom as he thought about Gayla. Then, he heard a recently familiar voice behind him; it sounded like Deputy Johnson. He felt his head move back and to the left as darkness again filled his sight.

"Have a nice nap?" Gayla inquired as the plane descended towards the runway.

"Of course. I was dreaming of you," Hephanaethus replied cleverly.

Gayla smiled as she felt "the old David" laying on his infinite charm.

"I'm so glad we're here. I only wish it were warm enough for the beach." Gayla said sadly.

"Maybe things will heat up a bit later," Hephanaethus said as he placed his hand on her knee and leisurely moved it towards her thigh. He winked at her. "How hot would you like it."

"Hot as fire," she replied teasingly.

"I believe I can accommodate your needs," he replied through a twisted smile.

"I'm sure you can," she responded oblivious to the murderous intentions of her mate. Gayla saw the trip as a second honeymoon. She had desires to be met and was eager to meet David's desires also. They needed to rekindle the romance in a setting unpolluted by either one's in-laws. Here, David couldn't take off to the lab. Emergency counseling couldn't bother her. This was both the time and the place for the fires of passion to burn out of control.

Chapter 11

David's eyes opened slowly. As he tilted his head he knew that he had been placed in a straightjacket and, according to a clipboard hanging from the wall, he was apparently being held for psychological evaluation at the local hospital. He twisted his neck to see the leg brace holding his knee rigidly at a slight angle.

Carefully, he listened to a conversation taking place outside the door.

"After he killed Michelle Macintosh, he apparently burned the laboratory. The body in the lab was burned beyond recognition. We need to leave him here until he cooperates and identifies the body."

"If he even knows, it was probably a random homicide. This guy is a real fruitcake. He said as clear as day that he intended to kill some other guy just a few seconds before we subdued him."

"What about his medical injuries? How long will it be before we can transport him to a normal prison?"

"I'm not concerned with his medical injuries. The bastard

got off easy for what he's done."

David wiggled about in the straightjacket. *How terrifyingly familiar*, he thought. *Now the "justice system" was responsible for Gayla. It's too late*, he thought as he looked at the clock. *Why bother. Existence is pointless from here on out if this is what it's going to be like.* David couldn't help but notice that the straightjacket was less confining than the cloth straps that Hephanaethus had restricted him with. *I can get out of this one too. They already think I'm crazy at this point. DNA evidence will convict me. The only woman I've ever really loved is now dead. I have nothing to lose.*

David wiggled the fingers of his left hand, gathering what loose material he could in a tight pinch. He knew that he had to remain focused on these single objectives as he had done the previous evening in the lab.

His concentration was broken.

"I see you're awake," announced the nurse, as she entered the room with two uniformed police officers following closely behind.

"Can you take me out of this contraption?" David made reference to the straightjacket.

The nurse looked questioningly at the officers behind her.

"Sure," replied the larger man, as he gripped the end of a stick attached to his belt. It was identical to the one responsible for the latest knot on David's head.

The nurse pulled the sleeves tighter to unfasten the buckles behind him.

David's arms fell to his sides as his shoulders spread widely again. He breathed deeply, preparing himself for hours of explanations. At this point he had to consider which edge of the sword was sharpest. He was being accused of an entire list of crimes, most of which he could blame on the clone. Alternatively, confessing to producing the illegal clone could still make him responsible for the clone's actions. He compared his situation to being stuck between a gas chamber and a lethal injection system as he contemplated "Arizona justice."

The policemen stood on either side of David and lifted him

from the bed to place him in the wheelchair below.

David wondered if the pain in his hips had gone away or if the sensation was merely dulled by the agony of his shattered knee coupled with the pounding, sore lump on the back of his skull.

"You would be well advised not to resist us this time, sir," an officer said arrogantly as he leaned him forward to place the handcuffs around his wrists behind him. The two men lifted him from the chair and helped him into the backseat of the police cruiser.

"When can I have my phone call?" David asked as he tried to grasp one last fleeting hope of Gayla's survival.

"Ask the investigator when we arrive at the station," an officer replied.

As she opened the windows, Gayla remarked, "This place smells so musty. I told you we should have come here last summer. Now we're going to freeze just trying to get some fresh air."

"So, let's drive around while the place airs out," suggested Hephanaethus. "I need to refresh my memory on what all there is to do around here anyway."

"Do you think its safe to leave the windows open while were just out gallivanting?"

"Of course. Are you afraid the *boogey man* will get you?" he teased.

"Watch your head," a policeman stated as he lifted David upward, intentionally banging his head against the frame of the car.

There was no wheel chair waiting for David here. This time, he would have to hobble to reach the police station.

Inside, a large Hispanic lady sat behind the counter.

As the officers pressed him forward, he pleaded, "Can I make that phone call now?"

"Not yet. Your name, sir?"

"David Brooks," he replied disappointedly.

"Your home address and your home telephone," she continued as she slid the forms and an ink pen across the desk.

"You'll have to fill it out for him, Maria," announced one of the policemen behind David. "It's probably best that he stays handcuffed as much as possible."

The hefty clerk seemed annoyed that the offender would cause her more work.

"Okay, Mr. Brooks. I need you to answer the following questions."

As Hephanaethus and Gayla explored the surrounding area, he paid close attention to the details of the town. He noted churches, supermarkets, department stores, and overpasses above all other landmarks. Schemes piled on top of each other as he contemplated the fun he would have when Gayla ceased to amuse him.

At the Boston laboratory, Jim Turner worked diligently in an attempt to fuse DNA from lung tissue with an unfertilized egg when Susan, the laboratory's receptionist, approached.

"Dr. Turner, you have a phone call." she stated grimly.

He was puzzled by the tone of her voice. She was typically very chipper, but he could tell that she had intentionally dampened her mood. He walked to the phone as he looked at her curiously.

"Hello?"

"Jim, I have some terrible news for you," Professor Cook stammered. "The laboratory in Phoenix exploded today. The rescue workers found what they think was a body and aren't sure whether or not another one might have been completely consumed in the flames. I've tried to call both David and Trevor several times now. Neither one have answered. I just thought that you should know."

Jim remained silent as he listened to the Professor's words. He wondered which one of his friends had perished in the fire, or had they both? He considered the fact that he might have died with them had he been there. His heart sank as he began to grasp the finality of their passing.

"The body," Jim started as his abdominal muscles tightened, " . . . when will they hold a funeral for it?"

"Not until after they have been able to identify it," Cook replied with a sigh.

"Good evening, David," the investigator greeted politely in an attempt to gain David's trust. "I'm Detective Gill, a member of the Arizona State Police Department. I'm investigating the alleged charges of the murder of Trevor Williams, the murder of Michelle Macintosh, the attempted murder of Charles Macintosh, the arson of Research and Developmental Pursuits laboratory, the assault on a officer of the law, grand theft auto, the illegal possession of a firearm, and the evasion of justice of which you are suspected." The detective paused to catch his breath before proceeding.

David grew numb as his situation worsened. *They left out speeding and reckless driving,* he thought sarcastically. He was now beyond the point of feeling sorrow for the family members of the victims. His mood grew calm, cold, and hopeless.

Detective Gill stared into David's eyes as he prepared to finish the advisement of rights. The detective saw no shock, no remorse, and no possibility of innocence.

Detective Gill continued, "I advise you that under the Fifth Amendment of the Constitution you have the right to remain silent, that is, to say nothing at all. Any statement you make, oral or written, may be used as evidence against you in a trial or in other judicial or administrative proceedings. You have the right to consult a lawyer and to have a lawyer present during this interview."

David debated over whether or not he should get a lawyer. Legally, he knew he needed one. He could spend the rest of his days imprisoned, most likely on death row for the offenses of which he was already certain to be convicted. On the other hand, requesting a lawyer would add several more hours to the time it would take to convince the police of the existence of the clone and to find out what had happened to Gayla.

"You may obtain a lawyer of your own choosing, at your own expense. If you cannot afford a lawyer, and want one, one will be appointed for you before any questioning. You may request a lawyer at any time during this interview. If you decide to answer questions, you may stop the questioning at any time. Do you understand your rights?" the investigator asked while anticipating David's motives.

David nodded his head and whispered, "Yes".

"Do you want a lawyer?" the anxious detective probed.

David continued the internal debate. *I can stop the questioning after I let them know about Gayla, then I can get a lawyer.*

He decided. With a slow shake of his head, David sighed and took a deep breath. "No," he replied dreadfully, hoping that he had made the right decision.

"Are you willing to answer questions?" asked the detective.

"I've already answered two," David replied impatiently, waiting for his turn to do some real talking.

The detective nodded, noting both anger and sarcasm in David's voice.

Thomas Pope hovered above Michelle's body as he searched desperately for any evidence that could prove "beyond the shadow of a doubt" that David Brooks was responsible for taking her life. His son, Joshua, had dated her for the last two years of high school. Joshua had mentioned to him three days ago his plans for marriage. Thomas was not a man known to show emotions, yet he cried with his son after sharing the news of her death.

Joshua blamed himself. He and Michelle would have been at the movies that night, like every other Monday night, if only he hadn't volunteered to work an extra night to acquire extra money. Monday nights were the only nights in which neither typically had to work.

"If I had not been working," he said, weeping, "she wouldn't have been there."

On the front of her teeth, her own blood and skin were wedged violently into the cracks near her gums. On the backside of her teeth, Thomas noticed something that could in theory be more helpful—tiny bits of bloody flesh between her teeth that most likely would not have been wedged in their current location from her mouth striking the bedpost. Based on the statement from Charles Macintosh, the only witness, this should be the skin of her attacker.

He knew the importance of his findings; he alone had to find specific evidence, not clues, not possibilities, but evidence that proved David Brooks had been the man that had taken Michelle's life. Sure, they had a witness, her father, an old man with such poor vision that he had been advised not to drive a motor vehicle. A man whom was suspected of showing the early symptoms of Alzheimer's. The testimony would be discredited by any *decent*—in this case he would use that word loosely—public defense attorney. Some called Thomas a perfectionist when it came to his work; in his own mind he was far from that label. Four years ago, Juan Cisco, a sex-offender walked freely out of the courtroom because Thomas had neglected to gather sufficient evidence to prove the guilt. The forensics had been plenty to convince Thomas but fell short of convincing the jury. The scolding he had received from the victim's father after the trial still echoed through his mind every time he conducted a new investigation.

While he continued piecing clues together in an attempt to form concrete evidence, both of his counterparts examined a more mysterious corpse, or at least what was believed to be a corpse.

Charles Macintosh knelt beside a large chunk of granite and

wept. On the gravestone was engraved the name of "EMILY MACINTOSH." The old man rubbed tears down his withered face as he spoke towards the stone. "I tried my best, Emily. I couldn't do it without you. I hope Michelle is with you now." Streams of teary snot flowed from the man's nostrils as he reached and grabbed the stone with both arms. Moving closer against the stone and clinging tightly, he whispered, "We'll all be together again real soon, I promise."

It seemed as if Charles was living though his worst nightmare. The night was cold and dark and he was left alone in the world. Charles stretched his form out on the plot where he had planned to rest his body for eternity, an eternity that he would gladly trade for the life of his daughter. His tear moistened skin chapped in the cool winter wind as he continued to share his despair with the cold, inanimate granite block.

"Who's body was in the laboratory?" Detective Gill asked.

"Trevor Williams," David replied.

"How do you know the identity of the body, David?"

"Because I saw the body before the lab burned?"

"Did you kill Trevor Williams?"

"No," David responded as he looked at the clock desperately. Suddenly, another faint glimmer of hope streaked through David's mind. "Can I call my wife?" he asked, "I'm worried about her."

"Can you wait until after the interview?" the detective asked before arriving at his next question. "Why are you worried about her?"

"I'm afraid she's dead," David said without even showing emotion at this point.

The detective looked at David's weary face. *Has he killed her too?* Detective Gill wondered. This was an interruption to his planned line of questioning, but it could reveal even more information if he went along with David's request.

As Gayla lay next to Hephanaethus watching the weather report, she pouted, "Fog tonight and rain tomorrow. It figures. We finally come back to Florida and we have record breaking cold temperatures. I certainly hope the weather has cleared up by our anniversary. We should've waited a little longer I suppose. I'm sorry, I shouldn't have pressed the issue. If we had waited like you wanted to, we could've enjoyed the whole vacation a lot more."

"Who said that I'm not enjoying it now?" Hephanaethus replied. "We can still have plenty of time together. You just relax and I'll go get us some snacks for later on, okay?"

"Don't you want me to come with you?" Gayla questioned, reluctant to let him take off and leave her lonely again.

"I'm just going to the store. I'll be back in twenty minutes, okay? I promise."

She nodded more in acceptance than in agreement.

As Thomas Pope carefully removed the last bit of skin from between the backs of Michelle's lower teeth, his beeper sounded. He ignored it at first, and continued with his examination as he looked for any skin or blood beneath her fingernails. As the beeper sounded again, he gently placed her hand back on the table by her side and jerked the annoying pager from his side. As he suspected, the number belonged to the police station.

"Ken," he called to one of the other detectives who had been examining a smaller, flaky, black corpse, "could you call the station for me . . . see what they want?"

The other detective nodded.

"Can't figure this one out," he informed his senior counterpart. "The bones were 'heat shrunk,' an' most of the teeth popped right out of their sockets before we could compare any dental records."

The younger investigator called the police station. "This is Ken Jones. Tom said you guys were trying to contact us."

"Yeah," Detective Gill answered. "I have a name for 'Mr.

Crispy.' Its Trevor Williams. I haven't had time to find out anything else for you though."

"Thanks for the name. It's more than we had so far," Jones admitted.

A detective listened intently as a phone in David's home rang.

In the interrogation room, Detective Gill stood near David. He had yet to see any sign of emotion from David and hoped that he would be able to deduce some hint of David's true nature as he watched his facial expressions.

The phone rang a second time. To the detective secretly monitoring the call, this seemed normal. Conversely, to David, hours seemed to pass between the rings of the phone.

David tried to convince himself that he had already accepted the cruel reality of Gayla's fate as the phone rang yet a third time. It wasn't working. Tears welled up near the inner corners of his eyes as the telephone let out its fourth morbid ring. Earlier that same day, David was convinced that he could not possibly shed another tear beyond those he already had. Hearing Gayla's voice on the answering machine had proved him painfully wrong.

"Hi, you've reached the residence of David and Gayla Brooks. We're not here right now, so leave a message."

As David blubbered, the detective reconsidered his guilt, at least for killing his own wife. As for the others, well, evidence was still pointing a stiff finger directly at David. Gill lowered his head, partly in confusion over David's disturbance by Gayla's not answering the phone, and partially to contemplate if David had a valid reason for concern.

Detective Gill stepped out into the hallway and motioned towards another detective.

"I need you to take a look inside this house," Gill stated as he handed the other man a piece of paper with David's address circled.

"I know it sounds flaky, but there may be a body inside the

110

house. We've got to check it out either way."

"Do you *actually* think that this place is going to turn out to be a crime scene?" Detective Harris questioned in a doubtful tone.

"Would you be willing to bet your career that it isn't?" replied Gill with an aggravated scowl on his face.

Chapter 12

A sign on the window advertised vegetable shortening on sale. Hephanaethus imagined how he could use this as part of his plan. He grabbed a shopping cart, strolled down the aisle, and proceeded to fill the cart with a case of vegetable shortening, three cases of motor oil, two boxes of large plastic freezer bags, and a quick selection of snacks to prevent Gayla from suspecting anything unusual.

As Hephanaethus approached the cashier with the odd assortment of groceries, he made an attempt to look away as much as possible, hoping that she wouldn't remember many details about his face. By morning, this combination of groceries would be a crucial piece of evidence for the most infamous tragedy to ever befall the panhandle portion of the state.

"Your total comes to one hundred twelve dollars and eighty-three cents, sir."

After paying for his strange arsenal, Hephanaethus handed the bag boy two folded one-dollar bills and said "I'll take them out, thanks."

"Thank you, sir," the youngster replied as he shoved the tip into his pocket.

Will it be the cashier or the bag boy? Hephanaethus wondered. *Maybe I'll just kill them both to be on the safe side,* he pondered. *They'll have to wait until I can make time for them.*

Hephanaethus placed the two bags containing the snack foods in the front passenger side seat and then opened the trunk of the car to stow the ingredients of the upcoming disaster.

Detective Harris rang the doorbell and waited. While he waited, he looked back at the driveway, which would have been empty if his own car were not parked there.

"What sort of killer turns the lights off and locks up?" Harris grumbled beneath his breath as he contemplated the usefulness of forcing his way into the house.

No further evidence could be found, Thomas Pope concluded as he surveyed the shapely corpse of the young victim. He peeled the thin latex glove from his hand.

"Have you got it figured out yet?" Pope asked the other investigators.

"Not exactly," replied Ken Jones as he raked his forearm across his curly, light brown hair. "But Gill gave us a name, and according to records at the hospital, this guy used to weigh two hundred forty-three pounds. Can you believe that?"

Pope looked at the small charred corpse and tried to imagine whether or not the man was alive when the fire began.

He lifted the phone and tapped at the buttons; he had the mortician's number memorized for years now, and it was a sure sign that the world was a foul and cruel place.

The door of the condominium bounced open as Hephanaethus fumbled two thin, plastic grocery bags filled with snack foods in his left hand while returning his keys to the pocket of his pants with his right hand. He sat the bags on the kitchen counter and strolled into the bedroom where he noticed Gayla lying soundly asleep. He returned to the kitchen and put most of the food away, particularly the perishables that would need to be refrigerated. He had to insure that she never grew suspicious of his trips, otherwise he would have to kill her and that would take some of the thrill out of his latest game.

He crept into bed beside her as he looked at the clock. *Eleven thirty four*, he noted. *Enough time to rest this frail human body before my busy morning starts.*

"You don't have keys to your own house?" Detective Gill asked suspiciously.

"No. They were in my pants, but my pants were stolen."

The explanation created more questions than it answered.

"We have a key hidden in the back, it's under a brick, just below the electric meter." David blurted, hoping to hasten the detective's entry into the house.

Gill raised the receiver from the cradle and pressed the blinking button, then proceeded to pass on David's directions to Detective Harris.

Detective Gill continued to imagine how this paranoia of David's would tie into the crimes he was allegedly responsible for. He peered into David's eyes as if he were attempting to examine his soul while he waited for some sort of news from his co-worker. Gill wasn't entirely sure this was even David's house, or more importantly, he wasn't even sure that this man was really David Brooks; he had no identification to prove it.

"Okay, I found the key." replied Harris. "But they apparently have an alarm system on the house. Does this guy happen to know the code?" he asked as if it might prove whether or not this was really David's house.

"The code for your alarm system?" Detective Gill asked as he continued to peer at David.

"It's zero, nine, one, nine, nine, two." David replied

anxiously.

"O nine, nineteen, ninety two." Gill repeated.

"Bingo," came the reply from Harris as the alarm silenced. The detective flipped a light switch on the wall of the living room, then turned off his flashlight. He called out

"Hello, is anyone home."

As he suspected, there was no response to his question.

Harris moved from room to room in the house looking closely for any signs of a struggle, but such signs did not exist—not on the first floor, at least. Then he crept up the stairs to the master bedroom. The bed was made perfectly and all the windows were locked. He continued his search.

Stopping in the hallway, before going down the stairs, Harris noticed a picture on the wall. He looked closely, it certainly appeared to be the same man that was at the station being questioned and the woman standing beside him was a beautiful brunette wearing a wedding gown. He removed the picture from the wall and continued to look at the other pictures.

"Why do you think your wife is dead, David?" asked the detective.

"I think my twin killed her," he replied blankly.

"Your twin? Do you have a twin brother?"

David breathed in deeply and said, "I *did*."

Again, Detective Gill grew more confused with every answer that David gave. "Okay, you *had* a twin, and now you believe that this twin killed your wife?"

"Yes"

"What happened to your twin?"

"He was killed when we were ten years old. He was buried in the woods and no one ever found him." Clearly, delirium had conquered David. He was no longer able to speak about a matter as complex as this during this time he needed to grieve his loss.

"Did you kill him, David?" Detective Gill asked as he contemplated the full scope of a possible life-long serial killer who had begun with his own twin brother at the age of ten.

"No," he whispered.

"Then how do you know where he's buried if no one ever found his body?"

"The man who killed my wife and Trevor told me," David replied as he looked forward to the questioning ending. He was extremely hungry and tired, and needed some time alone. Looking at the detective across the table from his position, he sensed that this man did not believe him.

The detective searched every closet, the garage, the basement, and still no signs of any sort of struggle.

"This idiot . . ." huffed Harris, as he looked at his watch, "caused me to work three extra hours tonight for nothing."

At this point, the detective would have been glad to find something, anything to prove he had not been sent on a wild goose chase.

A flashing light caught his eye. It was the answering machine. Harris could only hope that he would be able to learn something from a message left behind. Five messages had been recorded recently. Harris pushed the play button and listened intently.

The first message was Professor Cook's voice. "David, this is Professor Cook. Please call me and let me know that you're okay."

A second message. "Yes, this is Professor Cook again. Call me."

The last three messages were blank. Harris wished that this Professor Cook had left a telephone number so that he could call him and try to deduce some sort of information. This too, had turned out to be a waste of his time.

"Can we stop the questioning now?" asked David. "I'm starving. I just want something to eat."

"Sure," replied Detective Gill as he looked at his watch.

"We will have to keep you in custody until the questioning has been completed though. You'll have to spend what's left of the night in confinement and we will continue to try to locate your wife."

After embalming and then cleaning the body for its final time, the mortician prepared to clothe Michelle's lifeless body in the gown her father had selected earlier that day.

The beautician applied extra makeup to the round circular bruises on Michelle's cheeks. The blood in her right eye would not be seen after he closed her eyes again. The fake grin he placed on her face would hide the teeth chipped by her own bedpost. While the beautician knew she could never restore the beauty Michelle possessed in life, she would give it her best attempt.

David's answering machine began to fill up with new messages, not only from Professor Cook but also from Jim Turner. Jim called David and then Trevor every thirty minutes for the next four hours before going to bed after work.

Promptly at four o'clock the alarm sounded. Hephanaethus looked toward Gayla. Thankfully, she was a sound sleeper. He crept about the bedroom donning some comfortable clothes and proceeded out the door.

Two policemen entered the room. Detective Gill gave a quick and inconspicuous nod.

The officers led David out of the room to get some food.

Gill ran his hand upwards through the back of his short, sweaty bristly hair. He looked forward to ending his long day, but he knew as soon as David was ready to talk he would need to be back in the office again.

As he turned off the lights and started to pull the door shut behind him the phone rang. He was tempted not to answer it.

"Hello, Detective . . ."

"Nothing!" blared Detective Harris. "He's wasting our time." Harris continued.

"This guy is dangerous," Gill argued. "We need to follow up on *any* small clue we can get from him."

"Well, there's nothing here, but I'll bring these pictures in so we'll have something for the bulletin."

Detective Gill rubbed his jaw. "I don't know if it'll make a difference. Bring whatever you think might help. Be prepared. This case is going to keep us busy for months."

"Great," replied Harris sarcastically.

Two large paper sacks filled with empty oil containers leaned against the rail of the overpass. The night was dark and chilly. As the meteorologist had predicted, a heavy morning fog began to fill the landscape, substantially limiting the range of visibility. Hephanaethus watched as two dull spheres of light drifted through the dense cloud. The drivers could barely see the road through the mass of cold, apparently weightless, mist.

"This is going to be too easy," Hephanaethus spoke proudly, in anticipation of the upcoming tragedy.

He gathered the top edges of the plastic bag and tied them into a double knot. After loading the trash into the trunk of his car, he looked in both directions on the road below. There was no traffic coming; now he could finish his plan. One heavy bag after another hit the road below; some burst spilling their contents, others survived the impact harmlessly. Huge globs of the vegetable shortening splattered in all directions as each container emptied its contents onto the moist pavement below. All that was left for Hephanaethus to do now was wait.

As David put the last bite of his cheeseburger in his mouth the guards placed their hands beneath his arms to lift him upward. David had no idea where the guards would take him next, but he had lost any real concern. At this point he was sure that he could rest anywhere. It had been a long and painful day. He looked at the leg brace on his knee. *That was yesterday morning,* he thought. *It seems like it happened a month ago.*

The guards led David down the stairs. Already smelling the alcohol in the vomit of the nearest cell, he could only hope that this would not be where he stayed. Holding his breath as he walked down the hallway, he was relieved to see that he was being taken to a cell currently unoccupied.

After the casket containing Michelle's body was placed in the viewing room of the funeral home, the doors opened. The old man looked around the room as the undertaker departed. He was alone in the room; he was alone in the world, for that matter. The only surviving family that would be attending the funeral was his niece in Michigan and his nephew in South Carolina. It would be some time before they arrived. He knew that a few of his closest neighbors were sure to drop by to express their sorrow for him and probably several of Michelle's friends, whom he had considered peculiar at best, given the latest trends and fads that the youngsters followed.

All in all, two days from now he would be alone in this world. This was what he had feared most about living out his twilight years. His wife, Emily was nineteen years younger, yet he had outlived her. It seemed even less fair now than it had then. He looked forward to death; he needed a change from this dusty old earth anyway. Other than the grief of knowing he would never see his little girl again, beyond knowing that she would never have the opportunity to truly experience life, good and bad, he was, in fact, jealous of her. Two thoughts had kept him from committing suicide on the eve of Emily's funeral: one, he was a God fearing man, and wouldn't have the opportunity to ask for forgiveness for his final sin, and two, someone would have to see Michelle through those dreaded teenage years. *Now, I have one less reason*, he concluded as he began to question his own faith.

To the east, a globe of light illuminated through the fog. As it grew nearer and brighter, Hephanaethus clenched his fists tightly. He looked at his watch and estimated that the normal morning flow of traffic had to start soon. The illumination took an oblong shape, then split. "Perfect!" he hissed. As the first vehicle, a mid-sized sedan, approached, he knelt down and retrieved one of the empty vegetable shortening cans and tossed it over the opposite side of the bridge. Hephanaethus realized that the empty container would do no damage to the car, but it did have the desired effect.

As he drove through the dense fog, the driver concentrated on the road ahead. Suddenly, a loud clunk startled the driver as a large object tumbled down his windshield. Instinctively, he slammed on the brakes.

With a full stomach, David had slept well during his first two hours of confinement. As the barred door slid open he awoke. A large pale man entered the cell as the policeman closed the door behind him. A thin mustache covered his harelip, which in turn covered his massive gap toothed, overbite. His best features held a striking resemblance to a poorly drawn cartoon character.

He stood and looked at David's face as he summed him up. Despite the fact that David had not been able to shave for the last couple of days, he could tell that David was normally a clean-cut type, not the usual person he expected to see in the same cell as himself. He reared his head, crossed his arms and spoke.

"What are you in for, tax evasion?" he inquired in both a threatening and sarcastic tone.

David attempted to use his predicament to avoid another unfortunate one.

"Two counts of murder and stealing a police car," David

replied calling the larger man's bluff.

The large man quickly changed his threatening demeanor, he had heard about the incident that morning but expected someone capable of causing that amount of commotion to have a more hardened looking face. The man decided to take more time to observe David and his actions before trying to dominate him.

The treads of the tires filled with the greasy, white paste as they rolled through the splattered puddles. Plastic sacks filled with motor oil spilled their contents under the pressure of the automobile.

As the driver depressed the brakes, the wheels stopped but the car kept moving in random directions as the operator continued a rigorous series of maneuvers attempting to regain control of the vehicle. The red sedan spun around facing the vehicle that was behind it only seconds before.

A large white diesel truck hauling a cargo of fuel followed the red sedan through the thick fog. The driver was tired and weary; he looked forward to the end of his journey. He had driven for twelve hours straight. Ahead, he could barely make out whether the red sedan had applied his brakes or if the red glow was the typical amount of light produced by the rear lights. As he traveled beneath the overpass, he watched as the sedan zigzagged back and forth. He lifted his foot from the gas pedal, prepared to stop. The muscles of his jaws clenched tightly as he noticed the car change directions only ten yards in front of the large and powerful rig.

The large man watched David sleep. *So what,* he considered. *So he killed a couple of people. This is my fourth time in the "big house." He needs to learn some respect.* As he studied David's much smaller build, he knew he had to outweigh his cellmate by at least a hundred fifty pounds.

PSYCLONE

Hephanaethus watched in amusement as the large truck drew closer to the red sedan. *Killing a man in the flesh is no challenge; I have done it tens of thousands of times. It is so much more rewarding to kill a man's soul,* he decided proudly as he pondered what David's life would be like if he had survived the explosion somehow. He thought about the old man who had watched his daughter die at his hands. *What were his last thoughts as I crushed his skull,* he wondered sadistically.

The driver of the red sedan watched in terror as the lights of the large truck drew closer. He grabbed the handle of his door, instinctively attempting to flee the vehicle before the oncoming impact took place. As he heard the folding of metal, he looked down to see that the seatbelt across his chest and lap would prevent his escape.

The truck driver straightened his arms, pushing his back firmly against the seat behind him as his knee straightened, forcing the brake pedal within an inch of the metal floor. Through his peripheral vision he could see the gas-filled tanker behind him swinging widely to the left, barely clearing the banked wall on the opposite side of the underpass. Through the windshield, he watched helplessly as he gained a clear view of the sedan driver's distorted and terrorized face. In less than a second, he lost sight of the other man's face as the hood of his own vehicle eclipsed the less fortunate man's windshield.

Red metal peeled upward before buckling and collapsing. The moment moved in slow motion, yet he could not alter its outcome. He wondered how his children would react to the news when they learned of his demise? Would his wife remarry? Did he want her to? Who would raise his children? It would be a difficult task for her to take on by herself. Where would they bury his body? The red metal cracked through the glass. Was there a chance he would survive? *Maybe, but I would most likely be a paraplegic,* he deduced. The glass shattered, caving inwards; the steering wheel began to press against his chest. He blinked his eyes as a reaction to protect them; they would never reopen again.

The tanker behind the truck proceeded with its revolution around the truck's cab. Grease slung upwards through the air, oil splashed and then smeared along the path of the huge tires. Metal folded and crunched, glass shattered, and Hephanaethus smiled.

The tanker and the cab raked the compressed car from the road, into the field beyond the shoulder. The momentum of the trailer sheered off the metal hitch from the cab headed in another direction. The tanker tumbled to its side, crashing down on the sealed cap at its top.

Children argued over which Pokemon was the strongest and which teen music group was the best as the school bus crept through the morning mist.

The driver proceeded cautiously; she knew that the safety of the children was completely her responsibility until they arrived at school.

A man on a motorcycle raised the visor of his helmet to get a better look through the fog. He increased his speed slightly; he did not want to be late for work again. As he descended from the underpass, his wheel wobbled.

The school bus approached the underpass. In the distance, the driver could see a single headlight, though she could not tell if it were a motorcycle or a car with a light burned out. The tires of the bus, rolled through the oily paste unnoticed by the driver.

The man jerked against the pull of the handlebars and redistributed his weight. Normally, he could have averted disaster, but this was not a normal situation. He could see the headlights of a tall vehicle approaching from the east as his motorcycle slammed downward and sent him scooting across the slick pavement at a slightly different angle

Metal scraped against the pavement and a streak of sparks became a streak of fire. The man who had been riding on the motorcycle could see the wall of flames as it passed him. He rolled his body in an attempt to stop the sliding. The fire rushed closer as he tried to stand and flee. With both the pavement and his clothing being completely saturated in the slick and flammable mixture, even standing was a challenge. He had made it to a half erect position when the flames spread up his body.

The bus driver mashed the brake pedal downward. At her present rate of speed, she managed to stop the gargantuan vehicle with only a slight spin in the rear. She looked in confusion as a wall of fire split the road and widened before her. After hearing a thud against the bumper, she noticed that flames began to engulf the area just outside the main door. She leapt from her seat and instructed a child near the back to open the emergency door. There was no activity behind the bus and given her panic-stricken situation it seemed to be the best alternative.

The door was open and the first child, a third grade boy jumped free of the bus. The fire spread to the shoulder of the road and approached the leaking tanker.

Hephanaethus sat in his car and watched emotionlessly from the overpass. He drove it down the road, closer to the school bus, to get a better view of the destruction. From here, he could watch to see how many children would be spared.

The boy turned and stretched out his arms encouraging his little brother to jump.

A small girl with long blonde hair and blue eyes sat in her seat confused as to why the bus driver seemed so upset. She looked out her window; she couldn't see the burning man thrashing about on the road ahead, all she saw was a man sitting in his car. The window was rolled down and she saw the man smile. She smiled back at him gleefully and waved.

Hephanaethus stared back at the little girl until a deep red-orange, fiery cloud blocked her face out.

Debris flew through the air as the mighty explosion rattled the glass in the windows of his rental car. He was certain that no one had survived.

Charles Macintosh was exhausted. He had been awake for forty-three hours now, with the only exception being the two hours he had spent unconscious after the blow to his head from the strangers' heel. He stared sadly in the direction of the casket as friends and more distant family members tried to express their sorrow for him.

He approached the casket and gently rubbed Michelle's neck with the back of his curled fingers.

"Damn him! Why didn't he just go ahead and kill me too?" he growled painfully.

Several other mourners heard the remark, but none would attempt to answer.

Upon returning to his seat, he crossed his arms on the pew in front of him, rested his head on the cushion his folded arms had formed, and began to weep quietly.

The door to a green metal trash crate slid open. Hephanaethus tucked the oil-saturated bags beneath some of the other bags. While he considered himself above the confines of mortal law, he didn't want any evidence that would raise police suspicions. It wouldn't stop him but it might lead to unnecessary complications. He peeked into the trunk of the car again to make sure that all potential evidence was gone.

Upon his arrival at the condo, he washed his hands and crept into bed beside Gayla again, making sure to not wake her.

Chapter 13

The cot in the cell reminded David of the one that he had been strapped to before the laboratory had exploded. As he rolled over searching for a comfortable position on the urine stained mattress, he noticed that he was being watched closely by the large man slumped against the nearby opposite wall of the cell. To avoid his stare, David rolled over to face the closer wall. He couldn't sleep anymore; his guess of what the man was thinking made him nauseous. "I have to get out of here," he whimpered under his breath. While he had no desire to continue to live what was sure to be a life of painfully haunting memories, he didn't want to spend the rest of his life being a homosexual slave to his cellmates either. *They'll have to kill me*, he concluded.

Hephanaethus lay soundly asleep next to Gayla when she woke. He had just fallen back to sleep and needed another short nap before he resumed his day, knowing he would need plenty of energy to continue living his double life without drawing suspicions.

"So much for a romantic night, huh?" Gayla whispered to her sleeping mate. She placed her hand flat down on his chest and rested her head atop it as she slid her leg over the top of his. She wondered how long he would want to sleep before they could go out and enjoy their vacation.

The alarm clock sounded its shrill beep. Detective Gill didn't want to get started on his busy day again, but he did want to complete the interview with David as soon as possible. He reached over and silenced the alarm, then continued to lie in his bed considering how much of David's story might be true.

David had seemed to speak in riddles. *He has to be insane,* thought Gill, playing David's words over in his head: "My twin killed her." and "He was killed when we were ten years old." *He's definitely insane,* Gill confirmed; there was simply no other logical explanation. As he continued to consider David's position, he determined that he would have to insure that David obtained a lawyer. At this rate, he did not expect to get a truthful confession from David, not in the near future anyway, and maybe a lawyer could at least extract a believable statement from him, even if it was fabricated.

As Gill continued to lay in bed trying to convince himself that he had a true reason for getting out of bed today, a question formed in his mind. In fact, he was almost disappointed in himself for not coming up with this question earlier that morning. As he stared wide-eyed towards the ceiling above his bed, he mouthed the question softer than a whisper, "Where would Gayla have been at three o'clock in the morning?"

Forming numerous answers to this question, he sporadically jumped to several conclusions, none of which were connected to another.

Maybe she was having an affair, and David was going to kill her for it. Maybe David was right, someone had killed her then removed the body or maybe they had led her out of the house before they killed her . . .

Dozens of possibilities raced through his mind, none were the same and none bore any resemblance to David's testimony. They did however, give him the much needed adrenaline rush that would push him headlong into another busy day.

"Ya know, I'm in here for killin' somebody too," the fat, bearded cellmate announced to David, not caring if he was really asleep or not. "I shot a man at point blank range right in front of his family. Blew damn near half his head off," he continued as if he were a new rooster in the lot trying to take control of the coop.

David lay motionless in his bed. He could call the man's bluff with one of his own, or he could continue to ignore the man, but eventually confrontation was inevitable, this much, he still remembered from high school.

The sound of other mourner's entering the chapel-style funeral home woke Charles from his slumber. He looked toward the casket sadly, *If only it could have been a horrible dream*, he thought to himself as his focused upon the lifeless corpse.

He stood, then turned to hear a neighbor and a couple of other people he barely knew express their sympathies for him as they began to speak of the memories they had of Michelle's short life. He nodded politely and interrupted, "I need to get some fresh air." He paused. "I'll be back shortly."

Charles pushed open the glass door, walked down the narrow steps in front of the funeral home, and dug his hand into his pocket, retrieving the keys to his old, rusty Ford pickup truck. As he started the engine, he remembered how yesterday morning he had started the engine and seen a man down the road, a man that he should've killed.

After driving a short distance down the road to a local pawnshop, he sat outside looking through the bug-splattered windshield of his truck, then through the plate glass window of the pawnshop and toward the gun case inside. True, his vision wasn't what it used to be, but he wasn't blind yet. He glanced down at the dashboard of his truck and slapped it gently twice.

"They won't have to worry about old man Macintosh drivin' around in a couple of days," he whispered to his truck as though it would understand.

Without speaking another word, he opened the door and half fell from the driver's seat. Then he proceeded into the pawnshop.

Gayla looked at the groceries that Hephanaethus had purchased the previous night. *Nothing but junk food, that's David*, she thought as a stressful grin shimmered across her lips. She noticed the white plastic sacks cluttering the countertop; one was completely empty, the other contained a box of "Chicken in a Biscuit" snack crackers that he had neglected to put away, and a thin strip of paper—a cash register receipt to be more exact. Gayla didn't bother to see whether he had paid for the groceries in cash or written a check, but she knew that he was infamous for writing checks and failing to enter in the amount or bothering to balance the checkbook. She picked up the crackers and stowed them in the cabinet above the stove. Then she folded the register receipt and tucked it into the back pocket of her jeans. She didn't have time to balance the checkbook now, even if he did write a check; she was hungry and wanted to get to the store to buy some *real* food.

She picked up the sacks that lay on the counter and glanced at them almost mindlessly. They were white with red letters on them that read, "THOMPSON'S SUPERMARKET."

"I'm going to go get us some real food for breakfast," Gayla spoke towards her sleeping mate hoping he would wake up.

"That's fine," Hephanaethus replied as he rolled to his side and yawned before resuming his restful nap.

Again, she found herself growing frustrated with her mate. She grabbed the keys to the rental car and closed the door behind her.

As she grasped the steering wheel of the vehicle, she felt a slick, greasy residue. It seemed odd but she paid little attention to it at the time.

Charles focused his vision on the 9mm handgun near the center of the top shelf. He hadn't owned or even fired a firearm since before Michelle's birth. His wife had begged him to sell the weapons before they brought a young child into the home. Now he contemplated whether his current situation would have been altered, even slightly, if he had bought this handgun last week. He didn't really like handguns; they only served one purpose, but that one purpose was why millions were bought and sold every year.

"Can I help you, sir?" asked the short, thin man behind the counter.

"Do ya sell any ammo for that gun ya got there?" the old man inquired as he pointed at the black metal weapon.

"No sir, only the gun, and you'll have to get a permit for a handgun."

"Is that so?" Charles questioned, and then in the back of his mind he remembered seeing the issue discussed on television some time before. "What about that old rifle?" he questioned.

"That's a Winchester 30-30," the sales clerk stated. "There weren't many of this model produced . . ."

Charles waved his hand and said, "You can save your sales pitch. I'm going to buy a gun here today."

"Would you like to see this one, sir?" the clerk offered.

Charles grabbed the gun in his right hand. He didn't make any suicidal motions but the clerk had a feeling he knew the old man's intent for the weapon. *He's an old man and no telling what his circumstances are*, the clerk thought. *Besides, it's a legal sell*, he reminded himself.

Again, Jim tried to reach his former coworkers. Though he knew that he needed to get back to work, his mind was preoccupied. He unzipped a small black suitcase and considered packing it, but didn't. Yet, he was compelled to go to Phoenix, but then again wondered whether he should wait until the body had been identified.

Dr. Martinez stopped her work as she looked at the phone. Trevor hadn't called as he had claimed that he would. She wondered if she had ever really meant anything to him or if she had always and would always be less important than his work.

"See if he's ready to resume the questioning," Gill blared as he burst through the door of the police station.

"Who are you talking about?" asked an officer near the front desk.

"David Brooks. Go get him and see if he's willing to answer more questions."

With a quick nod, the officer spun and hastily left to retrieve the aforementioned suspect.

David stared at the walls, waiting for the news that someone had discovered Gayla's body. *Where could she be?* David wondered. His thinking was interrupted again, but this time it wasn't by his rotund cellmate; it was a different voice, one somewhat higher pitched and barely masculine.

"David Brooks," the short, thin officer called.

"Which one of you is David Brooks?"

David raised from his cot, part of him hoping that the young man would have some information regarding Gayla, part of him dreading the news because it would then be final.

"I am," David replied with a crackling voice. Then he cleared his throat and repeated louder and deeper, "I am."

"Are you ready to resume the questioning?" the officer asked.

David's head swung down as if he had been clobbered from behind with a baseball bat. The officer hadn't brought him any news at all. Instead they just wanted more from him. He knew that he would have to come clean about the cloning business. It was a no win situation. Either directly or indirectly, he would be held responsible for the crimes. He raised his head back up to make eye contact with the man again and then nodded *yes*.

As Gayla drove towards the grocery store she reached down to turn on the radio. The radio was only to break the silence, she was on her long awaited vacation, she was over two thousand miles away from her home in Arizona, but she felt just as lonely as usual.

As the volume increased she immediately recognized the words to one of her favorite songs, "Jesse's Girl." She moved with the music in spite of the seatbelt that pinned her to the driver's side bucket seat. The song dwindled as a news report took over the airwaves. She moved her right hand near the tuning knob to tune the radio to another station but stopped with a bit of morbid curiosity as she heard the words, "Twenty-one people died this morning in a multi-vehicle car accident which the police believe might have been started by a malicious prank."

As she pulled into the parking lot of the nearby supermarket—the same one Hephanaethus had visited late last night—her eyes fixed on a sign in the window that read, "Crisco Vegetable Shortening $2.59 48 ounce can" in large, black bold letters against a yellow background. Then, through the static of the radio, she heard the words; ". . . both lanes of the highway were covered by a thick layer of what appears to be motor oil and either lard or vegetable shortening, according to local police detectives."

Probably teenagers that don't realize the consequences, Gayla thought to herself sadly as she turned the ignition key, stopping both the car and the radio. Instinct told her that the items used to create the tragedy had been purchased in the same grocery store she was about to enter.

"I'll take it," Charles told the pawnshop clerk, as he looked him squarely in the eyes.

The clerk nodded as he punched the price into the cash register and added the taxes.

"Your total is four hundred seventy-six dollars and ninety-nine cents," the clerk replied.

The old man reached in his pocket. He wouldn't need to write a check for this purchase; he had stashed away several thousand dollars cash in the old farmhouse he used to call home. The point had been to have money for his twilight years so that his daughter Michelle wouldn't have to take on his financial burdens. None of this mattered now. Michelle was gone, and after he had insured that she had received a proper burial, his twilight years would come to a long awaited end.

Placing his frail hand on the weapon, Charles pulled the rifle from the edge of the glass top counter then looked at the clerk. Charles nodded at the clerk, said "Thank you," and for the first time since the stranger had arrived at his door, he smiled.

David hobbled through the open doorway of Detective Gill's office. His knee was still held motionless at a slight angle by the leg brace outside his state issued clothing, his head was lowered, and his hands were cuffed in front of him. A shave, a shower, and a chance to brush his teeth were much needed. The sour taste of his morning breath and a slimy, yet gritty, film coating his teeth made him hesitant to exhale through his mouth as he spoke. David knew he looked guilty as he slowly raised his head to make eye contact with Detective Gill.

The expression on Gill's face gave away his suspicions. "David, I feel that it would be in your best interest to attain a lawyer at this point," Gill stated blankly. He looked into David's eyes, or at least glanced into them, before David returned his gaze downward again. Gill didn't know for certain that Brooks was guilty of all the crimes he was being accused of, but he did know that David was guilty of some unspeakable crime.

David remained silent; he still had the right to do so. Contemplating his need for a good attorney, he doubted that the court appointed public defender would do as much for him as a lawyer receiving money directly from his personal bank account. Yet, for all the money that he had accumulated, he couldn't access it; his identity had been stolen. He felt like an illegal immigrant without a green card. There was no proof of who he was, no proof that he had not committed the crime, and now his decision had already been made by his sudden financial dilemma. At last he spoke. "I suppose I'll need a court appointed attorney."

Gill nodded, then replied anxiously. "I'll have you one here shortly."

David looked back at the detective and asked, "Will I have the opportunity to clean up soon?"

Gill looked back at him. Normally, he would have been given this opportunity as he was processed, but because of the haste the police department had taken, David had to specifically request even the basic elements of a normal day, even for a prisoner. The detective realized that this case was not being handled like it should have been, and the public defense attorney was sure to use the matter against the police department, himself included. Detective Gill nodded again. "Yes, I can arrange that for you, and by tomorrow you will be on a more normal schedule for such matters."

Looking upwards at the red letters centered near the roof of the supermarket she read "THOMPSON'S SUPERMARKET;" the name sounded oddly familiar. Then she remembered the thin, white plastic bags crumpled on the kitchen counter. Oh yes, this is where David bought the junk food last night, she remembered, still unsuspicious of her husband.

Charles slid the rifle behind and beneath the seat of his

pickup truck and looked across the road towards a strip mall. Squinting, he saw his next stop, a nearby sporting goods store.

"I would like to have a word in private with my client before we begin," John Wilson, the balding, middle aged, public defender told Detective Gill.

"Of course," replied Gill as he led both David and the lawyer into a small, windowless conference room, near the center of the building.

John opened his briefcase and removed a long yellow writing pad, then clicked the end of his ink pen. He waited to speak until Detective Gill closed the door behind him.

David felt more relaxed now that he had received a shower and the vulgar taste in his mouth had been replaced by a fresher one that had already began to grow stale again. Now that his face was free of the stubble, if not for the issued clothing that adorned his body, he would have appeared as normal as the average man on the street, perhaps better.

"David, the first thing that I need to remind you of is that I am *your* lawyer. I'm on *your* side. I need you to trust me. It's for your benefit and my own. I want you to tell me the *truth* about what happened. Don't leave out any details. Even something that might seem insignificant to you could have a major impact on what sentence you receive, if any at all."

His hands twisted wildly as he spoke, his fingers occasionally making prolonged jabs at the top of the table.

David could sense that John was nervous and he hoped that *he* wasn't the cause of John's nervousness. He also hoped that John's nervousness wouldn't be so apparent in the courtroom.

Chapter 14

Hephanaethus pried his eyes open, with the bedroom light still shining brightly from Gayla's earlier attempt to wake him from his slumber. Rising upward, he balanced himself with his hands turned backward, pressing into the mattress behind him, and called, "Gayla."

When he got no response, he twisted off the side of the bed and walked to the window, spreading the blinds with his fingers. The car was gone, and so was Gayla. His hands felt slick and he hoped that she wouldn't find any condemning evidence from his pernicious adventure, quite confident that she wouldn't. After all, he had several millennia of experience in covering his tracks, and he possessed an intellect far greater than most humans could even comprehend. The notion that she could actually catch *him* in a crime that he had deliberately tried to hide seemed ridiculous in retrospect.

While he waited, he turned on the television and scanned through various channels in search of a local news report. Eventually, he found a station that was broadcasting the news, but they weren't currently reporting the accident from this morning. Instead, the focus was on a racist incident that had occurred earlier that night. The picture in the background behind the reporter was that of burning cross. It reminded him of how he had started the tradition years ago. He remembered how he had convinced a group of weak-minded fools that it would scare away the blacks in the area.

They had begun this tradition to accomplish their own goals without putting any real thought into its sacrilegious implications. He had also convinced them to set ablaze their churches. In the days of forced segregation, the black people in the area would have no place to worship. Successfully, he had used racial hatred to his advantage. Then another symbol appeared in a caption behind the reporter; it was a swastika. Hephanaethus ignored the words of the reporter as he began to reminisce about another time.

Over sixty years ago, he had tried desperately to get someone else to utilize the concept of human cloning—a man named Adolph Hitler. He had spent even more time manipulating Hitler's life than he had David Brook's life.

After some Jews had slain his parents, little by little Hephanaethus had filled his mind with carefully planned ideas. Of all his manipulations, this was the one that he was most proud of. If only he had been able to sway more people into the notion of cloning the Arian race and creating an army to "cleanse" the earth, he would have had the same army that he hoped to build now.

A spotted, aged hand tilted the small, but heavy, box of bullets from the shelf of a nearby sporting goods store. The old man's eyes strained through his glasses as he read the package. It was exactly what he needed, though he had only needed a single bullet and in his own conservative mind, buying the whole box seemed to be a waste. He realized that first of all, the store wouldn't sell him a single bullet and secondly, such a request might draw suspicions to his purchase.

"Where should I start?" David asked as he prepared for a very long conversation.

John peered back, oblivious to the length of the story he was about to hear and shrugged his shoulders and stated, "Wherever you like, David"

David drew in a deep breath and started, "When I was born."

John already regretted his answer to David's question.

"I had a twin brother named Darryl. He was my *identical* twin. Less than a month after our tenth birthday, Darryl was kidnapped by a demon."

John listened intently and scribbled down Darryl's name, drawing a line. On the other end of the line he wrote "twin brother." He cringed, internally, as David spoke the word "demon," hoping that the cringe didn't show through his face, but he knew that it probably did.

"No one ever found my brother's body. For over twenty years now he has simply been listed as missing. Around the middle of December of last year, I decided to conduct an experiment. I drew DNA from my own blood and cloned myself. The clone was not meant to be a typical clone. I had altered the DNA strand to cause the clone to grow beyond the infant stage and to the same developmental stage as myself. Its never been heard of, but its not the first time I have cloned a mammal, though not another human, beyond the infant stage."

John continued listening to the story. So far, he had followed along okay, with the exception of one word, "demon." The lone word tainted the story to a point beyond the realm of credibility. From that word alone, he prepared to use an insanity plea for David's defense.

"I couldn't let anyone, even my own wife, Gayla, know about this clone. I knew it was illegal. For that crime, I am guilty. Anyway, as I was saying, I created this clone. I wanted so much to have my twin brother back, but not just for me, more for my mother. To this day, my mother still blames herself for Darryl's disappearance. I wanted to create him, fill him in on all the details of *his* past, and introduce him to my mother as Darryl. I wanted to give them something to believe in. Deep down, I knew they still wondered if he were out there somewhere . . . alive.

"After the clone was . . . born, so to speak . . . around the middle of last month, I had to put adult diapers on him. I raised him like my own child. I taught him things, and he learned exceptionally fast due to the enhancement I had made to my twenty-first chromosome. I still hid him from both my co-workers and my wife. I didn't want anyone, not even Darryl to have the full realization that he was a clone. At some point, and I'm still not sure when, he was possessed by this demon."

John had started to be drawn into the story. If David was a geneticist, it was possible albeit, doubtful, that the story contained some truth. Then, just as John started to believe portions of it, David used *that* word again, demon. It was like a scar on an otherwise beautiful woman's face. If only, it weren't there, but alas, it was.

"I can't remember the exact pronunciation of the demon's name," David continued. "And I'm not sure that I could even pronounce it correctly if I heard it again. But it sounded bizarre. Something like, 'heifer nasal.'"

A heavily built man with hair the color of pinesap slid the box of bullets into a small paper bag and handed them to Charles.

"Deer season's almost over in most states," he remarked, making the assumption from the caliber of the bullet.

"Oh, I'm just going target practicing. Going to shoot a few cans out in the desert," Charles replied as he contemplated whether or not this would be the final fib that he ever told.

Charles took the small sack and placed it carefully beneath the seat along with the recently purchased rifle. He then climbed back into the cab of his pickup and drove back towards the funeral home where the body of his daughter lay in wait of burial.

"The demon had possessed the body of Darryl and had escaped from the observatory room some time Sunday night. By the time I came in Monday morning, this demon had already killed my friend and co-worker, Trevor Williams."

John nodded his head solemnly, *Oh yes, the devil made him do it and it wasn't him, it was his evil twin.*

Statements like this would make him the laughing stock of the legal profession. Instead of making it to the cover of *Time Magazine*, he would more likely make the cover of *The Enquirer*, *The Weekly World News*, or a number of other tabloids. He continued listening to David's story, trying to decide which parts should be extracted safely for David's defense. Thinking it wise not to use the entire story, he needed some way to break the news to David to stay quite about the demon business if he was to piece together a viable defense.

David looked at his lawyer, sensing that John believed only part of his story, even though it was entirely accurate. He looked at the lawyer's pad where he had begun to doodle in its margin; it was a sure sign that John doubted David's testimony. He stopped and posed a question to his attorney. "Should I continue or just stop here,"

"What do you mean?" John asked, unaware that his thoughts were spilling across his own face.

"I know you don't believe me, and in a way I don't blame you," David rationalized. "But, it's the truth. I know the whole demon thing sounds . . ." he paused, looking for the appropriate word, "flaky."

John smiled apologetically. He realized that David had read his mind fluently; this he could not hide.

"Please continue," John Wilson replied.

"Then he gave me a shot of some sort of sedative. I'm not sure what it was. When I finally woke up I was strapped down so tightly that I couldn't move. He had removed all of my clothes, even my underwear. He was examining me . . . I guess for scars or tattoos. That's when he told me . . ." David paused and looked into the lawyers face, making sure that the man was listening without the earlier signs of doubtfulness.

"What did he tell you?" John asked.

"That's when he told me that *he* was the man who had taken my brother and how he'd tortured and killed him. That's when he told me where my brother was buried. He's been watching me my entire life. He said that all my discoveries in the scientific field were actually things that he had led me to finding. It's like every major event in my life revolved around his plans. He killed my brother, making me want to find a way to clone him somehow. He helped me research and learn about cloning, and all the while it was some sick game. Don't you see? My entire life, my utter existence, has just been a game." Again, David paused with a renewed sense of personal violation. A feeling of helplessness washed over him. The "why me" tone had taken control of his voice. Again, he grew nauseous at the realization of the truth.

John Wilson had listened closely to David's recollection. At first, he had thought David to be insane; now he wondered. He recognized David as being an intelligent man, and he was no more certain of the truth now than he had been before he'd heard David's story. Yet, for reasons that he couldn't explain, he was beginning to believe David's story. Now he waited for David to finish the story, intending to ask him for more details about Trevor's death.

"Did *he* . . ." John still refused to use the word demon, "tell you that he was going to kill your wife then?"

David closed his eyes, trying to remember the exact wording that he had been trying to forget since it had happened.

"Yes, well . . . no. He didn't say, 'I'm going to kill your wife.' He said it differently. He said he was going to relive the excitement from Darryl with Gayla. He said he was going to 'take care of her.'"

"Would you like to continue from the point that you learned about your brother's death?" John asked as he scribbled the phrases down the side of the page.

From another room in the same building, Detective Gill called David's home again. The same as before; the message came on. Gayla wasn't there. He tilted his head backwards, taking in a good view of the drop ceiling above him, and wondered if indeed, Gayla was out there somewhere, not dead, but dying, left for dead. Was something really wrong? Was David trying to save her from something else before he was trapped here? He sighed through his nose, then reached for the phone again.

Hephanaethus met Gayla just outside the door to help her with the heavy sacks of groceries. He looked into her eyes, trolling for any sort of knowledge that she might have of his escapade. Seeing none, he dismissed the notion entirely.

"Good morning," Gayla beamed, obviously in a better mood than she had been earlier.

"Good morning," he echoed. "I see that you didn't approve of my grocery list." Hephanaethus smiled as he kissed her on the side of the mouth.

Charles Macintosh trudged up the stairs and into the funeral home. Several neighbors greeted him remorsefully as he entered. Among those that greeted him were Thomas Pope, Teresa, his wife, and their son, Josh. They understood the protective nature that parents had over only children. In their own minds, though, none would say it; they knew he was alone in the world.

"She's in a better place, Charles," Teresa attempted to comfort him.

The words were no more comforting than the heel of Hephanaethus' shoe had been. He had heard them before a few years ago when Emily had died.

Joshua said nothing; instead, he turned away again, looking towards the coffin while he played with a flip top box in the right pocket of his pants. He stared at Michelle's motionless body knowing that when she was buried, so too, would be all the visions of his future—his family.

"After he told me about how he had killed my brother, then he told me . . . well . . . insinuated that he was going to kill Gayla. He left me strapped there on the cot. After that I don't know what happened. I had barely escaped the lab when I saw this truck and I waved my arms for help. The next thing I knew this old man was driving his truck straight at me, trying to run me over. I tried to get over, off the road, but the truck ran off the road. That's how my knee got busted up."

David patted his leg brace and took a deep breath.

John continued writing and David waited to finish the story until John caught up. John took in the sequence of events as he wrote. *If this story is true, or even parts of it*, he thought to himself, *David has endured more in twenty-four hours than anyone should have to in a lifetime.*

"Sounds like you had a pretty shitty day, partner," John said sympathetically.

They met each other's gaze. Though David's cheeks were dry, his eyes glistened with fluids ready to pour forth at any moment. For all of John's shortcomings as a lawyer, he had a saving grace that made up for his other inadequacies—instinct. He knew, by the end of their testimonies, precisely what they were lying about. Continuing his gaze into his client's teary eyes, John realized that if David was lying, David was the best liar he had ever met. David's story, especially the demon part, was going to be a stumbling block before the jury, but now John believed it and that would have to be good enough.

Joshua Pope stood back from the crowd of his elders while they consoled one another. When they were through speaking, he lowered his head respectfully and cleared his throat. Then he stepped forward toward Charles Macintosh, inserted his hand back into his pocket, and grasped the flip top box between his forefinger and thumb again.

"Mr. Macintosh," he started as he approached him closer. "Yesterday morning, before I found out about what had happened to Michelle, I bought something for her. I was wondering if you would let me give it to her now." Pulling his hand forth from his pocket, he introduced a gray velvet box. He slid his thumb to the front edge of the box and popped it open, revealing an engagement ring with a dainty diamond crowning its top.

Charles instantly exploded with a wail of grief, more powerful than any other moment in his long lifetime. Stretching his arms forward, he pulled the young man tight against him. Charles sobbed as if he had just relived the moment of his daughter's death again, clinging to Josh as if he were Michelle herself.

"Yes," he spoke between gasps, as he accepted the young man's proposal for her.

"Hello. Phoenix Counseling Center. May I help you," answered a young feminine voice on the far end of the line.

"Yes, ma'am. This is Detective Gill from the Phoenix police department, and I need to contact Gayla Brooks immediately."

"I'm sorry sir. She is on vacation in Florida right now. Could I refer you to another psychologist?"

"No thank you," Gill replied in confusion before repeating, "I need to speak with Gayla Brooks. Do you have a cell phone number, a beeper number, a number that I can reach her at in Florida . . . anything like that?"

"Mrs. Brooks asked me not to give out her beeper number, but I could relay a message for her if you would like."

Gill breathed deeply, wondering how much of the conversation the receptionist seemed to miss. His patience was thinner than usual today; he had to work quickly.

"I repeat. This is Detective Gill from the Phoenix police department. This is an emergency and I need to speak with her myself."

The words, spoken slower and more harshly, delivered a sudden epiphany to the receptionist. She surrendered the beeper number to the detective without further questions.

Without saying another word, Gill pushed another button on the black phone on his desk and entered the numbers he had recently scribbled on his desk calendar. After listening to the short message, he tapped in his own phone number and replaced the handset back in its position. Folding his arms, he continued staring at the phone as if he could somehow make the call come sooner.

In the darkness of the Phoenix airport's parking garage, a red light blinked. A small device vibrated wildly and uselessly. It was Gayla's beeper, beeping like a tree falling in the forest with no one to hear the sound.

Chapter 15

Hephanaethus looked at the paper sacks filled with groceries. They bore a striking resemblance to the paper sacks filled with empty oil jugs and empty Crisco cans which he had thrown into a nearby dumpster earlier this morning.

Gayla sat the brown paper bags on the table and turned toward Hephanaethus. "I realized something when I started into the grocery store this morning."

"What's that?" Hephanaethus asked wondering when he would have to end the charade.

"I've lost my beeper somewhere. I know I put it on before we left yesterday morning, but I don't know where it is now. Do you think I should call the office and see if they need anything?"

"Nah," Hephanaethus shook his head. "Wait until Friday, at least."

He was growing tired of this game and intended to kill her before Friday, at the latest. Even so, he didn't want her to figure out anything beforehand. The only reason he had allowed her to live this long was so the wound on his genitals would have a chance to heal so he could rape her as she died.

"If you hadn't slept so late today, I was going to suggest we take a trip to Orlando. Or maybe go to Sea World or Busch Gardens in Tampa Bay. I was hoping we could spend the night and do something romantic for our anniversary."

A smile formed on his face as she made suggestions as to the scene of her own destruction.

"Tomorrow morning, I promise I'll be ready."

Again, Gayla mistook his remark for the sweet sincerity of her husband.

"Well, like I was saying, the old man's truck busted up my knee. The next thing I knew, he clobbered me on the right side of my head," David paused as he rubbed the knot, showing John where the can had collided with his head.

"Then he turned up the gas can over my head, trying to splash gas on my clothes and into my eyes, babbling about what I had done to his daughter. I'd never met this man or his daughter before . . . never in my life," David emphasized.

"He lit a match and tried to burn me alive. Then I saw this deputy sheriff's car come by. I thought, 'great, now maybe he can get this old coot off me and get me to my house to see if Gayla is still alive.' But, it didn't work out that way, before I could speak; the old man told the cop that I killed his daughter. From my perspective, my wife's life depended on whether or not I could make it to rescue her. I guess you could say that I didn't have time for any more bullshit that morning. I could tell that the cop wasn't going to take me to my house but instead to jail. I could tell that he didn't care anything about my side of the story. So, I did what I had to do. I knocked the cop over and I took his gun. I knew I had better have a decent sort of weapon if I intended to face down a demon and save Gayla."

John wrote feverishly. He still wondered about the cause of the fire at the lab and the details of Trevor's death, but he wasn't going to stop David, not now. As the story unfolded, John repeatedly found that he kept placing himself in David's shoes. Over and over, the actions that seemed so hideously criminal were being explained by a desperate man's logic.

"From the moment I escaped the lab, everything centered around me getting home to check on Gayla and I'll always wonder if I could have saved her life if I had been able to make it home. It was at least fourteen or fifteen hours later when I convinced Detective Gill to let me call home just to see if she was still alive. I don't know when he would have killed her and I'm not really sure I want to know." David concluded his story. It had been an abridged version and he knew he would have plenty to clarify now, but for the first time he had been able to tell the full story. He knew that his own accounts would send him to prison, but the story was out and it felt good.

John abruptly finished his notes and looked up to face David again. "And Trevor?" he inquired.

"When I found Trevor, his throat was already cut. He was already dead. The clone had killed him before I got there. I wish I could give you more details, but . . ." David shrugged his shoulders.

"What about the lab? Apparently it didn't explode until after you escaped," John mentioned, hoping that David could explain that one away as easily.

"The clone took a bucket and concocted this nasty little mixture that we had tested for the military late last summer. It was a form of plastic explosives. He had an electric wire, one that had come from one of the florescent lights overhead. The mixture foams and when it gets an electrical charge it explodes. It was sort of a random time bomb. I was just lucky that the foam stayed away from the wire as long as it did. If it had taken me another five minutes to escape, I wouldn't be talking to you, except through a psychic or a Ouija board."

John nodded satisfactorily. He had gotten hundreds of people off the hook, but he'd never used the old demon story on any jury. This would be a first. But what God fearing person would say that demons didn't exist, "beyond the shadow of a doubt."

Detective Gill slammed the phone down against the receiver. Gayla had not returned his call yet and he had just made his forth attempt.

"What the hell is going on here?" he growled as he flung himself backward in his chair.

He slapped his palm against the desk and ran a hand back across his hair. He looked at the silent telephone again. He needed an answer. If Gayla wouldn't call back, maybe he should get an answer from David. He walked down the hallway toward the conference room where he had led David and John.

"John's probably pumping him full of a bunch of lies like he did with that Cisco bastard." Gill growled toward Detective Harris, as he approached to ask if Detective Gill had heard any news. "I don't think this guy is even who he says he is. Gayla Brooks is supposedly in Florida with her husband."

"Didn't you see the pictures I brought back from the house?" Detective Harris asked.

"No. What pictures?" Gill replied with a dumfounded look.

Harris motioned for Gill to follow as he walked toward the front desk.

"Do you think I have a decent case . . . I mean as far as the whole human cloning issue goes?" David asked.

"Honestly, I don't know where to start yet. What we need is a witness to . . . well . . . something."

David sighed as he looked at the flabbergasted lawyer. He knew that the lawyer was being partial to him. As for the jury, that would be a different situation.

Detective Harris slid a deep drawer out of the filing cabinet. He reached into the drawer and removed a thick stack of framed pictures. Harris cradled the pictures down to the floor and spread them out. After he worked his way to the wedding picture, he handed it to Detective Gill.

"That's him alright," Gill confessed as he returned the picture to Harris. A quote echoed in Gill's mind suddenly; it was David's voice, "*My twin killed her.*"

A small diamond engagement ring twinkled from inside the casket. Josh stood above Michelle's body, caressing the same hand that he had placed the ring on.

"Charles," Thomas Pope said softly, "I can tell you need to sleep in a normal bed, at least for a few hours. Let me drive you home. I can bring you right back out here whenever you like."

Charles looked back at him. It was true; Charles was still miserably tired. He decided to accept Thomas' offer. "If you're sure that it won't be too much of a burden," Charles replied as he contemplated driving himself again.

"Not at all," Thomas said as he patted him on the back.

Two detectives walked down the hall.

"I've got to find out where in Florida. John Wilson's had plenty of time. Plenty of time to concoct the best lies anyway," Gill huffed, harboring a four-year grudge.

At the end of the hall, the detectives stopped and Gill struck the door rapidly three times with his knuckles.

David sighed while shaking his head in sorrow. "There were no witnesses to anything."

The conversation ceased at the sound of a triple tap at the door.

"Come in," replied John.

Detective Gill popped into the room.

"David, had you planned any trip to Florida with your wife."

"Yes, we were supposed to leave tomorrow. I wanted to take her there for our anniversary," David replied sadly.

John looked at detective Gill and studied his facial

expressions. The two had worked with each other or, more accurately, against each other for over eight years. He sensed that the detective had some sort of news that he would not share with him, especially in David's presence.

"Brian," John addressed detective Gill by first name now, "I think we'll need to postpone the interview until tomorrow or later this evening at the earliest."

Gill looked back at Wilson suspiciously. Wilson gave an inconspicuous nod of his head while David continued focusing on Gill.

"Fine," Gill replied at last. "Detective Harris, could you insure that Mr. Brooks is escorted back to his quarters?"

Harris gave a quick nod of his head and placed his hand loosely on David's forearm as he stood.

"Why?" David finally asked curiously. "How did you know about Florida? Has someone seen Gayla?" By now David had begun trying to link together the question to what the detective had learned. He knew that Gill was hiding something, although he did not know exactly what.

"No," Gill said, without revealing any further information.

He turned and watched David continue down the hall.

Wilson approached the door and motioned for Gill to step further inside the room before he closed the door.

"How much did Brooks tell you before he requested an attorney?" John inquired.

"Why the hell didn't you ask him yourself? Why did you want to talk to me if you weren't finished interviewing him anyway?" Gill barked.

"Look, I know we've had our differences, Brian" John started before being interrupted.

"Differences! Let me tell you about differences. After you got that Juan Cisco bastard free, he raped and killed a five-year-old child. *You knew* he was guilty. It took me three months to gather enough evidence to get him off the streets and *you* got the son-of-a-bitch off because the proof was illegally attained. If there was any *real* justice, I would be arresting *you* right now for accessory to the crime," Gill blared as he pointed a shaky forefinger in Wilson's direction.

"I didn't *know* that he was guilty." John defended himself from the detective's accusation. "It was my job to represent my client to the best of my ability. My job to insure that he had a fair trial. Okay, I admit, I was wrong and that's something I'll have to live with . . ."

"No, that's something that little girl's parents will have to live with, or in the case of their daughter, live without."

Gill released his anger that had stewed for four years. His fists clenched tightly, wishing he could punch John in the mouth without destroying his own career.

"Davis lost his job when he corrected your mistake," Gill continued.

"You call emptying a revolver into someone's temple 'correcting a mistake?' He should have lost his job *and* been thrown in prison. That was murder."

"It was self defense," Gill argued as he lost control of a devious smirk.

"David didn't kill the girl," John stated as a matter of fact, turning the conversation back to the original subject.

Gill rolled his eyes, in the presumption that he was trying to free another guilty man just to win the case.

"Forensics will determine that," Gill stated calmly and confidently.

"DNA evidence is useless in this case," John protested.

"What?" Gill screamed giving John Wilson a look of total incompetence.

"Didn't you read Brooks' profile? He's a scientist. He cloned himself. His clone, which has the exact same DNA, committed the crimes. He's guilty of cloning a human, but not of murder," John blurted, already regretting the fact that he had given away the entire basis of his defense in the heat of a conversation that should have been forbidden in the first place.

A clone, Gill considered, *"my twin killed her."*

Without concluding his argument with John Wilson, Detective Gill reached a conclusion and found that he needed one more piece of vital information. He turned and opened the door, walking directly towards his office. John Wilson was not yet satisfied with the discussion. He had yet to learn of Brian's recent revelation. He followed closely behind the detective waiting for some type of response and hopefully some information helpful to David's case.

Wilson knew that Gill would not easily reveal information to him. He knew that Gill despised him, not only did he oppose the detective's testimonies in court, he was his ex-brother-in-law. Gill was aware that Wilson was following behind him.

Wilson quickly slid to the side through the doorway just before Gill slammed the door shut behind him. The detective said nothing to the lawyer, not even the typical "Get the hell out of my office," response in which the lawyer had grown accustomed to hearing. He shuffled through papers scattered across his desk, knocking some to the floor until he found it. "It" was the number for Gayla's receptionist. He grabbed the phone and kept his back to the lawyer.

Thomas had not mentioned it, but as the two men neared Charles' house, Charles asked, "Did you do the forensics on Michelle?"

Thomas paused and swallowed forcefully as he prepared to respond to the question. "Yes," he answered at last.

Charles nodded but remained silent.

"Charles, are you sure, I mean one hundred percent sure, that the man you saw on the road later that morning was the same man that took Michelle's life?" Thomas questioned, hoping that he wouldn't sound doubtful of his long time acquaintance's allegation.

Charles removed his thick glasses from his face. "I'm not blind yet. And even if I was, I will never forget that voice."

Thomas nodded in acceptance. "I did my best. I collected all the evidence there was. We'll get him. There won't be any doubt in any jury members mind this time, I give you my word on that."

"I know. I appreciate it," Charles acknowledged as the

vehicle pulled into the shallow gravel driveway.

"Just give me a call when you want me to drive you back, okay."

"Okay," Charles replied just before closing the passenger side door.

David received a long overdue meal before being taken back to his confinement. As he ate the bland, under-seasoned food, his paranoia began to take control of his mind again. *What is to keep this demon from possessing my lawyer or the judge or jury foreman on the day of the trial? For that matter, he could possess that big, hairy cellmate at any given moment. He has followed me since childhood and he won't stop here.*

As he swallowed the last bite of food, a guard drew closer to lead David back to his cell. Paranoia tightened its grip on David as he focused on every person he passed, wondering who *he* would be next.

The large bearded man whom David shared cell quarters with, grinned as he noticed David's approach. To his surprise, David glared back at him fearlessly.

The larger man continued to grin as he prepared to intimidate David into submission.

"Hello, again," Detective Gill beamed into the phone needing another bit of information from the receptionist.

"This is Detective Gill from the police department. Earlier, you had mentioned that Gayla Brooks went to Florida. I just needed to know one more thing. Did she mention anything about whether anyone else was going with her?"

"No . . . well . . . ah . . . not besides her husband anyway," the receptionist responded.

"Great, thank you again," Gill replied, being more courteous this time, in the event that he had to contact her again.

Gill dropped the phone and turned toward Wilson. He was far from an expert on the issue of cloning, but he saw truth in what John had said. He had not heard the full story, which David had confessed to John, but it was enough for him to draw vivid conclusions.

"Well?" John asked expecting to hear the answer Brian had received.

"Well?" Brian echoed sarcastically, then continued. "Well, get the hell out of my office."

"If she's supposed to be in Florida with her husband, Brian, then she's in danger and you've arrested the wrong man. I'll leave when I get an answer," John negotiated.

"You'll leave now," Brian replied as he pointed at the door. "Investigating crimes is *my* job, freeing guilty people is *yours*."

Chapter 16

"You think your pretty tough, don't you?" asked the cellmate.

"Just shut up, I'm not in the mood," David replied, deciding he might as well adjust to prison life.

David's remark was loud enough to draw the attention of two men in a similar cell across the hall. The cellmate could not let the smaller man demonstrate his insubordination in front of the other captives that had just heard the remark.

"Let me show you a better use for that smart mouth of yours," replied the large man as he stepped closer to David, preparing to tackle him.

His strong arms wrapped around David, pinning both of David's arms against his own torso. The onlookers cheered not caring who won.

David was not a fighter. He hadn't been in a fight for fifteen years. But what he was, was an angry man and further, he was a doctor, a man who understood human anatomy very well. He forced his hand up, along the other man's sternum and plunged his thumb deeply into the man's throat.

The large man gasped and lowered his chin instinctively

trying to protect his throat.

With a twist of his wrist, David extended his forefinger and middle finger and drove them up into his opponent's eye sockets.

The man howled out in pain. David really hoped that it was Hephanaethus; he wanted revenge.

Only two guards were responsible for this temporary holding facility today. Both rushed in at the sound of the commotion.

David grabbed the other man's throat, nearly silencing him. He squeezed on both the esophagus and the trachea as he shifted his position and used the large man's own weight against him, shoving his head into the corner near the floor.

The guard in front fumbled the key into the keyhole of the cell door. By the time the guard could unlock and open the door, David pulled downward on his cellmate's esophagus, inducing a gag reflex. With his head still pinned in the corner the man's undigested lunch could not escape his mouth fast enough. Some of the vomit streamed out his nostril but more flooded into his lungs.

One guard grabbed David by the collar and pulled him back; the other rushed in over the man on the floor.

"He's dying!" the young guard panicked.

The guard who held David turned in response to his partner's words.

David seized the opportunity and pushed the guard forward over the top of the other, then turned and fled out of the cell and down the hallway. His braced leg swung outward in an ungraceful arc as he swung it frantically down the corridor.

David rounded the corner of the concrete blocked wall, leaving the secured area, and charged on into and through the unsecured portion of the building. Here he had an escape. With only a hope and a prayer that another police officer or detective was not currently occupying it, he clomped hastily through the swinging doorway of the men's room. With his good leg, he stepped up on the sink and lifted a tile from the drop ceiling above him and slid it back on top of the tile behind it. Placing his hands on the concrete partition, he pushed himself upward and wrapped both legs and an arm around an overhead water pipe connected to the sprinkler system. Then he reached over and pulled the ceiling tile back to its previous position a single second before the door swung open again.

The guard drew his radio. "An inmate has escaped. We need assistance," came the message as he jogged down the hallway. As the guard rounded the corner outside the secured area, he thought he caught a glimpse of the men's room door closing. *That's a stupid place to hide,* he thought, as he moved to investigate. Abruptly but cautiously, he opened the door. The room looked vacant. After checking each individual stall, there were still no signs of David or anyone else for that matter. He didn't have time to waste on something he wasn't sure of, so he proceeded to check other areas of the building.

Agent Gill had lowered the phone after another futile attempt to reach Gayla's pager when he heard the commotion in the hallway outside his office. He got up to soothe his curiosity.

"Brooks escaped," Harris hollered down the hallway. "They think he's still in the building but we can't find him anywhere."

David crawled along the water pipe hand over foot. Small beams of light from seams and holes in the florescent lights below split through the darkness providing enough light for him to see how to navigate over the rooms. He looked back to the place where he had managed to enter the ceiling and attempted to get his bearings straight. A broken corner on a ceiling tile revealed a concrete wall about thirty feet away.

Hanging in a sloth-like fashion, he contemplated Detective Gill's question.

"She's alive," he whispered joyfully to himself as a wave of intuition washed through his mind. He twisted around the pipe at a nearby T-intersection and continued his journey towards the concrete wall with a new inspiration.

From here, he could hear people running around frantically below shouting, "He's not here," and "I already checked there."

"If he were still here, we would have found him by now," Detective Harris said angrily. "Alert all units that we have an escaped suspect and then give . . . what ever his name is . . ."

"Macintosh," Gill interjected and finished the command for him. "Let Mr. Macintosh know that David has escaped. Don't call. Go there and offer him protective custody, just in case."

Gill had begun to doubt David's guilt, but he wasn't going to bet the old man's life on it.

"Thomas, can you take me back out there?" Charles asked.
"Sure, I'll be right over," Thomas replied.

David pushed several coils of flexible metal tubes, which encased the electrical lines, out of his path and continued his journey toward the faintly illuminated concrete block wall. He had to creep along now as the ruckus below had settled. Now anyone below could hear him as easily as he had heard them. He locked his feet tightly around the water pipe and continued to inch his way to a prospective freedom.

Upon reaching the area where the light had shone through, David looked down into the office below through the broken corner of the ceiling tile. He could see the back and top of a balding head in one direction; from another he saw an office window, not a plate glass window but one that could be easily opened. Here he would wait for his opportunity to regain his freedom and find a way to Florida.

A cool and salty breeze blew the tiny droplets of rain into their faces as they ran for the front door of the condominium. Hephanaethus reached for Gayla's hand as they leaped under the overhang and into the dryness.

A gentle smile formed from beneath Gayla's rain moistened

dark hair as it hung heavily in her face.

"We had better make the most of our day tomorrow. It's supposed to be the only sunny day this week."

Hephanaethus put his arm around her waist and said, "I'm sure we'll have a blast." He unlocked the door and opened it for Gayla as he stood back practicing the etiquette of a true gentleman.

She unbuttoned the front of her blouse and peeled it off her back. "Would you mind drying me off?" she purred erotically.

Hephanaethus smiled back at her but would continue to refrain from any passionate moments until his wound had healed completely.

"You're ovulating again, aren't you?" he asked with a grin.

"Maybe," she replied, keeping her smile in place.

David perched from the thick metal water pipe. He had been there for less than twenty minutes but it had seemed like an eternity, as he clung tightly to the pipe. His right foot felt like it weighed ninety pounds due to the additional weight of the leg brace, but he held it in place on the top of the pipe. At any moment he was sure that his strength would give way and his foot would crash trough the brittle tile beneath, revealing the position he had maintained for the past hour and a half.

David closed his eyes and contemplated how he, a mortal man could defeat a demon. The man in the cell had been too easily defeated to be possessed by the ancient spirit. Though he estimated that the cellmate was not an innocent man, he was far from the demon he prepared to do battle with. He peeked through the broken corner again and saw a dry, aged hand place a wooden ruler on the desk. He wondered how much longer he could maintain his position.

His eyes closed tightly as he squeezed his grip with the last bit of his strength, then he began to do something he hadn't done in nearly a year—he prayed. He prayed that Gayla was still safe. He prayed that she had escaped. He asked forgiveness for his cloning, for what he had done to the man in the cell, for not spending more time with Gayla. He prayed for a sign and some direction in which way to go when he lost his grip on the water pipe. He asked for help in stopping the demon.

His chain of thought was interrupted as he heard a woman's voice, one that sounded a lot like Gayla's voice.

"Are you staying late tonight, Fred?" the voice asked.

"No, I was just leaving," the man at the desk replied as he tossed his wooden pencil carelessly to the side and stood up from his chair.

Through the triangular hole below David and above the desk, David watched as a yellow wooden pencil fell across the wooden ruler on the desk. From his current position, he could see a perfectly shaped wooden cross on the desk as the man left the room yielding an escape route.

His ankle slipped from the pipe, despite all his desperate attempts, but went unnoticed as it crashed through the ceiling tile; the thud blended with the sound of the door slamming shut behind its other occupant.

Upon his arrival at the Macintosh house, the officer noticed that it was vacant and decided to return to the funeral home to inform the old man of the impending danger. He raised his radio to his lips, "Has anyone found Brooks yet?"

Three other officers responded nearly simultaneously, "No sign," "Negative," "Still looking."

Hooking his fingers through the broken corner, David removed the tile and twisted his body so that he could exit the ceiling feet first. Replacing this tile seemed pointless when he looked at the tile two feet away that was broken from side to side, near its center, by his foot's descent.

David looked through the window of the dark office from where he stood. He was reluctant to approach closer to the window due to his fear that someone would see him clearly. He looked down the street. On the far corner on the opposite side of the street, he could see a dingy sign with dark letters. The sign read, "LAUNDROMAT COIN OPERATED." Looking down at his issued garb, David planned his first stop of the evening.

Charles entered the funeral home again and joined the other mourners in despair. After a few somber minutes passed, a policeman approached Charles.

"Mr. Macintosh, I regret to inform you that the suspect, David Brooks escaped from jail around two hours ago. I feel that you should seek protective custody until we can recapture him."

Charles scowled at the policeman's remark. "I wouldn't have left my daughter's side before over him. I have absolutely no reason to leave her now. If you want to protect somebody, you get back outta here and find him before he kills somebody else. Don't you worry about me."

The officer looked around the room; half of its occupants were men, most of which seemed strong and of able body.

"If you change your mind, call this number," the officer replied softly as he handed Charles a small card with his own duty number and other emergency numbers printed on it.

David turned the clasp locks on the window inward to unlock it. He knew that he would be unable to close the window after he left and regretted the clear path that he left behind himself. He looked directly below the window, calculating where he would land when he sprang to freedom. Regardless of the direction, angle, or speed at which he left window, the dense patch of holly bushes below would break his fall. Already, he writhed in pain as he imagined the sharp prickles piercing his skin and the blunt pruned stubs gouging and scraping as he plunged through them.

He drew a deep breath and raised the window.

Quickly, a small voice in his head reminded him, *you don't want anyone to notice.*

He propped his stiff leg on the windowsill and bent his good knee to align his feet side by side as he prepared to slide feet first down the brick wall into the prickly hell that waited below.

His landing was no less painful than he had imagined and he bit his lips until he drew blood to keep from screaming and drawing attention to his location.

"So *now* you need me, huh?" John Wilson remarked with satisfaction as he approached the open door of Detective Gills office.

"Your *innocent* client nearly killed another man before he escaped, in case you haven't heard. Or did you put him up to it, I should say?"

"What? You're talking about David Brooks?" John stammered back in surprise.

"Okay, here's what I need and you'd damn well better not be holding out on me here. I don't care what kind of client confidentiality you claim to have, I'll arrest you if you don't cooperate and you'll just have to sue me later," Gill said in a threatening and demanding tone. "Do you know where in Florida David had intended to go? Did he say anything to you about it?"

"No, the subject never came up until you asked him about it at the end," John replied.

"Did he mention that he intended to escape?"

"No, not at all."

"John, I need any information you have before more innocent people get hurt."

"I didn't know anything about it! Honestly! I didn't even know that he escaped until I walked through the door."

"Do you know who does his taxes?"

"Now how the hell would I know that? Don't be stupid."

Gill leaned back in his chair, eyed Wilson suspiciously, and said, "Fine, that's all I needed to know."

John turned to leave and Detective Gill reached for the phone again.

"Yes, I need to speak to the tax assessor," Gill spoke into the phone.

No more than fifty feet from Detective Gill's office window, David crept through the bushes, wincing as the sharp edges dug shallow grooves in his skin. Near the last stretch of holly bushes, David lay flat on his stomach and waited for the dusky sky to fade into total darkness before proceeding.

Agent Gill studied a road atlas as he spoke on the phone. "I need a ticket to Panama City, Florida."

Detective Harris stood by the doorway waiting for him to finish his telephone conversation.

"Early afternoon tomorrow."

Harris looked at Gill strangely now.

"Great," he nodded, "you too."

"Surely you're not actually planning to go to Florida? We don't have any jurisdiction there."

"No, but I can identify Brooks a lot better than they can with nothing to go on but a few pictures," Gill replied rationally.

"Have you notified the local police department and asked them to find Mrs. Brooks?"

"What would I tell them? They can't arrest her for anything. If, on the possibility she is with this clone, and Brooks' story has any truth to it, we could endanger her by letting her hear second hand that her husband was arrested in Arizona. Look, it doesn't sound very realistic. If she says something to this man she's with . . ."

"You actually believe this crock of shit story, don't you?" asked Harris.

"I've put some thought into it," Gill replied philosophically.

Harris shook his head in disappointment.

"So, how did you find out where in Florida to go?"

"He owns a condo and claims tax deductions every year. Figure it out, *detective*." Gill replied haughtily as he walked out the door, donning his jacket as he went.

164

Chapter 17

"John, how have you been?" remarked a smiling African-American man from behind counter. He drew his hand from the pocket of the pants of his uniform and reached outward to shake John's hand. The man had been a former client of John Wilson's and felt greatly indebted to him. John smiled back as he clenched the other man's hand tightly.

"Mike, do you remember telling me that if I ever needed anything that I could count on you."

"Of course, anything."

"I'm trying to prove someone else's innocence, and I need your help. I need to see if you can find the ticket stubs for David and Gayla Brooks on . . ."

Mike raised his hand, holding two thick pieces of paper. "Is this what you're looking for?" Mike asked with anticipation.

"Well, yes. How did you know?"

"Some guy from the police department called up and said that these would need to be taken as evidence. If you had been much later, I probably couldn't have been able to help you. They're on their way down here to pick these up now."

"Make me a copy if you don't mind."

"You know, John, I wouldn't be bending the rules for anybody else. I'm not supposed to do this, but I *do* owe you one."

The first star, which was not really a star at all, but a planet, began to shimmer as it was enveloped by the surrounding darkness. David lay back staring into the vast and endless darkness above him. His faith had never been stronger before. It only stood to reason that if demons existed, so, too, did angels, along with God and Christ the Savior. He wondered if Trevor had had any last second revelations. Gayla, he knew, believed that God existed despite the fact that they rarely went to church, but was her faith strong enough? He closed his eyes again and prayed for his wife's soul if not for her life.

Several more distant specks of light poked through the sable sky when David saw Detective Gill getting into his car and leaving. He rolled over onto his belly again and considered the signs that would make his identity apparent to the typical observer. He looked at his clothing; that was one thing that he could change after he reached the laundry mat. His stiff leg that caused his obvious limp was also a dead giveaway.

He carefully removed his shirt and poked his fingers through small holes gashed open by the holly bushes and ripped the material at the seams giving it a sleeveless appearance, at least from a distance. He raised upward and peeled the Velcro strips from the leg brace. Then, he reached for the bottoms of his pants' legs. He folded and rolled the material carefully until they took on the appearance of shorts. Then he tucked the bundle of excess material and up inside the bottoms of his newly formed shorts. He relied on the darkness to hide the distinct color of his clothing during his brief stagger to the laundry mat on the opposite side of the street.

Again, he regretted the obviousness of the trail he left behind as he tucked the metal rods and Velcro straps of the leg brace beneath the prickly holly bushes in a frail attempt to hide them.

Detective Gill followed the directions to David's house. In his experience, an escapee was likely to retreat to his home, if not for a hideout, extra clothing, money, or food. According to the visitor's log, David had not had even a single visitation since his arrest; he apparently didn't have family in the nearby area and as for Gayla . . . well . . . who knew? David had been trying to get home when he stole the police car. It seemed only logical that he would now want to investigate his home for himself before he journeyed towards Florida, if he was really headed for Florida. Again, this was Gill's own unsupported conclusion.

Without a trace of conspicuousness, David limped into the laundry mat.

A young woman chased after her three-year-old daughter and hardly noticed David's entrance. The washers were motionless and quite. It seemed logical that the clothes in the four large dryers belonged to the woman.

He contemplated his next move. It would seem a little bold to prowl through her clothes in front of her, hoping to find men's clothing near his size. He proceeded with a slow trot directly to the back and into the bathroom. With the door shut behind him, he stood and waited, listening carefully for the sound of someone else to arrive or for the woman and her daughter to leave.

Through the thin, hollow wooden door, David heard the young mother's voice call out, "Come on Jenna, we have to go next door to get some change."

David waited a hasty ten count and opened the bathroom door, glimpsing the mother and daughter as they left. He limped to the nearest dryer and opened it. As he had hoped, some of the clothes in the dryer were men's clothing. Unfortunately, they were considerably large for David. He continued digging through the warm heap until he found a pair of sweat pants;

these were smaller and possibly belonged to the mother but he was desperate. A plain gray T-shirt caught on his thumb as he removed the sweats.

"Good enough," he spoke softly to himself as he closed the glass door of the dryer and hobbled back to the bathroom.

Detective Gill walked around the perimeter of David's home. He checked to see if Harris had replaced the key under the brick. He had. Gill left it in place and replaced the brick. He concluded that if this was the only key David had to the house, then David would have to retrieve this same key to enter his own house when he arrived. Gill stepped back into the darkness behind the garage and sat on the ground, crouching behind a large rubber garbage bin.

After an abrupt change into the short-legged sweat pants and over-sized T-shirt David resumed listening to the little girl squawk and cackle as she played while her mother finished folding the laundry. Impatiently, he waited for the mother and daughter to leave. He didn't want to risk the remote chance that the woman had seen him earlier, dressed in different clothing or the fact that he was now wearing their clothing. He heard other voices; he couldn't make out the details as to what they were saying since they were speaking in Spanish and David's knowledge of the language had lapsed over recent years. Yet, he could understand them well enough to know that they would be here for awhile.

"Mommy, mommy, I need to go potty," the little girl hollered from outside David's recent hide out as she rattled the knob of the locked door.

"Wait just a minute," the mother said. "Come help me load the clothes into the car. I don't like for you to use public toilets unless it's an emergency."

"It *is* a 'mergency," the toddler replied.

The knob rattled harder.

168

"It's locked. Somebody else is in there. Let's go. You can go potty in a minute."

David breathed a breath of the odiferous air deeply into his lungs. He was relieved that the mother had not waited for him to leave the bathroom. It would have been a face-to-face meeting that could have cost him his freedom and Gayla's life.

His mind continued to change from minute to minute as he speculated on Gayla's chances of survival. He figured that *if* she were still alive, her life expectancy was growing shorter by the second. He was relatively certain that Hephanaethus would not allow her to live long enough to return to Phoenix and learn the truth as to what had happened. Still, as he had opened his eyes after praying earlier, he was certain that she *was* still alive and that she was in Florida with Hephanaethus.

The voices of the mother and daughter had faded into nothingness now. David balled his state issued clothing under his arm and hobbled to the trash can. The can was nearly full with empty fabric softener and bleach bottles and large, bulky detergent boxes. He wished that the clothes could have been buried beneath the other trash but decided not to arouse the suspicions of the Spanish-speaking couple on the opposite side of the row of washing machines. His trail continued to be more and more noticeable.

It wouldn't take much of an investigator to determine where I've been, he considered as he approached the door, almost expecting the police to be waiting for him to exit the building.

Gill crept out from his shadowy hiding place and back to his car.

"Has anyone seen Brooks yet?" Gill asked over the radio.

"Negative," answered an unidentified voice over the airwaves. "You'd think somebody would've noticed a guy hobbling around in a jail uniform with a leg brace, but we've asked nearly every cab driver and bus driver in Phoenix and nobody's seen anything."

"Dr. Brooks," David said quietly into the telephone receiver while he waited for the automated system to place the collect call.

He could only hope that someone at the lab would be there to answer the call; someone that would accept the charges. In Boston it was after midnight; they were likely to be short staffed, if anyone was there at all.

At last, an unfamiliar feminine voice answered, "Yes."

"Hi, I'm trying to reach Dr. Jim Turner."

"He went home a couple of hours ago and probably won't be in until Saturday. Can I help you or take a message?"

"No, this is Dr. Brooks, a friend and former co-worker. I need to speak to him. Could you give me his home phone number?"

She hesitated, it was against policy to release the number but she was speaking to a fellow doctor and she had heard his name before. He was a minor legend in the cloning realm.

"Didn't you work at the Phoenix lab?" she questioned as she made the connection.

"Yes, and that is what I'm calling Jim about. This is an emergency," David stated impatiently.

Without further questions, she surrendered the number.

Gayla stared sadly into the mirror above the bathroom vanity. She pondered how much beauty she had lost as the years had rolled by. For two consecutive nights her husband had refused her. This had never happened before. Less than a week ago, he had made love to her so passionately that it seemed as if they had never done so before. In her own mind, she exaggerated how the beauty that she had once possessed had fled her, leaving her unattractive and undesirable.

On the other side of the wall, Hephanaethus lay in bed resting his head on his crossed arms behind him as he plotted. He thought about the past; about how he had joined Satan before they were cast out of heaven. He remembered the victory he had felt as he helped corrupt the world before the great flood. The crucifixion, which he participated in as a Roman soldier, was the most triumphant of all memories. The lives that he had taken amidst the greatest and bloodiest wars from the height of the Roman empire, to the ruins of Serbia, where people were slain for religious beliefs, he had claimed countless thousands of lives, killing as slowly as possible—the more suffering the better.

He thought about the present, about how he had consistently manipulated David, unawares, to submit to his desires. He looked forward to this weekend, when Gayla would beg for hours for him to end her pain by taking her life, still convinced that he was the man she had married several years ago.

He thought about the future; about how he would manage to become the antichrist and then whether he should overthrow Satan before or after challenging God himself.

"Yes, I'll accept the charges," muttered a surprised and confused doctor.

Jim boggled drowsily while he held the phone wondering why his former mentor would call him collect at his home in the middle of the night.

"Jim," David gasped, "you've got to help me, please. You're the only one that can help me now."

"Dave, I've been trying to reach you since the lab exploded. What happened?" Jim inquired as his concern drove him completely from his slumber.

"I'm in trouble, Jim. I need your help. I can't give you any more details than that right now. I need you to catch the next flight out here. It's a matter of life and death and don't let anyone know that you've heard from me or that you're coming to see me. When you get here, meet me below the bridge on Central Avenue, the one that goes over the Salt River." David blurted out quickly as he looked in all directions making sure that no one overheard his conversation.

"Which side of the bridge?" Jim asked as he stood up from

his bed and put on the pants he had removed before getting into bed.

"South side. Please Jim, not a word to anyone," David repeated.

"Okay, I'm on my way to the airport now," Jim said in a reassuring voice.

"Thanks, Jim," David replied as he hung up the phone and proceeded towards the rendezvous point. He knew it would take time for Jim to reach the airport and even longer to get a ticket for the next flight. He was also aware that the flight would take precious hours. But at his current rate of travel, he would have to rush just to make it a few miles away to the bridge before Jim arrived.

He hobbled through the darkest passages hoping to avoid any of the less pleasant people that would be sharing his route. *One thug is enough for the day*, he thought as he limped along, hoping his irregular gait wouldn't draw any unwanted attention.

Chapter 18

The sun had not yet risen but Gayla had.

"Happy Anniversary!" She whispered loudly into the ear of her sleeping mate.

"Happy anniversary," Hephanaethus repeated as a grin formed from the side of his mouth.

"Come on, get in the shower, Orlando's waiting," Gayla whispered as she tugged on Hephanaethus' arm.

He raised and smiled at her, "Okay, I'll be ready in a few minutes."

David was exhausted from the trip and he was not even half way to the bridge. He sat down and leaned against a large metal trash bin and remembered a conversation that he'd had with Gayla the last time they were in Florida. She had wanted to get a phone for the condo but David had discouraged the idea, arguing that this was their get away and it would be more relaxing if no one could disturb their peace and quiet.

"If only I had listened . . ." he sighed aloud before finishing the rest of the sentence quietly in his mind. *I could call her and warn her of the danger.*

"Happy Anniversary," David whispered with a pitiful tone of sarcasm as tears filled his eyes. Closing his eyes, he rested his knee on the pavement savoring the sweet memories that filled his mind until he fell asleep.

By now, it was apparent to Detective Gill that his prediction of David's return home was inaccurate. He stood up, stretched his legs, and walked back to his vehicle.

"Any signs of Brooks yet?"

"No, but we're still looking," came the reply.

David woke up shivering against the cold metal. The frigidness reminded him of Gayla's home state, Vermont. Pain shot in all directions from his knee. If not for reminding himself that he might still be able to save Gayla's life, he'd lay and wait for the police to find him and take him back to the cell. While the smelly mattress was not his idea of comfortable, it was better than where he currently rested. He tucked his left leg beneath his body and tried to put as little pressure as possible on his right knee while he stood up beside the large trash bin.

With a muffled growl of anguish, he continued to stagger towards his destination as he looked forward to Jim's arrival. Most of all, he looked forward to the luxury of traveling in a car instead of hopping clumsily on his path to Florida.

The formal ceremony was scheduled to start in an hour. Friends whom she had known from high school filed in through the pews to the back of the large room. He looked at the mountains of flower arrangements, which were placed around her throughout the night. *She was truly beloved*, he realized. For just a moment, he paused his grieving to notice how many other lives the stranger had disrupted by his cruel deed.

Jim looked out the window of the plane and down toward the surface far below as he tried to imagine what had happened to David and what kind of trouble he was really in. Despite the expenses that he wasn't entirely sure David would reimburse, he was partially flattered that David would call him in his time of need.

Charles sat silently as he listened to the words of the eulogy. He wondered if Michelle and Emily had been reunited in their afterlife. He wondered if he would see them later on this evening. He imagined the joyous reunion until tears of joy washed away the tears of pain that streamed down his cheeks.

A small, black suitcase lay open on the bed. Detective Gill quickly packed the clothing he would need for the next few days. Running late as the long night he had spent hiding behind David's garage had taken its toll on him, he considered the fact that David had not "followed the rules" by not returning home. He wondered if David might indeed surprise him further by escaping to somewhere other than Florida. This trip could very well be a waste of time and money, he realized.

Pausing for a second, he looked into the mirror on the wall above his dresser. *I don't look crazy, do I? Should I call ahead to let the local police department know? How am I going to word this when I do get out there? No, I don't have enough information. I don't know what I'm dealing with here. I have to see the situation first hand, and then I can take him—if he even exists—into custody for suspicion.*

Gill shivered and shook his head, as if trying to shake the false portions of the story from the mental pictures in his mind.

He lifted the phone again and called the Fort Walton police department.

"Let me speak to your head detective," Gill demanded.

As he waited for the telephone transfer to take place, he wondered how he should word his portion of the conversation.

"Detective Carson speaking, can I help you?" answered a firm scratchy voice.

"Yes, this is Detective Brian Gill from the Phoenix police department. I'm coming in tonight around nine o'clock to try and locate a suspect. Who can I contact to assist me with the apprehension?"

"Well, that depends. What is this person suspected of?"

"Two counts of murder, kidnapping, and arson"

For a moment, silence consumed the connection as the detective in Florida tried to grasp the nature of the suspect.

"I can be available myself. In the meantime, could you give me the suspect's name and fax me a picture?"

"Unfortunately, that won't be possible at this time because I'm already running late to get to the airport but I will have that information for you tonight when I arrive."

"Okay, I look forward to seeing you, Detective Gill," the other detective replied before terminating the connection.

Gill had considered giving them David's name in case he was stopped for a speeding ticket or other random violation, but he had to make certain that it was the clone and not the real David Brooks. Furthermore, it wasn't so much that he didn't trust the police department in Florida, but on this case he didn't trust anyone.

". . . 3592," John finished as he replaced his credit card back into his wallet.

It was only obvious that John would be losing money on this case, but it was not the usual case. He had only a bizarre alibi for his client's only defense and he would have to put some real effort into proving David's innocence, if such was the case. John had become interested not only in David's defense, but also in the existence of this clone. He could only hope that David had not told him the most believable, however peculiar, lie he had ever heard. He wondered about the interaction of a demon. John had always had a firm belief in both God and the Bible.

If the Bible says that demons exist, then surely they do, but . . . always that but. *The excuse, "The devil made me do it" has become entirely too cliché. It's a prelude to ridicule.*

His gaze into the mirror ceased as the ring of the telephone startled him into reality and the present.

"Hello," Gill answered.

"Brian, Brooks was still in the building last night."

"How do you figure?" Gill interrupted anxiously.

"Chris Enslow came in this morning and found his window open. He said he hadn't opened that window in over a month. A ceiling tile was broken two feet away. We checked that men's room more closely and noticed some white chips and dust from the ceiling on the counter. Then a couple of guys found his leg brace in the bushes. He's still here and there's no way he can make it out of Phoenix without us catching him. I really think you're wasting your time and money going to Florida. He's here."

"I'm not going to Florida for him. I'm going there for her. I have to find out what is really going on. We can't afford to make assumptions here. Not this time."

"Suit yourself. I just thought you'd be interested."

"I am, thank you, Doug."

Detective Gill looked at his watch as he hung up the phone. *If I had more time, I would swing by his house again. He has to show up sometime. But I don't have the time.*

He zipped the cover shut and lifted his bag.

Contrary to the advice of others, Charles had insisted on driving himself to the burial ceremony. No one had wanted to upset the stubborn man during his already difficult time. Tears further blurred his weak vision as he followed behind the black hearse. He debated to himself whether it would be most appropriate to take his own life at the cemetery or in his own home. As he brought his truck to a stop at the cemetery, the box of bullets slid from beneath the seat. Charles looked down between his feet at the crumpled paper bag containing the bullets and kicked them back under the seat,

"Don't rush me," he grumbled.

John could see Detective Gill standing in front of him at the pre-boarding counter. He had hoped that the detective would not find out about his own trip to Florida, but with both men traveling on the same flight, John was sure that Gill would notice him. He wondered what Gill's intentions were. The two had a mutual distrust for one another.

Jim stood up in a crouched position as the plane came to a halt. He anxiously awaited some sort of explanation from David, whether it was good news or bad. Judging from David's voice he was strongly inclined to believe that it was bad news. He wondered what he could do for David that David was incapable of doing for himself. As the elderly couple that had been sitting between Jim and the aisle merged into the traffic of exiting passengers, Jim stepped forward and turned to retrieve his own bags from the overhead luggage compartment. It was a small bag that had been hastily packed. Jim wondered how long he would need to stay in the Phoenix area and if he should have brought more clothing.

Jim walked through the tunnel and into the building. Once inside, he maneuvered around several people amidst their joyous reunions and then between two men that seemed to be exchanging harsher words. Jim couldn't help but pick up small portions of their conversation.

"What do you think you're going to accomplish, John?"

"I'm going to prove that David Brooks is an innocent man. That's all you need to know," John Wilson replied.

Jim Turner side stepped from the narrow walkway and grabbed his ticket stub, making an effort to not appear to be eavesdropping on the two men's conversation.

"So help me, if you interfere with police business, I'll have you thrown in the same cell with the last person whose case you lost."

"Stop, just stop with your idle threats, Brian. You've got a job to do, so do it and let me do mine."

Jim pieced two interesting bits of the conversation together: "David Brooks is innocent" and "police business." Jim now feared even more about what David had managed to get himself into.

Realizing that the conversation had paused, Jim tucked his ticket stubs back into his pocket and proceeded towards a sign that read "CAR RENTALS." He hastened his steps and wondered if David would still be able to meet him at the rendezvous point.

Gritty dirt sifted from Charles' hand as he hovered over the grave of his daughter. He breathed deeply and looked towards two men with shovels that then began to pile the dirt in quickly. Beside Charles was Joshua Pope. The old man looked at the younger one and they contemplated what the loss had meant to each other for a moment.

"Charles, would you like to come and stay with us?" asked Thomas Pope who was directly behind Charles.

"No, thank you," Charles replied solemnly. "I have to go home and pack Michelle's belongings. I would rather be alone to think, but thank you again."

From here, David could see the massive bridge in the distance. Pains from his leg shot in opposite directions with every step now. The pain altered direction from shooting up near his hips to the soles of his feet. His knee buckled at the slightest bit of pressure and he wondered if he would have to continue his journey doing a belly crawl.

Jim waited for the attendant to hand him the keys while she proceeded to discuss the mileage and gas prices with him. He nodded and looked at his watch.

"Well, I can see that you're in a hurry, so here are your keys, sir. Have a good day."

Jim nodded politely and resumed a brisk walk to the area of the parking lot the lady had mentioned. Once he saw it, he increased his pace to a jog until he arrived at the car.

Strips of sod unwound atop the barren soil that covered Michelle's grave. Charles waited for the other mourners to file out and he waved to some as they left. When all had departed, he looked at Emily's head stone and winked. Moving closer to the stone, he whispered, "Will they take me?"

He contemplated forgiveness and suicide one more time.

"Will I see you again? Is she with you?" Charles raised and started towards his truck.

Checking the time on his watch, he decided to wait until later on in the evening before taking his own life. He would use these last few hours to write down his intentions for the family's possessions.

Jim pressed his foot firmly on the accelerator, increasing his speed to eighty miles per hour only a few seconds after leaving the airport parking lot. Then he remembered that he would not want to draw suspicions or get pulled over and lose even more precious time.

David continued his stumbling towards the bridge. He looked up at the sun and tried to estimate the time. He was sure that Jim had already arrived and wondered how long he would wait. In the distance he could hear a familiar sound. It sounded like a pickup truck in desperate need of a new muffler. David looked behind him, his face filled with terror as he saw an old man stretching his head out the window of the same truck that had busted his knee.

At the first glimpse, Charles wasn't sure if this was really David or if he was having an emotionally induced hallucination. He watched the man limp away frantically. It reminded him of the way David had limped on his way to the police car. He pressed on the brake pedal as he focused harder on the limping man. As the truck came to an abrupt halt, the stock of the 30-30 rifle beneath the seat slid outward and banged against his heel. The bullets slid between his feet. Charles took this as confirmation.

Jim Turner parked his car on the shoulder of the road near the south side of the bridge that David had specified. He hoped that David would be waiting for him, eager to find out why David had needed him but dreading the news as well. He had always prided himself on being a law-abiding man. How could he help his friend if he was a fugitive? On the other hand, how could he refuse to help David? No matter what the situation turned out to be, Jim was confident that he was about to face an internal struggle and be forced to make a difficult decision . . . perhaps the wrong one.

David felt a sense of deja vu as he saw the pickup truck drive over the sidewalk and onto the rough, patchy field. David considered his options. They were limited—nonexistent to be honest. If the police did show up this time, his situation would be altered but not necessarily improved. He continued limping towards the bridge but felt no comfort in arriving there. At this point it would change nothing. He could see a man in the distance walking down the steep slope from the side of the road. He hoped it was Jim, but then again did it really matter now?

Charles drove the truck over the rough clumps of grass that

speckled the field, stopped about forty feet away from David's present location, and opened the door of the truck. Climbing out, he dragged the rifle outward with one hand and emptied the brown paper sack containing the box of bullets with his other hand.

David looked back as he noticed the truck stop, continuing his frantic efforts to flee, and trying desperately to ignore the pain in his right leg. His face moistened with sweat and his blood pounded through his veins until he could hear his own pulse as he contemplated the shortness of his life. As he glanced back at Charles, the first bullet was being injected into the rifle. Then he looked at the man coming down the hill and screamed, "Jim!"

Jim could barely hear the distant voice, but he could tell that it was David. He looked back behind David. He could see Charles loading the rifle and engaging a bullet into the chamber as he worked the lever. He hastened his pace towards David but his stomach clenched as he wondered what he should do. Logic convinced him that he did not want to be too close to David when the shot was fired. Still, he rushed closer, taking his chances with the unknown and unpredictable hand of fate.

Charles raked the remaining bullets off the seat and climbed behind the wheel again. He continued towards David without bothering to close the truck's door. The truck rolled along lazily at a speed of about ten miles per hour but still closed the gap quickly.

David looked into the cab of the truck and saw Charles holding the rifle across his lap with his right hand clenching near the trigger. Again the truck stopped, and David saw no point in attempting further evasion, he stopped to face his destiny.

Jim lost his balance near the bottom of the slope and continued the rest of the distance in a clumsy roll. He sprang back to his feet and proceeded toward David and the truck. As he hurried, his mind filled with fear, not only for David but also for himself. He evaluated his own courage as his speed decreased.

"I hope that God will forgive me for what I'm about to do," Charles began after stopping the truck and climbing out of the seat one last time. "But if he doesn't," the old man continued, "then I guess I'll start hunting you down again when we get to hell."

Charles raised the rifle to his shoulder. David, frightened, tried to overcome the paralysis in his legs as he attempted again to evade the old man. Charles lowered his head to rest his cheek on the rifle as he raised the business end and took aim at David's back. He peered through the thick lenses of his glasses; his eyesight was not what it used to be, but he had been a marksman during the Korean War. He didn't intend for the first shot to be fatal for David; that would be too easy and more than what he deserved for what he had done to Michelle. Charles lowered his aim to David's hip and squeezed the trigger.

David's right knee collapsed under his weight as he made his reckless leap and he fell downward. A loud and thunderous roll caused him to lose the remaining control he had over his bodily functions. The split second of time that it took for him to fall toward the ground seemed to last an hour. He knew that by the time he heard the sound of the shot it would already be too late. Yet he didn't feel any pain from the bullet at this time. He lowered his head to examine the damage that the bullet had caused. The stolen gray T-shirt took a maroon hue at his side.

Jim watched as David fell. He felt both sorrow for David and fear for himself. He heard the echoes of the shot through the lower lying areas around the river. It seemed as if the morbid roar would never fade from existence.

Charles flipped the lever and expelled the smoky brass casing. He approached the stranger whom he believed to be the man who had taken his daughter's life.

David rolled to his back and clenched his side as he realized that the bullet had only grazed his side and scorched the fatty skin as it had passed. He looked up into the old man's eyes as the old man moved the barrel to within a foot of his face.

Charles' jaw tightened and twitched as he raised the wooden stock close to David's face, again. His right hand began to tremble and his left hand lost all feeling making it harder to follow the position of David's thrashing head. Blood surged though the old man's head as he could still feel the bruise caused by the stranger's heel. His sight dimmed still further and Charles knew that this was not caused from his old age, nor from the tears he had recently cried. He knew that his own time had come, and it seemed like a reward. Again, he daydreamed of the joyous reunion he would have with his wife and daughter as he raised his head upwards and silently asked for forgiveness as he forgave the stranger at his feet. He lost his grip on the weapon and it fell to the ground beside David only an instant before the old man did. Charles raised his hands to his temple, inhaled deeply one last time, and smiled.

As David rolled over, he considered his own bizarre "luck;" he considered also the fate of the man. He considered whether or not he could save him and whether or not the old man would want to live any longer. From his last statement, David guessed that the old man might have been planning on committing suicide. He looked closely at the bruise on the man's temple. He wondered if he had had a stroke or a brain aneurysm or possibly a heart attack. He thought of the irony, five minutes earlier and David would have never known of the old man's fate. Five minutes later and he would have been dead anyway.

David raised up and looked toward Jim who continued to stand in confusion at a distance. David regained his stance.

"Can you bring the car around to me? I haven't been in much of a mood to walk lately."

David smiled facetiously, feeling a comfort that he had not felt since before he'd created the clone a few months ago. Jim nodded in wonder and proceeded back up the hill towards his car.

Chapter 19

The smell of salt water filled the air even though they were nearly forty miles from the ocean. Gayla smiled with amazement as she watched the dolphins leap from the water and into the air.

Hephanaethus looked across the lake as performers dressed in pirate costumes prepared for a show. It brought back fond memories of his past. He looked at Gayla and wondered if he should kill her here. He imagined drowning her or slashing her arm and throwing her into the shark tank.

"What's wrong?" Gayla questioned as she looked into his eyes.

"Nothing. Everything is perfect," he replied as he gave her a bright smile.

"What's going on around here? What are you in trouble for David?" Jim asked.

"Just drive. I'll explain on the way. We can't go to the Phoenix Airport, though. We'll have to take the next flight out of Tucson."

"Don't you want to go to the hospital? You've been shot."

"The bleeding has almost stopped. Trust me, I'm a doctor, too, remember? We have to get moving fast, though."

"Where are we going?"

"Ft. Walton, Florida. Oh yeah, you'll have to buy both tickets in your name and we'll have to take different flights on two different airlines. I'll pay you back as soon as all of this is over."

"All of what?" Jim asked again.

"Well, they think I killed somebody, but I didn't, but I know who did."

"Wait a minute. *Who* is *they*?"

"The Phoenix police department and the old man that was trying to kill me."

"So why are we going to Florida?"

"Because that's where Gayla is. That's where *he* is."

"He who?"

"The guy that killed Trevor and destroyed the lab and killed the girl. The guy that's got Gayla."

The full impact of David's statement fell on Jim like a ton of bricks. "Trevor is dead, the lab was intentionally destroyed, and Gayla has been kidnapped," Jim clarified in his own mind. "But why do they blame you?"

"Because," David hesitated as he remembered vividly how much Jim had opposed cloning a human being in their argument proceeding his experiment. "It was my clone," David eventually confessed.

Jim turned his head and gazed sadly at David.

Through the sympathetic expression, David could also see another message in Jim's face. It was the "I told you so" look.

"I know I shouldn't have, but I didn't know then, not really. I never imagined how bad this would turn out. Believe me, I've paid and will continue to pay for my mistake, but now I have to save Gayla. Please Jim, I'm depending entirely on you."

Jim sighed. He felt like an accessory to the crime by helping David in any way, but Gayla's life depended on it. He feared making any decision because he knew he would regret making the wrong one. Jim knew there was more to David's story but he didn't know if David was ready to tell it yet. Furthermore, he didn't know if he was ready to hear it at this point. He drove his car down the ramp to I-10 south and remained quiet as he tried to grasp what had happened. He felt remorse for David but was unable to show it as he tried to determine what would make such an intelligent man make such a ridiculous decision.

John Wilson and Brian Gill stared blankly at each other from across a lobby while they waited for their connecting flight at the Dallas/Ft. Worth airport. Each man wondered about the other's intentions and both considered the possibility that this time they both sought the same thing—truth.

Detective Gill reflected on all the grudges he had held against the defense attorney. He reflected back to when they had started the grudge, which had been near the end of his failed marriage with John's sister. He remembered the days when the two had been friends despite their differences in courtrooms.

John stared back and reminisced on the same moments from his own perspective. Deep down he was confident that this was not a "witch hunt." He believed that Brian had only the interest of Gayla Brooks in mind. Despite their recent quarrels, John considered Brian to be a good and honest man. He wondered if they would still be friends if the marriage hadn't failed.

The detective looked at the lawyer and spoke,

"We're on the same side this time, John."

"I know," John replied as he stretched forth his empty palm, silently requesting a truce.

Brian looked back and nodded with a small grin as he accepted the unspoken truce with a handshake.

The silence in the car had become ironic. David finally had someone he could talk to but there was nothing to say at this point. Finally, he broke the silence as he posed what might have been a rhetorical question to Jim.

"The clone was possessed by a demon. It's immortal. How could I stand a chance?"

Jim listened closely to David's words, closing his eyes in a long blink, before responding with, "Well, I think everyone is immortal in a sense. Just as sure as there is life after life. Do you believe in heaven?"

"Yes,"

"Well, congratulations. Welcome to immortality," Jim replied with a voice of assurance.

David didn't understand Jim's reply in entirety at the time, but it was still comforting to hear.

Jim continued his thoughts on the matter to further clarify his point to David. "Life on Earth is just a test. Now is when you make the decisions that determine your life in heaven or well . . ." Jim intentionally left his last statement open ended.

Jim looked at his speedometer, then his watch. "We made pretty good time and I'll get us tickets out of here as early as possible. I'll help you however I can," Jim committed himself.

"Thanks. You're a lot smarter than I ever gave you credit for, Jim. I wish I had listened to you before."

The funeral homes were booked solid in Niceville, Florida. Parents and other relatives were grief-stricken and wondered who could have committed such a horrible crime. Some families had lost their only child, while others had lost two children in the early morning explosion that had claimed the lives of four adults and seventeen children. Rumors had spread throughout the town about some teenagers that might have been responsible for the accident not realizing how tragic the outcome would be. Now those rumors were being cast aside for a much truer set of rumors. The newer rumors involved a man who appeared to be in his late twenties or early thirties. A cashier and a bag boy from a nearby grocery store argued about the man's appearance as the police sketch artist had drawn a picture that only vaguely resembled Hephanaethus. Both had paid notice to the bizarre purchase and had easily linked the two events together. The sketch that was being shown over the local news had a different jaw line and nose shape than Hephanaethus. They could neither remember nor agree on the man's eye color. Already, police had taken three other men in for questioning. Neither was positively identified by either grocery store employees and all had flawless alibis.

The recent news and the police sketch were unknown to Gayla as she stood beside the man she believed to be her husband. She caressed the wet, slick top of a common gray dolphin and wondered what it was thinking as it looked back at her. She knew they were capable of communication between themselves and she imagined what they might be saying to each other through their shrill chirps. She wondered if they were as fascinated by the people outside the water as the people were by them and their environments.

The dolphin looked at Hephanaethus. Her animal instinct told her to stay away from this person. She could sense evil intentions, deceit, and danger. The dolphin looked back at Gayla helplessly, wishing she could somehow communicate a recognizable warning to the less threatening human that was making physical contact with her now.

In the shadows of the airport parking garage, Jim dug through his small bag quickly and removed one of the few shirts he had packed in his haste as he had prepared to leave Boston. It was a button-up shirt and it looked even more peculiar with the short-legged sweat pants that David wore, but David had insisted that he didn't want to waste any time and risk not getting one of the last remaining tickets for the next flight out to Florida. David's clothing combination was quite the fashion statement, but at least the newly donned shirt didn't have the suspicious looking bloodstain at the side. David ripped a strip from the gray T-shirt and formed a bandage to tie around his waist to keep some pressure on his wound and to continue to suppress the bleeding.

His friend had been murdered. His mind had been reproduced. His knee had been shattered. His side had been shot. His wife had been taken. His heart had been broken. In the last three days, David had aged thirty years. He had been tormented, assaulted, chased, arrested, interrogated, and finally, shot. He felt like he imagined an old Vietnam veteran would have felt.

"Go on, hurry up, and get the tickets. I'll meet you inside," David urged Jim.

"Are you sure you'll be alright?" Jim inquired.

"Jim, I made it a long way on my own. I think I can handle the trip inside, just go. I'll meet you there," David insisted as he hopped along, bracing himself from one car trunk to another, hoping not to set off anyone's car alarms. Jim turned back to check on David's progress as he proceeded out of the garage alone as David had instructed. David waved impatiently at Jim to continue as he stumbled ahead.

Once inside the airport lobby, David sat back inconspicuously in one of the seats joined together in a row near the outside entrance. He watched quietly as Jim left the counter of one airline and proceeded to the counter of another airline to buy another ticket for the same location. As he watched Jim scurry about the airport, he caught a glimpse of a wheelchair and began to formulate a plan. Not only would a wheelchair help him to maneuver around with less pain, he would seem less conspicuous also. Fewer people would notice his condition and those who did would only take pity on the handicapped man. He stood and began to stumble towards the vacant wheelchair moments before an overweight, slothful woman in her late forties walked capably to the chair and sat down in front of him. Yet another plan foiled, he considered.

Looking further down the open room, he could see yet another unoccupied wheelchair. He increased his speed to the best of his ability with only a hope and a prayer that no one else would claim the chair before he reached it. Hobble after stumble, he made his way to the chair. By the time he reached the wheelchair, Jim had purchased the other ticket.

"We have to hurry," Jim said. "The first flight leaves in twenty-five minutes."

David gripped the rims of the wheels and started to wheel himself towards the security checkpoint. He had never considered, before now, how much strength was required to keep a wheel chair moving.

Jim noticed his struggle and began to push David forward from behind.

"I'll let you take this first flight, but you'll have to wait another hour and ten minutes for my flight to arrive when you reach Ft. Walton."

"I can't go far without you," David assured him.

Brian Gill looked at his watch again. He knew that time was running short, if it had not run out already. He looked up the rows of seats and across the aisle; he could see the top of John's balding head. He wondered what information David had given John. More importantly, he wondered how he could get John to reveal this information to him.

I've got to convince John that I'm on David's side—that I believe David is innocent.

Brian closed his eyes and leaned back again wondering how much of his argument would be true. Conclusions were risky and sometimes career threatening when proven wrong. He was unsure of how much he wanted to believe at this point.

After clearing the security checkpoint, Jim and David rushed down the corridor to catch David's flight. They arrived just as the door started to close.

"Hold the door!" David yelled from his wheelchair as Jim pushed from behind at top speed.

The man at the door swung the door open again,

"Are both of you traveling?" he inquired.

"No, just me," David replied as he extended his arm and presented the ticket to the flight attendant as Jim brought the wheelchair to a stop.

Once inside the airplane, David positioned his injured right leg comfortably and closed his eyes. He knew that no amount of his own efforts could make the plane arrive faster in Florida. All he could do was wait and hope and pray. But now he had more peace in his mind. He felt comforted that Jim was helping him. He realized that it would be a debt that could never be repaid, even after he reimbursed Jim financially.

Jim was taking a chance for him—a risk that could cost him his freedom as well.

Jim looked out the large window at the DC-9 airliner as it backed away from the building. His flight would be leaving in less than an hour and he would take to the skies again; only hours after arriving from the opposite side of the country, he would be flying across it again. He closed his eyes briefly and said a quick prayer. When he opened his eyes again he saw the plane begin to speed down the runway. Then his eyes closed again as he said another quick prayer. Neither prayer was for himself; the first was for Gayla, the second for David.

"Do we have to leave now?" Gayla asked.

"It's a long drive back," Hephanaethus replied.

"Well then, let's spend the night here," she suggested.

"I don't know if we could even find a vacant motel for tonight, but I'll tell you what, when we get back tonight we'll call and make reservations for the Disneyland motel for next week, okay?"

Again, Gayla wasn't getting her way, but the proposal was even better than her request. She nodded eagerly and smiled back at Hephanaethus.

Hephanaethus was not concerned about Gayla's plans for next week. He intended to kill her tonight anyway, but after much deliberation, he had determined that the condo would be the most appropriate place to do so. His intuition had told him that David had survived the laboratory explosion. Eventually, someone would check the condo in Florida and David would know for the rest of his life that Gayla had been brutally killed in their "sacred retreat."

Jim stood anxiously near the door as boarding began. Regardless of how quickly he boarded, he knew it wouldn't make it's connection any sooner in Dallas, but it would make him feel better just to be on the plane.

Chapter 20

The plane rolled at a snail's pace towards the building and then stopped. As soon as the long metal tunnel contacted the hull of the plane, people stood up and gathered their belongings and attempted to get off the plane as early as possible. Brian and John looked at each other impatiently. For these men, every second might count; it might mean the difference between life and death. Then again, it might not matter; it might already be too late. Either way, they both wanted to know.

On a different plane, a different man grew impatient and wondered whether or not Gayla was still alive. If she was, how long did he have to arrive there? He rubbed his knee and wished that he still had the brace that he had tucked under the bushes outside the police building.

He wondered for a moment why he had a demon that had followed him for years and yet had not had an angel to protect him from the demon's destruction. He wondered if demons were actually stronger. Suddenly another revelation occurred to him. The demon had trapped him in the lab, but he had escaped before it exploded. The old man had tried to kill him, but he had survived. He had been in confinement, but he had escaped. The old man had tried to kill him again, and again he survived. Gayla had been taken away by this demon, but David was somewhat confident that she was still alive. He felt comforted that he indeed had a guardian angel that had helped him overcome so many obstacles. He realized that being a mortal, he would have otherwise had no chance to survive the demon's attacks. Despite all that the demon had done, he had still survived, maybe because the angel had protected him by laying out his own countermeasures.

"Do you need me to drive for awhile?" Gayla asked.

"No, that's okay. I just want to get you home," Hephanaethus replied with his devious grin as he rested his hand on her knee and slid it up her thigh a few inches.

"You're being awfully presumptuous, aren't you?" she replied with a wide smile.

"Call it a prediction," he answered slyly.

"I should have us home in less than three hours, if we can avoid getting a speeding ticket that is."

"Well, we've made good time so far and I can tell that you are obviously in more of a hurry to get back than I am. I do have to wash laundry tonight though."

"Well, while you're doing laundry, I'll go pick up some Chinese food for dinner."

"Ooh! That sounds good. I'm in the mood for something spicy."

"So am I," Hephanaethus replied with another innuendo and grinned.

He continued playing the role of her husband and she continued to believe whole-heartedly that he was David. Proud of this charade, he would remember it as one of his best performances.

John waited near the door for Brian to get off of the plane. As Brian burst through the crowd, John asked, "Do you want to share a car? We're going to the same place."

"Sounds great, but can we put it on your card for now and I'll pay you back later. Your sister seems to have all of my money."

John smiled at Brian's sarcasm, but admittedly, it was a true statement.

"Let's go," Brian urged, as his gait became increasingly more brisk.

After acquiring a car, the two dashed out to the parking lot and threw their bags into the back seat of the Dodge Neon they had rented.

"I'll drive," Gill said as he reached for the keys. "That way if we get pulled over for speeding, I can explain that it is police business."

John hesitated but tossed Brian the keys to avoid wasting precious time bickering.

"We should be there in about an hour," Brian said as he looked at his watch again.

"Do you have an address?" John inquired.

"Yes, but we'll have to stop by the police station first. I don't have jurisdiction here and I'm going to need some sort of back up if we really do have a psycho on our hands."

"I think 'Psycho' is an understatement this time, Brian. David described him as a 'demon.'" John volunteered.

"A demon?" Brian mocked as John had suspected that he would.

"Yes, I know. That one has been a little hard for me to get over. But he said it with such confidence. He said it even had a name."

"I think I'll leave that part of the story out when I talk to the local police," Brian said with a smirk.

Hephanaethus and Gayla continued to speed down the

highway when Gayla reached down to tune in a radio station. Eventually, she found a classic rock station playing "Stairway to Heaven," A few melodies later, a news report came on. Again, she reached down to change the station but paused when she heard the words, "Police now have a suspect for the terrible early morning tragedy that claimed the lives of twenty-one people yesterday morning. Two employees of a local supermarket reported a man buying an excessive amount of vegetable shortening and motor oil less than eight hours before the four-vehicle pileup occurred.

As he listened to the words, Hephanaethus debated whether to kill the witnesses after he had finished with Gayla.

So they have a suspect, that don't impress me much, he altered the lyrics of the song that had just started playing on the radio.

David waited with great anticipation as the jet airliner pulled away from the ground. Soon he would know; either good or bad, at least he would know. He closed his eyes tightly and again he prayed that he would see Gayla alive. He hoped that she had figured out the true nature of Hephanaethus and managed to escape. He had taken for granted that Gayla was in Florida. For a moment, he considered what he would do if he had been wrong.

What if Gayla wasn't even there? Then what?

It would be the same situation he had dealt with when his brother had disappeared. For years he had dreamed uselessly of the day he would find his twin. He wondered if he would be better off to find Gayla dead than to not find her at all. At least he would know.

The sun appeared to sink into the fluffy floor of clouds below. Jim looked out the window and attempted to ease the intense pressure he felt by enjoying this natural beauty. Subconsciously, he had been ripping a small foil bag into tiny slivers. The dust from the honey roasted peanuts which had been in the bag had scattered across the thin tray and onto his lap.

An old, prudish woman beside him brushed the crumbs from her sleeve as she gave him a cold scowl.

"I'm sorry, I've been a bit fidgety lately," Jim said as he raked the trash into his small cup.

The woman did not reply but continued to look ahead sourly. Jim wondered where David was now. More importantly, he wondered where Gayla was now. He hadn't asked David how he'd found out that Gayla was in Florida if he hadn't spoken to her since she had left. He also wondered about the whereabouts of the two men he had heard discussing David and arguing.

Traffic came to a screeching halt on Highway 98. Traffic had backed up from the one lane bypass near the scene of the accident that Hephanaethus had caused the previous morning. As cars began to form a line behind Brian and John, Brian considered the possibilities of turning around and taking an alternative route.

Surely, this won't take more than half an hour, he estimated.

The suburbs surrounding Tallahassee were behind them now. Gayla wondered why her mate seemed to be in such a hurry, but never questioned it. Instead, she tilted the seat back and rested her eyes. It was getting late and she needed a nap if she were going to stay up and wash laundry later in the night.

His estimation had been wrong; nearly an hour later, Brian had moved less than two miles. He could see the traffic stopped ahead and a man wearing an orange vest directing the traffic.

John looked at Brian and asked, "Do you believe in heaven?"

The question seemed peculiar to Brian; besides, John knew that he did. Brian had gone to church regularly with John's sister prior to their divorce.

"Yes, of course," Brian replied softly.

"What about hell?"

"Yes," Brian repeated.

"You believe in angels too, don't you?"

"Yes," Brian answered, his patience wearing thin.

"Then, why not demons?" John asked.

"It's not that I don't believe in the existence of demons, I'm just sick of everybody dodging responsibilities for their actions with the excuse that 'the devil made me do it.'

"For years now, we've both heard every crime in the book blamed on drug addictions, rock music, mental illnesses and role-playing games, but never, *never*, do they want to accept the responsibility for their own actions."

"But don't you think it's possible that every now and then, a demon could wreak havoc on earth? Would you bet your soul that this clone was not possessed by a demon?" John interrogated.

Brian remained quite; he wanted to dismiss John's words as he had done so many times in the past, but this time it was a little harder to do. Perhaps it wasn't beyond the realm of possibility that the clone was possessed by a demon, but it was definitely on the edge of that realm.

The plane descended and so, too, did David's expectations. He had risked everything on Gayla being here and now his pessimistic views were convincing him that like all his previous efforts, this too would be in vain. He wondered if waiting for Jim was really his best option.

I could take a cab, David considered before remembering that he didn't have even a single penny with him.

The hour that he would have to wait for Jim would seem like an eternity. He was not even on the ground yet and he was already tired of waiting.

Gayla woke up as the car stopped.

"Where are we?"

"We just got off of I-10, and now were on 285," Hephanaethus responded. "We'll be home soon. Just relax and get some rest. You'll need it for later on."

Gayla took the remark as one of those countless innuendoes of David's. She could have never imagined what Hephanaethus truly had planned for tonight, her last night as a living human.

Two cars remained in front of Brian when the man in the orange vest held up the stop sign and signaled for the traffic from the opposite direction to proceed. "I can't believe this! She'll be dead of old age by the time we finally get to her!" Detective Gill fumed in frustration.

He watched as the wave of headlights went past and wondered if the clone was in one of the cars that passed by him.

The airport at Fort Walton was tiny in comparison to the Dallas-Ft. Worth airport that David had recently rolled through in his wheelchair. He resented the injury to his leg even more now. It prevented him from pacing as he normally did when he became anxious. He rolled the wheelchair back and forth; it didn't have the same effect. In less than two minutes, he had traveled around the entire terminal. The only thought that gave him comfort was the fact that he knew he would see Jim as soon as he arrived. He checked the flight information on the screen. Jim's flight was scheduled to arrive on time.

Brian stayed close to the bumper of the car in front of him as they proceeded through the narrow bypass. It was obvious that the car in front of him couldn't go any faster than the car in front of it, but Brian still tagged closely behind as if it would somehow force the traffic through quicker.

"I'll just drop you off here and go get the Chinese food now while you get the laundry ready, okay?" Hephanaethus suggested.

"Sounds good. I'm starving. Can you get me General Tso's chicken?" Gayla asked.

"Sure. Do you want egg rolls or crab Rangoon?"

"Both. I'm splurging tonight."

"Consider it done," Hephanaethus replied.

He had no intention of getting the Chinese food; it was merely a reason to have time to prepare for Gayla's upcoming violation. He winked at her as he backed out of the parking spot and turned the vehicle around.

It had been a close call for Jim. His plane had arrived late in Chicago and he had to run at his top speed to catch his connecting flight to Fort Walton. It seemed as if the pilot of this flight was ahead of schedule however. The plane had already begun its descent thirty minutes prior to its projected arrival time.

Once again, Gayla was alone. Out of habit she turned on the television just to have that comforting bit of background noise. She didn't care what program was on, just as long as there was noise.

Detective Gill sped past the car in front of him and continued to race toward the local police station. He looked at the address on the map he had attained from an Internet web site.

"I think I can get us there in another ten minutes."

"Are the local police going to come with us?" John asked.

"Yes"

"What about a search warrant?"

"I'll have them start it when we get there. If we're lucky, we won't need one."

If Gayla doesn't answer the door, then we'll play it by ear. Don't expect this one to be played by the book."

"I never did. And *if David is innocent,* I'll never mention the legality of attaining proof."

"Of course not. You're not in this business for justice. You're in it to win," Brian remarked sarcastically.

"Don't condemn me. You're in it to win too, Brian. You forget how far we go back."

"This time, you're right. I do want to win. But if I win, the families of the victims also win. That is justice."

"That's revenge," John corrected.

Hephanaethus parked along the dark side of a hardware store.

An employee had keys in his hand and was about to lock the door as Hephanaethus opened it.

"We're about to close, buddy," the young man announced.

"I'll only be a minute," Hephanaethus replied carelessly.

The employee was irritated but decided to give the customer a few short minutes to make his purchase.

Chapter 21

Six young gamins patrolled the parking lot. They were looking for trouble but could not conceive the amounts that they were about to find. One car in the parking lot stood out from the rest; it was a rental car. It was well known in their profession, if thievery could be called a profession, that rental cars were far less likely to be equipped with car alarms or other protective devices. Also, rental cars typically identified tourists, which decreased the chances of getting caught. Walking near the front and center of this pack was a lanky, pale-skinned teenager. His hair fell in a long, tangled dirty blonde mass.

"Hey Stone, over there," one of the other urchins whispered.

"Yeah, I see it."

The arrival time of Jim's flight on the monitor appeared earlier than the time Jim had previously told David. David rolled the wheelchair into a small lobby near a window. He wasn't a smoker, he hadn't even smoked a cigar in recent years, but he was nervous, and this was quite possibly one of the last airports in the civilized world that would allow someone to smoke indoors. He looked over towards a man sitting alone at a table in the lobby and asked, "Excuse me, could I bum one of those from you?"

"Sure," the old man answered as he handed a cigarette to David. The old man looked at David's legs. He was curious about what could have happened to the young man but thought it polite not to ask. Instead he asked a different question. "Have you had a rough day?"

"Rough week," David replied through an overwhelmed sigh.

David could see a plane touching down on the runway and wondered if it was Jim's plane. His anticipation rose as the flight was announced.

"Can I trouble you for a light too."

"Of course," replied the smiling stranger as he reached forth and lit David's cigarette for him.

David breathed the toxins deep into his lungs, then expelled them forcefully with a cough. Blood rushed to his head; the sensation was hauntingly similar to that which he had experienced while he had been trapped on the cot before the laboratory had exploded. The sudden rush had made him dizzy and he was confident that if he had been standing, his knees would have grown weak and buckled beneath him.

Fifty feet of nylon rope and four elastic cords slapped against the counter.

The irritated store clerk rang up the merchandise as Hephanaethus handed him a fifty-dollar bill. After the exchange was complete, Hephanaethus strolled out the door and around the corner to where he had parked his car only minutes before. He was almost amused to see the dysfunctional youth unlocking his door.

"It's easier with the key," Hephanaethus announced as he held the keys in the air and dangled them from his finger.

Stone and the other members of the gang were surprised that this lone man walked towards them so confidently without even a trace of fear.

"Do you boys need a ride?" Hephanaethus offered politely.

"No, we need a car," Stone replied as he reached under his shirt and pulled out the handgun that had been tucked inside his pants. He held the gun at a slight angle as he pointed it at Hephanaethus.

Hephanaethus smiled fearlessly at the youngster. "All you had to do was ask. But now you've *complicated* things haven't you?"

The tires squealed in front of the police station. Brian swung open the car door and sprinted through the doorway. He looked at an officer standing next to the doorway. "I need to see Detective Carson," he said in a loud and demanding voice.

"I've been waiting."

A rugged looking older gentleman with snow-white hair stated as he donned his jacket.

"I'm sorry, I got caught in some sort of detour . . ."

"That wasn't just a detour," Detective Carson interrupted. "That was the remnants of the most horrible prank ever pulled around here. Twenty-one people burned to death, most of which were young kids. They're still trying to get the greasy residues off the highway. Anyway, do you have a picture of this suspect for me?" Carson asked.

"Yes," Brian answered as he opened his briefcase and removed two photographs he had brought from Arizona with him. He handed the photos to Detective Carson.

Carson adjusted his glasses and examined the picture closely then walked over to the counter at the front desk and compared it to the sketch of the man who had been seen purchasing the large quantities of motor oil and vegetable shortening. The two didn't match exactly but a considerable resemblance was noted.

As she piled the laundry into the basket, Gayla reached

inside the pockets and removed the lip balm, change, and other miscellaneous items that always seemed to find their way into the dryer. She tossed two quarters, a nickel, and three pennies on the counter and then checked the back pocket of the jeans she had worn the previous day. She pulled out a long piece of white paper that had been folded in fourths. At first, she couldn't remember what this piece of paper was or from where it had came. As the paper unfolded she remembered; it was the receipt from the thin plastic bags she had found on the counter. Along the top it read "THOMPSON'S SUPERMARKET." She looked at the bottom of the receipt. The total of a hundred twelve dollars and eighty-three cents seemed a bit outrageous for the snack crackers and squeeze cheese bundle that had been brought back. The bill had been paid in cash and she would not need to add it into the checkbook. However, she was very curious to learn where the extra money had gone, and scanned over each individual item on the receipt.

While Jim was trying to squeeze his way past the other passengers, David rolled the wheelchair next to the metal doors of the building.

David could barely see Jim's head behind the slower moving people obstructing his path when he yelled, "I'm going to go find us a cab. I'll meet you outside."

"Okay. I'll be there as soon as I can get by."

The remark seemed to irritate several of the passengers in front of him but they did step aside to let Jim rush past them.

David spun his wheelchair around and pushed it forward as fast as he could.

Jim nearly had to sprint to catch up with him by the time he got to the doors leading out.

Several cabs lined the sidewalk. David looked at the drivers before deciding which one to get into. This time he would discriminate. Wanting someone who would drive fast out of instinct, he headed directly to the cab with the youngest driver. He had already waited too long and would easily lose his patience with a slow driver here at the end.

Jim helped David into the car, slammed his door, pushed the airport owned wheelchair towards the wall, ran around to the other side of the cab, and jumped in.

Once they were all in the car and David had given the driver the address, David leaned forward near the driver's ear and urged, "Get us there as quick as you can and I'll make sure you get a good tip."

Jim said nothing, but sat in silence as he noticed how freely David was spending, or at least promising away, *his* money.

The cab driver checked his mirrors and looked around for cops before accelerating to a speed that made David comfortable.

David inhaled deeply and fell back against the seat. He hoped that Gayla was all right, whether she really was here or not. He wondered what the clone was doing now.

Hephanaethus looked at the youngster with as much pity as he had to offer. For several decades during his many lives in the eastern portions of Asia, he had practiced and mastered martial arts maneuvers. The vessel that he currently occupied was not toned well enough for him to use all of his abilities, but he was certainly more than this young punk could handle.

With a quick step to his right, Hephanaethus grasped Stone's right arm with his own right hand. He brought his left hand up from beneath the weapon and grabbed the barrel quickly. As he forced the barrel in an arcing motion, Stone's finger slid from the trigger before he could squeeze it. The forefinger straightened as the barrel rose higher. The bone snapped and the knuckle separated when the barrel reached a high noon position.

Still confused as to exactly what had taken place, Stone howled in pain. "Ahhhgh," he screamed with his mouth wide open and his eyes blinking with reflexive tears.

Hephanaethus kept the gun in his left hand as he flipped it around to a pointing position then plunged the barrel of the gun into Stone's mouth and deep down into his throat. With his right hand, Hephanaethus ran his fingers through the tangled dirty blonde hair. He smiled as he reminisced about the last time he had held blonde hair in his hands like this. But unlike the incident with Michelle, he didn't intend to kill Stone. He had bigger and better plans for him and his small pack of friends.

Stone began to gag on the barrel and tried desperately to gasp for air through his suppressed trachea. His eyes widened with fear as he met Hephanaethus' gaze.

Hephanaethus pulled the gun out of Stone's mouth for only an instant to let the vomit escape. While he allowed Stone to finish expelling his stomach's contents, he slung the weapon back towards the other members of the gang and stated calmly, "Don't move or I'll kill everyone of you."

As the weapon rotated it slung bits of undigested food and droplets of Stone's saliva across the others. They didn't move. They were paralyzed by fear and they knew that Stone always kept the magazine at its full ten-bullet capacity.

Stone gasped a quick breath of air less than a second before the barrel plunged down his throat again.

Hephanaethus shoved the youngster into a stoop and slid the barrel back and forth only often enough to let the vomit escape. Finally, Hephanaethus released him and dropped him to the pavement.

Stone lay on the cold pavement attempting to catch his breath between his dry heaves. He shivered and then expectorated.

The other gamins watched silently. They had never seen anyone do anything like this to Stone. They wondered if this man was actually tougher than Stone. They wondered whether or not he was another gang leader that had stolen the car from someone else. Among other issues, they considered the possibilities of being part of his gang.

Without removing the fully loaded magazine, Hephanaethus released his grip on the handle of the weapon and kept his finger in the trigger guard. The weapon dangled from his forefinger in the exact same manner that the keys to the car had done previously. Like the car keys, he held the weapon out in front of himself as if he were offering the weapon to anyone who would take it.

No one stepped forward to take the weapon; they all feared the consequences that Stone had already paid.

"Take it," Hephanaethus said as he slapped the gun flatly against the chest of "Slam," one of the teenagers in the front of the group. "You do have enough intelligence not to try to use it against me, don't you?"

"Uh, yes, yes, sir," he babbled.

"Good. Now how would you boys like to have some fun?"

They looked at Stone lying on the ground coughing and then looked back and forth at each other. Neither was anxious to offer up an answer.

"Well? You do like to have fun, don't you?"

"Yeah," they said quietly and nodded.

"You like girls too, right?" Hephanaethus inquired.

They smiled pretentiously and nodded again.

He removed David's wallet from his back pocket and opened it up. He gave a quick nod to Stone as he regained his feet and extracted a picture from his wallet and showed it to the teenage thugs.

"This is my wife. She has a fantasy of being gang-banged. I was wondering if you young stallions would offer me some assistance in this matter."

The youthful urchins looked fiendishly at each other; for them, it was like a dream come true. Even Stone was beginning to like the man that had almost killed him moments before.

"Hey man. Is this a setup of some kind?" one of the bolder and more cautious thugs asked.

"Not at all," Hephanaethus smiled as if he demanded their trust.

"Okay, all right, we're there. Where is she anyway?"

"Back at our condo. I'll go in and prepare her for our little scenario and then you guys can come in about five minutes later. Don't bother knocking. Just come on in."

"Do you think all of you could pile in the car for about half a mile?"

"Given the situation, I think we'll manage," Stone replied as cockily as before being gagged with his own weapon. Then he turned to face Slam and demanded, "Hey, gimme my gun back."

Without an argument, Slam returned the gun back to Stone.

"I wouldn't try that again if I were you," Slam whispered.

Stone didn't reply. He figured that he would eventually find a better time to get his vengeance on the man who had embarrassed him in front of his friends.

"Do you have an address?" Detective Carson asked as an uncharacteristic panic filled his voice.

"Yes," Detective Gill affirmed.

"Then let's go."

Without another word, Brian turned and proceeded out the door towards his car.

"Come on, I may need some backup," Carson commanded as he looked at two officers standing nearby.

The older detective jogged to the car and climbed into the back seat.

"Wait just a few seconds. I want these guys to follow us," Carson requested.

The marked car pulled behind them and Gill began to accelerate as he threw the map to the seat between himself and John Wilson.

"The guy in that picture looks a lot like our suspect that caused the accident. I may need to do my own questioning before we can release him to you."

"I'm sure we can work that out later," Gill replied.

"What accident would that be?" John inquired.

"Someone put Crisco and motor oil all over the road yesterday morning. Seventeen kids and four adults died because of it."

John thought to himself, *That sounds hideous. How could anyone do something so cruel?* He considered the demon story;

it sounded like the work of a demon.

"You said your suspect looks a lot like our suspect?" John asked for confirmation.

"Yes," Carson replied solemnly.

"It *is* a clone, Brian. Yesterday morning David was still being held in Phoenix," John whispered.

Brian swallowed hard. Every portion of David's testimony had seemed to be correct so far, and he dreaded learning the potentially fatal truth about the existence of the demon. He feared that for once he might indeed be going after a suspect that was above the law. One that he could not catch or beat in any other way.

Chapter 22

Gayla's eyes focused on one line of the receipt. The abbreviation seemed to stand for Crisco vegetable shortening. Above that line was another item brought to a considerably high total by the quantity of thirty-six; it appeared to stand for Quakerstate motor oil. This seemed peculiar, not only because of the size of the purchase itself, but she knew that David had always refused to use that particular brand of oil. However, the connection between this purchase and the car accident she had heard about on the radio the previous morning wasn't immediately obvious to her unsuspecting mind. Then she glanced towards the television.

"Turn up here," David bellowed as if the cab driver were thirty feet away. Blood raced through his veins, he was merely minutes away from learning the truth, or so he hoped. No matter what the outcome, he was confident that he would learn something in less than ten minutes. His fingernails dug into the seat as his mind filled with anticipation.

The ten o'clock evening news aired their report on the fatal accident and then showed the sketch of their suspect. Gayla grew numb as she looked at the sketch. It wasn't a perfect description, but she knew that the sketch was supposed to be of David. She grew weak as she tried to imagine how the man she had married and loved for several years could have done something so horrible. She didn't want to believe it. She wanted to believe it was someone else but she held the proof in her own hands. She debated whether to confront him about it before calling the police. Surely he wouldn't hurt her. If she knew him at all, she knew he would never harm her. Then she reconsidered; if she really knew him at all, he couldn't have been the man who was responsible for killing nearly two dozen people. She decided wisely that the smartest thing to do would be to confront him about it after he had been taken into police custody. He had been acting strange lately, and he had spent a considerable amount of time away with no explanation of where he had been.

Gayla turned the television off and decided to run for a safer place from which she could call the police. She opened the door quickly and started to flee, but planted her face firmly into Hephanaethus' chest as she spun around the wall beside the door.

"Hi there," Hephanaethus remarked, oblivious to her recent revelation.

She stepped backwards to open some distance between them, then stopped as her back bumped against the opposite facing of the door. Gayla tried to hide the fear and panic in her voice, forcing a smile to her face as Hephanaethus placed his arm on her shoulder and gently urged her inside. She didn't even notice the mob of teenagers standing near their car.

"So where's the Chinese food?" Gayla asked, spotting a plastic bag from a nearby hardware store in his hand while desperately thinking of an opportunity to escape.

"They said it wouldn't be ready for thirty minutes and then

they're going to deliver it to us," Hephanaethus lied as he closed the door behind them. "In the meantime, how would you like to get a little kinky?" he asked as he removed the nylon rope from the plastic bag in his hand. He estimated that his time was running short before the anxious young men would burst through the door.

"Uh, I've got a headache and I really have to get this laundry done," Gayla explained as she tried to force a convincing smile to her face.

Hephanaethus looked down at the cash register receipt that was growing limp in her hand from the moisture of her sweating palms. Suddenly, he realized that she had pieced it all together. Well, maybe not all, but enough to know that he had been responsible for causing the accident.

He didn't say another word; instead, he ripped the rope from its container and moved closer. He knew that dialog was useless from this point forth.

Gayla backed away further, looking for some way to escape, but there was only one door to exit the condo and he was standing in her way. Her only hope was to make it through the bedroom window and that would take time. She remembered from her studies of handling crisis situations that situations of this nature would be best if resisted; it was highly unlikely that she would ever live to be freed from the rope.

"No, get away!" she screamed as she backed towards a lamp in the corner.

Hephanaethus tied a slipknot in the rope as he moved closer to her.

Gayla reached back, grabbed the lamp by its base, and swung it forcefully at Hephanaethus, ripping the cord out of the wall as she went. He blocked her attack as her forearm pounded solidly against his own. Before she could draw her hand back, the slipknot had wrapped around her wrist.

Rotating his arm above her head, he spun her around, facing the opposite direction. Pressing his chest solidly against her back, he drove her into the wall. His fingers wrapped around her wrist and before she could resist, her other hand had been

ROGER SHARP

forced behind her back and looped snugly against the hand
which had previously been bound.

With both hands behind her back, she could only use her
legs to resist now. Wildly she kicked behind herself with all her
might, but the pain didn't even slow Hephanaethus.

He stepped back and waited for her heel to raise again.
When it did he seized the opportunity and pulled it upward
behind her, pinning her body almost motionless against the
wall. After placing a quick knot around one ankle he proceeded
to repeat his actions with the second ankle. All extremities were
now bound, but she still screamed, hoping that some neighbors
might be home and hear her struggling.

He threw her bound body to the bed and ripped her shirt
open. With a piece of the torn material from her shirt he made a
gag and suppressed her protests. With several feet of rope
remaining, Hephanaethus pulled the rope entangling her left
foot downward and tied it to the bedpost at the foot of the bed.
Then he reached the rope underneath the bed and brought the
rope back up to bind her right foot to the bedpost on the
opposite side.

Now Gayla lay spread eagle and face down on the bed with
her hands still tied behind her back. Her clothes were still on
with the exception of the front of her shirt being ripped open.

Hephanaethus removed David's pocketknife from his
pocket and cut the rope. Then he began binding her hands to the
top of the bed, leaving only enough slack in the rope to make
her resistance more interesting.

At last she had been completely bound, so he took the knife
and slid it inside the waist of her pants.

Gayla ceased her squirming momentarily out of fear of
being impaled by the knife. She lay still and tried to grasp the
concept of how the man she had loved for years could be doing
such a horrible thing to her. She had offered up her body
countless times to him in the past. She knew this couldn't be a
sexual thing. She wondered helplessly what he was about to do
and, more importantly, why he was going to do it. For years she
had been completely convinced that he loved her. David had

215

never been physically or even verbally abusive toward her.

The point of the knife pierced through the denim material of her jeans near the seam. He pulled the knife back out of her jeans and split them at the seam all the way down to her bound right ankle. He repeated this on her left side and then cut through the narrow strip of denim circling her waist. He flipped the rear of her jeans to the right side, revealing her narrow backed mock-thong panties beneath. With a single forceful tug he removed the shredded jeans from beneath her.

Tears rolled from her eyes as she still tried to deal with this confusion and betrayal. When she heard the door open, she felt a sudden sense of relief, wondering if it was the police. Had the neighbors heard her struggling? Had the police come to investigate her screams for help? She turned her head as her heart filled with hope. When she saw the group of teenage boys standing at the door, she assumed that they must have been passing by when they heard her and now they would help her out of her desperate situation. This optimistic view, along with several others, faded as she saw a smile come across Stone's face as he unfastened his own pants upon approach.

Stone began to remove his pants as he followed Hephanaethus' lead. The other boys noticed and followed the example.

Stone looked at Gayla lying stretched out on the bed. She was even more beautiful than the picture had revealed. The black lace panties that adorned her well-shaped buttocks sent his already overactive sex drive even higher. Lying down on the bed, he ran his arm beneath her as he maneuvered the rest of his body into position.

Hephanaethus eased his fingers beneath the lace trim of her panties and grasped both sides of the crouch seam at the bottom. With a quick tug, they ripped apart at the seam.

As Stone slid beneath her, Gayla tried to comprehend her husband's actions. In the last ten minutes, everything that she had always believed about her husband had turned into a complete lie. She knew that if he had loved her at all that he wouldn't allow other men, or in this case teenage boys, to have sex with her. And of all days, he picked their anniversary to do such a hideous thing. The sound of the door closing again seemed to be the sound of her life coming to an end.

From the backseat of the cab, David could see the door of his condo closing. That, at least, meant that *someone* was there. He looked forward to seeing Gayla again, but he was reasonably confident that he would have to face the demon clone, one on one, before having the chance to hold her in his arms again.

"Help me out here, Jim," David requested as he opened the door waiting for the cab to stop rolling.

Jim had already removed the money from his wallet and he threw it into the front seat as he reached for the handle of his own door.

An adrenaline rush numbed the pain momentarily as David began to sprint in an awkward gait toward the door.

Jim ran as fast as he could, trying relentlessly to keep up with his previously lame friend.

From the opposite side of the parking lot, he could see another car being closely followed by a police car, approaching. The lights atop the police car were flashing but the siren had been muted. Jim wondered if they were going to find this clone or if he would become David's cellmate.

Fear turned to fury as David opened the door.

Hephanaethus prepared to force Gayla into sodomy as he heard the door open again. Stone, who was beneath Gayla, fumbled through his underwear as he prepared for a violation of his own. Another five scantly clad teenage lowlifes surrounded the bed waiting for their own turns.

Gayla couldn't see who had opened the door, but imagined it was even more people that had come to partake in the mass assault upon her body.

"There he is. That's David!" John shouted.

Brian jerked the steering wheel sideways and brought the

car to a halt in front of the condo. By the time his door had swung outward to its full extent, Brian had removed a blue steel .45 from its holster inside his jacket and inserted a fully loaded magazine.

John turned to notice Detective Carson taking the same actions from behind him. Both men approached the condo rapidly while John followed closely behind and hoped that his client didn't get shot in the process.

Inside the condo, David vaulted toward his evil clone. His adrenaline rush had made him faster than he had ever moved before. He remembered as he hurled himself towards Hephanaethus how he had nearly killed his cellmate during his disillusioned state. He wanted to repeat his same actions here but with every intent to finish the kill.

Despite Hephanaethus' greater speed and superior fighting ability, he had been taken off guard by the sudden arrival. It was unexpected timing to say the least. But a wicked satisfaction flashed through his mind as he imagined the anguish that David had endured when seeing seven naked men gathered around his wife.

David's thumb plunged deep into the clone's throat and he tried to shove his hand upward to insert his fingers into Hephanaethus' eyes, but Hephanaethus' reflexes were much faster than those of the fat cellmate. He leaned back as David's hand slid harmlessly up his face, grabbed David's wrist, and was preparing to break David's arm when Jim's fist jabbed just behind his jawbone from the side. The location of the blow caused Hephanaethus' Eustachian tube to collapse making the vessel inoperable.

Stone was nearly to the point of penetration when he peeked beneath Gayla's outstretched arm and noticed Hephanaethus being bested by a man that looked identical to him. Despite his lust, he abandoned his quest for Gayla's body in favor of trying to save his own life. Feverishly, he dug at the side of the bed in an attempt to escape from beneath Gayla.

Gayla twisted her neck to see behind her. What she saw gave her a bit of hope through the confusion. It appeared to be

David fighting with David. Her mind filled with questions, but she was oddly relieved that one of the David's behind her seemed to be trying to save her from the other one. She shook her head trying to wake up from the nightmare she was sure she was having. This was impossible and therefore indicated that it had to be a dream—it had to be.

Just wake up, she told herself.

There was no waking. However strange, it *was* reality.

The other gang members turned and reached for their clothing. They weren't sure exactly what was going on here but they were expecting someone to die, perhaps even themselves.

Stone slid from beneath Gayla and tried to put his pants on hastily. His gun fell from his pocket as he pulled them upward to his knees. He reached down to retrieve the weapon.

"Hands up! Police," shouted detective Gill as the detective duo entered the doorway and saw more people inside than they had expected.

Detective Carson could see in his peripheral vision a gun being raised as Stone tried to pull his pants back up to his waist. Without time to decipher the gang leader's intentions, Carson turned and fired two shots into Stone's head.

Through the gag in her mouth Gayla's shriek sounded like a deep roar as she saw the rufescent wall behind Stone. His head fell back against it, just below the splatters, and streaked a wide patch of dark red blood down the wall.

The sound of the double blast had drawn everyone's attention besides David's. He continued swinging wildly at Hephanaethus. The blows were coming in faster than the disoriented immortal could defend against. He fell backwards and rolled to the side to get away from David.

The teenagers took their chances as they tried to rush past the detectives and avoid criminal charges. The two uniformed policemen just outside the front door of the condo shortened their journeys.

Brian became distracted from the battle between David and Hephanaethus as he attempted to determine Gayla's physical condition.

Hephanaethus tumbled and leaped through the window of the bedroom. Shards of glass fell in several directions as they sliced through Hephanaethus' skin. It was not a pleasant exit but one through which he predicted the vessel would survive.

Following Hephanaethus out the window was not a sane idea, and David's sanity was returning as he looked back at Gayla on the bed. Even stronger than the hatred he felt for the demon, was the love he felt for his wife.

Jim turned and screamed, "The clone is getting away!"

The uniformed policemen continued handcuffing the thugs while the detectives went out the front door and split up to go around the condo in opposite directions. They hoped to catch the clone before he could evade them again and terrorize the citizens of other cities.

David found his open knife lying on the floor near one of the bedposts and began sawing the ropes that bound Gayla's hands.

Jim untied the gag from her mouth while David freed her hands.

"I'm so sorry Gayla. I thought I would never see you again," David said as he finished cutting the ropes. He then threw his arms around her.

Gayla wrapped her own arms around David and clung to him tightly. She didn't know what had just happened, but she could tell that this was the *real* David, the man whom she had fallen in love with and married. For a reason that she couldn't understand, much less explain, she felt guilty, as if the attack had been partially her own fault.

Jim pulled a blanket around her before she realized that she had been exposed to him.

"Can you get me those shorts and my robe?" Gayla asked David as she pointed towards the overturned basket of clothes that had been lying in the middle of the floor prior to the assault.

David retrieved the shorts and handed them back to her. He wanted to know what had happened while they had been separated, or at least he thought he did. He felt almost obligated to ask but he was also sure that the answer would haunt him for the rest of his life. He wondered if this had been the first time she had been subjected to a gang rape. Did he save her from a close call or had she endured this on a daily basis while he was still in Arizona? Questions continued flooding his mind yet he feared answers as he had trained his mind to expect the worst over the past four days.

Jim stepped back and looked at David with relief. David had been right and now Gayla was safe. He felt that his job was done now, with one exception . . . the clone still ran free.

"I'm going to go now. I'll see if I can help track down the clone."

The clone, Gayla considered, she had heard Jim use the term earlier but had put little thought into it. She had been with David's clone, for how long she did not know.

Jim walked over to look out the broken window. He could see the rare patches of weeds that speckled the sandy slope up to a parking lot behind the condo. The bright white sand made a set of footprints clearly visible under the security lights. From his position, Jim could trace Hephanaethus' trail to the exact point of the parking lot where he had escaped. To either side, he could see the plain clothed detectives holding their weapons ready to fire on sight. He turned towards the man he had seen at the Phoenix airport and motioned him closer, then pointed to the path.

Gill nodded and motioned for Carson to follow him. John Wilson also followed behind. Since his arrival he had yet to see David, Gayla, or the clone. He still needed to see some sort of evidence helpful to David's case.

"I think the clone got away," Jim stated softly as he turned back towards David and Gayla.

"Are you okay?" David asked Gayla.

She nodded, but wasn't entirely convincing.

"Gayla, I've done something terrible. It's *my* fault. I brought this clone into the world and it's my job to take him back out of it. If I don't, he could kill thousands of other people. I have to go now but I'll be back," David explained, fully realizing that even now, in Gayla's most desperate hour, he was abandoning her again.

"I understand, but this time, I'm coming with you," Gayla stated solidly, as she leaned over and picked the weapon up off the floor. The detectives had forgotten to retrieve the handgun that Stone had been holding, and now Gayla sought her own vengeance against this clone.

The detectives looked behind every vehicle as they searched, and their eyes dashed across the parking lot trying to pick up some slight movement.

The uniformed police officers called for backup needing more room for the teenaged would-be sex offenders. They also needed another pair of handcuffs. The young troublemakers were still in too much shock from Stone's fate to put up much resistance, but the officers knew that the sheer number could present a problem if that situation changed.

Chapter 23

Two trios formed in the parking lot. Both wanted to find Hephanaethus, and every one of the six people had a serious desire to see him captured. Detective Carson wanted the man responsible for causing the accident that had claimed the lives of twenty-one people whom he had sworn to protect. He wanted the clone dead—no chance of parole.

Detective Gill wanted the man who had killed Michelle and tried to rape Gayla. If convenient, he would prefer that the clone resist arrest so that he could kill him in self-defense.

John Wilson wanted evidence; Hephanaethus was his link to David's defense. As an experienced attorney, he preferred to have living witnesses, one's that could talk and, hopefully, convict themselves.

Jim Turner wanted the clone eliminated. He wasn't sure how, but he knew that if this clone was actually demon possessed, great destruction lay in his path.

Gayla wanted the man who had subjected her to the mental anguish she still suffered. She knew that he had caused her to doubt the one thing she believed in most—David's love for her.

David wanted Hephanaethus for more reasons than he was even aware of at the moment. Still, he wasn't sure what had happened to Gayla in the past week, but his imagination filled his mind with a hateful jealousy beyond that which words could express. Needless to say, he wanted Hephanaethus dead, but not only dead in the flesh—he knew that would be useless—he wanted Hephanaethus dead *forever*. He was positive that this would be an issue in which he would prove incapable of accomplishing, but it was no less what he desired.

While the detectives looked for clues as to where the clone might have escaped, David handled his search differently. He said nothing to Gayla as he hobbled along as briskly as possible. He could feel the pain again in his legs but even this did not slow him down. He continued to hobble directly into the darkest place he could see from his current location. David didn't care where he was; he knew that Hephanaethus would come to him as he had been doing for over twenty years. As for Gayla, at least he knew that she was safe again. Now his life's purpose had changed again; destroying the demon was all that mattered.

"Blood," Carson pointed to a fresh red smear along the side of a car.

Gayla overheard his words and began drifting in the same direction as the detectives hastened their pace towards a nearby alleyway where Carson had thought he had seen some sort of movement in the shadows.

Jim followed with Gayla and motioned for David to follow but did not look back.

Unnoticed by the rest, David continued hobbling straight ahead to the darkest of the alleys. He knew that Hephanaethus had mastered the art of deception, and he knew that Hephanaethus could escape from them all if he tried. But most importantly, he knew that just as Hephanaethus had always followed him before, he would do so again.

The detectives held their weapons in both hands in front of them as they drew near the alley. Their forefingers formed tight seals on the triggers of their weapons and they were a mere flinch away from firing.

Gayla hid the weapon she had recently acquired beneath her robe as she followed behind.

John Wilson and Jim Turner greeted each other with a nod as they also moved in closer.

John noticed that among the people he saw in front of him, Jim was the only one he couldn't identify. Since his arrival he had yet to see David up close. "Where did David go?" John asked.

"He's right behind," Jim started as he turned around to point, then suddenly realized that David had not followed.

David stepped into the darkness alone, but he knew that he was not *truly* alone and he never would be. He didn't raise his guard to prepare for a sudden ambush from Hephanaethus because it just wasn't Hephanaethus' style.

Hephanaethus was more patient. He enjoyed watching people suffer too much to end it so quickly. Even as he heard the devious cackle, David didn't flinch.

"You are truly a glutton for punishment aren't you, David?" the voice from the deepest shadows said in a loud whisper.

"You'd find me anyway," David replied in acceptance of his fate. "I'm not going to give you the pleasure of dragging it out any longer. Go ahead and take me now. This life is nothing, and the sooner you kill me, the sooner I become immortal. I *will* win in the end," David stated as his previous epiphany matured to its full extent.

David had stunned Hephanaethus again, but unlike in the condo, this had nothing to do with his physical weaknesses. This time he stood up to Hephanaethus on his own ground. His spirit was not afraid of the demon, but welcomed his attack, as if daring him. The confidence with which David had spoken the words, along with the truth behind the statement, had dazed the wicked spirit. For once, Hephanaethus had no way to turn David's words against him. He remained silent as he debated how to best make David doubt the words he had just spoken.

"We've got to find David. He's gone!" Jim blurted.

On his first impulse, Detective Gill wanted to ignore the fact that David was lagging behind, but he realized that David and Hephanaethus were linked and that this was not his, but rather, David's battle with the demon.

The small mob of clone hunters turned and began to retrace their footsteps.

Jim pointed to where they had been the last time he had seen David. In the surrounding area, there were only two possible places that seemed likely for David to have gone.

Gayla jogged on her bare feet. She kept her hand tucked into her white terrycloth bathrobe and dashed desperately in what she felt would be the right direction.

She screamed, "David."

David could hear Gayla calling his name from the distance. He was aware that she had a gun with her. He was aware that the two detectives also had firearms of their own, but this was his battle, and no number of firearms could win it. Remaining silent, he stepped forward, drawing closer to where he had heard the loud whisper of the demonic clone.

After putting some considerable thought into the subject, Hephanaethus accepted that he had lost a spiritual battle. He acknowledged that even through the tortuous past that David had lived, he had only become stronger, and now he was . . . it was a word that sounded vulgar to his ears . . . saved. It was too late to kill his soul. The only pain he could inflict on David in the future would be physical. He backed away, drawing David closer as he prepared to make the best of his situation.

In the darkness of the alley, David couldn't see him, but he could hear him. Then Hephanaethus backed into an intersection of alleys and David could see the silhouette of his own face. He rushed forward, but Hephanaethus beat him to the first devastating blow. With a kick to David's diaphragm, Hephanaethus knocked him breathless and incapable of calling for help. Another blow struck him in front of his right shoulder and displaced the bone from its joint.

David screamed away what little breath he had regained. But the scream was so weak that it couldn't be heard more than fifteen feet away.

With a lightning fast jab, Hephanaethus dislocated David's left shoulder.

David staggered forward, trying to keep his balance despite his wounded knee. He could move neither arm nor could he scream for help. Still, he was not afraid.

Just as he had slain Michelle, Hephanaethus placed his right hand on the back of David's skull and cupped his left hand around David's chin. In a final attempt to weaken David's newly strengthened faith, Hephanaethus looked at him and slurred in a louder voice. "So, you think you'll be immortal huh? Well then, ask yourself one question, Where is your God now? Why doesn't he strike me down to save you? Where the hell is the thunder?"

At that moment, Gayla, Gill, and Carson each aimed their guns, knowing that it was now or never, and simultaneously fired. A thunderous roar echoed down the alley after three bright flashes of light momentarily illuminated an area to the right of the clone.

"God works in mysterious ways," Gill remarked coarsely as he stepped from the shadows of the intersecting corridor.

Behind him were Detective Carson and Gayla. The detectives had been unaware that she had been hiding her weapon, but given her circumstances, Detective Carson simply extended his hand to remove the weapon solemnly as she stopped and stared blankly at the dying man who looked so much like the man that she loved.

Blood streamed from the three wounds that had been inflicted on Hephanaethus. Gayla's shot had entered near his right shoulder and exited through his left, while darker blood began to soak his collar as it ran from the wound inflicted by Detective Gill's shot. He felt sick as the blood poured into his stomach from the hole created by Carson's bullet.

PSYCLONE

David knelt down beside his dying clone. By the dim light reflected down the alley he could just barely see the change in the clone's face as the demon Hephanaethus escaped the dying vessel. A look of innocence filled the clone's face and his eyes became soft again.

"What's happening to me?" Darryl asked with a child-like ignorance to the world's cruel reality. "I hurt. Will I stop hurting?" he gasped desperately, as blood bubbled up from his mouth and spilled down his chin.

David looked back at him with mixed emotions. Despite his wounds, David thought that he might have a chance to save him. But did he really want to? If the clone were saved, he couldn't stop Hephanaethus from possessing him again. But this was *his* clone; it had been like recreating his brother. Even more so, David had remembered feeling like Darryl's father as he taught him things and cared for him. This was like letting his own son die while he watched, not even attempting to save him.

"Yes," David answered before swallowing hard. "You'll stop hurting soon," he said as he tried to raise Darryl's head up closer to him. David's fingers slid through Darryl's bloody hair and he could feel the back of his skull about to collapse as he comforted the clone in his last breath.

Gayla watched quietly. She couldn't, or at least she didn't understand David's attachment to this creature that he now comforted. Despite all her knowledge of how the human mind works, she didn't know why her husband would be actually devastated to see the end of the horrible clone. But she had never met Darryl and didn't know what David had experienced and then hid from her. Furthermore, she knew nothing about Hephanaethus or how he had arranged every situation in David's life to be a decision on what he was *least* willing to lose.

John Wilson looked directly at Detective Gill and silently nodded. They knew that David's story had been an accurate one. They didn't discuss the issue any further; both had decided that there was nothing more to say about it.

Across from them, Jim and Detective Carson had also

chosen to remain quite as David began to weep and babble about Darryl. Carson was sure that this was the man who had been responsible for the accident, as for the demon, he, like Gayla, remained ignorant.

David felt a slight warm breeze on his hand as the last bit of air trailed out of Darryl's lungs. The memories of his young twin brother, and those of the clone two weeks ago, began to blur together as if they had actually been the same being.

"Darryl," David babbled, "it was my fault again. I'm sorry that you had to suffer . . . again." He wondered what had happened to the mind of Darryl while he had been possessed by the demon. He wondered if he had just been trapped in nothingness or if he had been forced to helplessly bare witness to all of the demon's foul deeds. It would remain a mystery to him for as long as he lived, and again he wasn't sure that he truly wanted to know the answer.

Chapter 24

David removed his wallet from the back pocket of his deceased clone. Then he reclaimed his keys, watch, and wedding band. He felt like a grave robber but these things had been very important to him. After removing his checkbook, David wrote Jim a check for four thousand dollars to cover the expenses that Jim had charged on his credit card.

Jim was tempted to say no and rip the check in half, but he had spent a considerable amount on the three one-way next flight tickets and he would need to return to Boston after he attended Trevor's funeral back in Phoenix.

"I'm just glad that I could help you, Dave. If you ever need me again, you know that I'll be there."

David grinned sadly and nodded.

John Wilson whispered to Brian Gill. "Do we have to take him back into custody now?"

"He's still going to have to face charges for illegal cloning, assaulting an officer, and stealing that patrol car. I'll see what I can do to dismiss any charges related to escaping confinement though. I don't have any choice, John, it's my duty." Brian replied as he rubbed the palm of his hand up his face.

John couldn't argue the response.

Gill turned to face Carson and extended his hand. "I appreciate your help here. I need to take Mr. Brooks back to Arizona now but I'll need to examine the body also. My forensics guys we'll be in touch with you by tomorrow morning."

Carson nodded satisfied.

"Thank you. I'm still not quite sure what's going on here but I suppose I can wait for that explanation until after I ask the witnesses if this was the man that we've been looking for."

John Wilson approached David Brooks from behind.

"I knew that you were being honest with me, David. I have every reason to believe that you will continue to be honest with me. When we get back to Arizona, we'll have to answer a few more questions, but I think your case looks pretty good." He didn't want to mention any of the charges that would continue to be pressed against him. David had come too far to jeopardize the case by attempting to flee again.

"You'll have to return to Phoenix on the same flight as Detective Gill and myself, but you'll be a free man. We will only be there as an escort," John continued.

Gayla wiggled her fingers in between David's and led him away from the clone's corpse.

"Happy Anniversary," Gayla whispered to her true husband.

David looked up at her sadly and nodded. The day had been so long and stressful that he had forgotten its significance. He closed his eyes and mouthed the words "Thank you" as he pulled her close again. He wasn't replying to Gayla's remark or even speaking to her when he expressed his gratitude.

Gayla was aware of this but understood.

They walked blindly down the sable alley and back towards their condo.

Brian Gill, John Wilson, and Jim Turner followed a respectable distance behind the couple. Detective Carson walked in the same general direction so he could get a ride back to the police station and end his long evening.

As they neared the condo, Gayla could see a stretcher being carried out the front door. There was a lump beneath the white sheet, and a dark red patch of blood had already begun to soak through the sheet near the top. The gangly youngster that had been so close to sexually assaulting her was dead. So, too, was the man that had looked like her husband. Yet, she still felt scared. Even David's presence couldn't relieve the trauma she had recently experienced. She needed time, and she was sure that she would need to take some time off from her job. How could she be a good psychologist when she couldn't deal with her own feelings? The last thing she needed now was to constantly deal with other people's problems.

As had became habit for him, Brian looked at his watch and considered what he had accomplished today and how much he still had to do before he could rest easily tonight. He didn't even know where he would sleep tonight and he had hours of work ahead of him. Legally, he should've had David in custody; he was still a suspect for a list of crimes, but again he considered Gayla's best interest. Both had been through a great deal of stress and they needed some time together before he took David back to Phoenix. If David escaped, he would have a lot of explaining to do. It was a chance he would take under the circumstances.

"Do your friend a favor," Brian spoke quietly as he turned to Jim. "Don't let him leave the area until I get back here in the morning. I'll be here around nine o'clock. He'll be okay as long as he doesn't try to run again."

Jim nodded.

The police had left the Brooks' condo marked off as a crime scene. David and Gayla would have to sleep elsewhere tonight.

When morning came, John Wilson, Brian Gill, and Jim Turner accompanied David and Gayla to the airport. They would all be taking the same flight back to Phoenix. David wondered if everyone in Phoenix would learn of the destruction caused by his clone. He wondered if he would be despised by all of the other residents of the city.

After their flight back to Phoenix, David and Gayla accompanied the detective back to the police station; John also went with them. Jim proceeded to the mortuary to attempt the grim task of trying to positively identify the charred corpse as Trevor's remains.

John and Gayla sat on either side next to David as he answered the detective's questions and made his official statement.

"We'll have to have a trial to determine your bail, but in the meantime, if you need to do anything, I'll bend the rules and escort you wherever you need to go."

Brian was taking a huge risk but he had reason to trust David now. His mistake had cost around two-dozen lives, but Brian realized that it was a mistake that humanity had been destined to make at some point in time. David had not been the first to promote the idea; he had only been the first to carry through with it. At any rate, he had decided to be uncommonly lenient with David until his trial took place.

After taking David's statement, Detective Gill called the local sheriff's office near White Horse, Pennsylvania and requested a search for the remains of a nine-year-old boy in a wooded area to the south. He knew that from the vagueness of the information that David had relayed to him that the search would likely be a long one.

"Can I see what happened to the laboratory?" David asked as he thought about all the achievements he had made in the past five years and wondered if they had all been totally destroyed.

"Yes," Gill answered softly with a sense of sympathy for David's situation.

The detective stood up and walked to the door. "I can take you there now if you'd like."

PSYCLONE

As David and Gayla stood in front of the scorched heap of remnants that had formerly been David's beloved lab, he hung his head remorsefully in remembrance of Trevor. While he looked down, he noticed a small, short white-haired mouse crawling across his foot. David leaned down and scooped up the mouse. Gayla watched in wonder as he flipped the tiny rodent over and examined one of its rear feet. David said nothing; he only nodded.

The mouse was indeed, Rambo. He knew that Rambo would always be a survivor, genetically superior to others of his species. This mouse had been the only mortal witness to the events that had happened in the lab. If David could extract the mouse's thoughts, perhaps he could use the accounts to clear him. But David realized that the peculiarities and events that had taken place in this laboratory would be best forgotten, rather than remembered.

David leaned close to Gayla and wrapped his arms around her waist. He gave her a gentle kiss and wondered how long it would be before they could return to a normal life. He wondered if normality was a thing of the past, like a quickly fading memory. He had prayed that these painful memories would fade, just as the joyful memories from college had already grown hazy. As he drew back from her, David took a deep breath and turned to face Detective Gill, who had been waiting in the distance. At least as much uncertainty filled his mind about his legal status as had his marital status. He walked slowly towards him and extended both hand's palms down.

"I'm ready now," David said softly.

"That won't be necessary," Gill said, as he motioned for David to relax his arms.

234

Epilogue

Four days after his request, Detective Gill received a phone call from a sheriff in Pennsylvania.

"By chance, a guy with a metal detector found a small skeleton that we believe is the one you were looking for," the sheriff announced with a grim tone of confidence.

"Thank you. I'll need to contact the mother of the child and get back with you after we've determined where to bury it," Gill replied.

Three closed caskets sat at the front of the funeral home. One contained the decayed remnants of a nine-year-old boy; it was Darryl Brooks, David's *true* brother. Another contained the charred remains of his close friend and co-worker, Trevor Williams. In the last casket lay the body of the nearly dismembered clone. David blamed himself for all three of the deaths. He knew that Hephanaethus would feel no remorse for their demise and that, in reality, he was the one who had taken their lives.

Approaching the casket containing the youngest corpse, David removed a small toy car from his pocket. "I've been waiting for years to give this back to you," he spoke softly to the remains as he placed the toy atop an ornate wooden coffin. David's mother stood beside him; she too wept, but she had accepted Darryl's fate sometime ago. Although she missed her other son, she had not had any hopes of bringing him back through some bizarre experiment. It had been a long time since they had seen each other and they both regretted the unfortunate circumstances that they were forced to deal with at a time that should have been a joyous reunion.

Gayla watched David closely. She wished that there were something she could do to ease his internal pains. She knew that he had remained hopeful for years that he would someday find his brother alive. David had been faithful to a fault in his pursuit to find him. She almost understood why he cloned himself. She could imagine his pain, or at least she thought she could. But regardless of how hard she tried, she knew that she was helpless to lessen his pain.

The funeral proceeded with only a small gathering. David and his mother were the only surviving family of the small child. Few knew that the clone even existed, and Trevor had neither living family nor any close ties to anyone except Diana, who would never learn of Trevor's fate. After the funeral was over, Detective Gill allowed David a few hours to visit with his mother at home. While the two consoled each other and reminisced about a more pleasant past, Gayla excused herself and retreated to the bathroom.

Gayla held her breath as she watched the home pregnancy test finish with a positive indication. She wondered when she had conceived. Was it with David, while they were at her parents' house in Vermont? Was it with the clone, after they had returned to Phoenix? David and the clone had the exact same blood type and DNA structure; maybe she would never really know. Of course, neither would David. Perhaps, it shouldn't matter, but it did. The child would share some of David's genetics either way, but would the spirit of a demon alter them somehow. Biologically speaking, no, but only time would tell the truth of the matter.

In the small dark one-bedroom apartment that Hephanaethus had rented in South Phoenix, three large containers were placed evenly across the room. Each of these containers was filled nearly to the top with amniotic fluids. What made one of the containers unique from another was the content. Different human shapes formed within each of them. In the first container, a large-framed man with dark skin lay nearly motionless. The second container held a statuesque woman with dark hair and cat-shaped aqua-colored eyes. In the last container, a clone, identical to the original clone that David had created, began to curl up comfortably. Other than the clones in their respective tanks, and a few choice supplies taken from the laboratory before the explosion, the room was empty. Other than the clones of Trevor Williams, David, and Gayla Brooks, nothing or no one else could be seen; but in the seemingly empty apartment, three dark entities slumbered, dreaming of the distant past:

The time was irrelevant; it was the beginning. The location was also irrelevant; it was all that existed. His forces were outnumbered two to one. As they retreated down the shimmering golden streets, Lucifer realized that he was not as well prepared for this confrontation as he had thought. He looked at the two seraphim with him as he prepared for the retreat.

Hephanaethus and Erin now regretted their allegiance to Lucifer who led the rebellion against God. Now they could only hope to escape the wrath of their creator, whom they had betrayed . . .

Hephanaethus awoke and smiled. He realized that even though he had waited a long time for this, his wait was almost over. Soon, these vessels, these empty husks, would be occupied . . . very, very soon. . . .

The End.........For Now

A Spectral Visions Imprint

Now Available

Riverwatch
by
Joseph M. Nassise

From a new voice in horror comes a novel rich in characterization and stunning in its imagery. In his debut novel, author Joseph M. Nassise weaves strange and shocking events into the ordinary lives of his characters so smoothly that the reader accepts them without pause, setting the stage for a climactic ending with the rushing power of a summer storm.

When his construction team finds the tunnel hidden beneath the cellar floor in the old Blake family mansion in Harrington Falls, Jake Caruso is excited by the possibility of what he might find hidden there. Exploring its depths, he discovers an even greater mystery: a sealed stone chamber at the end of that tunnel.

When the seal on that long forgotten chamber is broken, a reign of terror and death comes unbidden to the residents of the small mountain community. Something is stalking its citizens; something that comes in the dark of night on silent wings and strikes without warning, leaving a trail of blood in its wake. Something that should never have been released from the prison the Guardian had fashioned for it years before.

Now Jake, with the help of his friends Sam Travers and Katelynn Riley, will be forced to confront this ancient evil in an effort to stop the creature's rampage. The Nightshade, however, has other plans.

Ask for it at your local bookseller!

ISBN 1931402191

www.barclaybooks.com

A Spectral Visions Imprint

Now Available

The Apostate
by
Paul Lonardo

An ancient evil is spreading through Caldera, a burgeoning desert metropolis that has been heralded as the gateway of the new millennium. As the malevolent shadow spreads across the land, three seemingly ordinary people, Julian, Saney, and Chris, discover that they are the only ones who can defeat the true source of the region's evil, which may or may not be the Devil himself. When a man claiming to work for a mysterious global organization informs the trio that Satan has, in fact, chosen Caldera as the site of the final battle between good and evil, only one questions remains…

Is it too late for humanity?

Ask for it at your local bookseller!

ISBN 193140132

www.barclaybooks.com

Night Terrors
by
Drew Williams

He came to them in summer, while everyone slept....

For Detective Steve Wyckoff, the summer brought four suicides and a grisly murder to his hometown. Deaths that would haunt his dreams and lead him to the brink of madness.

For David Cavanaugh, the summer brought back long forgotten dreams of childhood. Dreams that became nightmares for which there would be no escape.

For Nathan Espy, the summer brought freedom from a life of abuse. Freedom purchased at the cost of his own soul.

From an abyss of darkness, he came to their dreams and whispered his name.

"Dust"

A Spectral Visions Imprint

Now Available!

Spirit Of Independence
by
Keith Rommel

Travis Winter, the Spirit of Independence, was viciously murdered in World War II. Soon after his untimely death, he discovers he is a chosen celestial knight; a new breed of Angel destined to fight the age-old war between Heaven and Hell. Yet, confusion reigns for Travis when he is pulled into Hell and is confronted by the Devil himself—the saddened creature who begs only to be heard.

Freed by a band of Angels sent to rescue him, Travis rejects the Devil's plea and begins a fifty year long odyssey to uncover the true reasons why Heaven and Hell war.

Now, in this, the present day, Travis comes to you, the reader, to share recent and extraordinary revelations that will no doubt change the way you view the Kingdom of Heaven and Hell. And what is revealed will change your own afterlife in ways you could never imagine …

Ask for it at your local bookseller!

ISBN 1931402078

www.barclaybooks.com